PRAISE FOR JENNY CARLISLE

Saddle up and hold on tight for a rip-roaring good time at the Caldwell Family Rodeo. While Carlisle's steadfast heroine determines to honor and keep her mother's legacy intact, her bungling big-hearted hero strives to live up to the shadow cast by his big brother and clean up his messes while he's at it. Through twists and turns, they never saw coming, both learn what's really important when they let go and let God handle their happily-ever-afters.

— SHANNON TAYLOR VANNATTER, AWARD-WINNING, MULTI-PUBLISHED AUTHOR OF CONTEMPORARY CHRISTIAN ROMANCE

This debut novel immediately makes you feel like you've known the characters and town forever. The sweet story is full of laughter, tears, and a reminder that even though it isn't easy to relinquish your hold on the reins of life, by letting God take them, only good will follow. Jenny Carlisle's first book has me looking forward to more to come.

— AMY ANGUISH MULTI-PUBLISHED AUTHOR OF CONTEMPORARY CHRISTIAN ROMANCE

Real-to-life characters and a setting that brought back precious memories of my cowboy daddy's amateur rodeo days made Jenny McLeod Carlisle's debut novel, *Hope Takes the Reins,* one that I'll read over again. Filled with believable family angst plus outside conflicts kept me rooting for the family, yelling at the troublemakers, and swooning over the sweet interwoven romance. If you like modern-day westerns, you'll love this one. And even if contemporary fiction is not your cup of tea, try this one anyway. It will leave you wanting more.

— JULANE HIEBERT MULTI-PUBLISHED
AUTHOR OF HISTORICAL FICTION

Hope Takes the

Reins

CROSSROADS BOOK ONE

Jenny Carlisle

Scrivenings
PRESS
Quench your thirst for story.
www.ScriveningsPress.com

Published by Scrivenings Press LLC
15 Lucky Lane
Morrilton, Arkansas 72110
https://ScriveningsPress.com

Printed in the United States of America

Paperback ISBN 978-1-64917-189-4

eBook ISBN 978-1-64917-190-0

Editors: Elena Hill and K. Banks

Cover by Linda Fulkerson, www.bookmarketinggraphics.com.

For Bliss, Chessica, and Sherry

"For I am persuaded that neither death nor life, nor angels nor principalities nor powers, nor things present nor things to come, nor height nor depth, nor any other created thing, shall be able to separate us from the love of God which is in Christ Jesus our Lord."

~ Romans 8: 38-39 NKJV

ACKNOWLEDGMENTS

Praise God from whom all blessings flow. With the assurance that faith in Jesus gives me, I can live every dream.

I am so grateful that God placed James Carlisle in my path at Bryant High School. His support and love during 45 years of marriage have made all the difference in my life. So thankful for the positive energy of all of our kids and grands as well.

When two pillars of the Arkansas Chapter of American Fiction Christian Writers became the founders of a new publishing company, Scrivenings Press, I finally had the opportunity to get my stories into publication. Special thanks to Linda Fulkerson, who has also helped immensely with my website. Shannon "Dream Crusher" Vannatter encouraged me to abandon the tired old story I had been promoting and reach back for this one that had captured me years ago and wouldn't leave me alone. Crushing that old dream to replace it with this new one was the best possible move for me. With Elena Hill as the editor who really connected with my characters and their story, I was finally set to bring it to life.

There is more than one community in Arkansas named Crossroads, but none are incorporated as a town. My town of Crossroads and all of its businesses are entirely fictional. There is no television station located in the Arkansas River Valley and plans for a casino there are still underway. During my research I found that there is a Caldwell Rodeo in Idaho, but this had no influence at all on my fictional Caldwell Family Rodeo.

Thanks to the Hull and Porterfield families for introducing me to competitive horse shows and the high quality young people who participate.

Thanks to Megan Earnhart for her help in coming up with some dastardly actions taken by the new business in town.

Here's hoping that your visit to small-town America brings you hope for your journey. Jeremiah 29:11.

PROLOGUE

O.D. Billings slid into his delivery truck. Why would Dad text mid-day?

Come home if you can. Mom needs us.

Blood drained from his face as his stomach went queasy. Since Mom realized there was an information blackout from the Middle East, all their thoughts were concentrated on his older brother. No confirmation, no details, no relief from the dread hanging over the Billings house. If they didn't hear something soon, it would be a long, hot summer in the Arkansas river valley.

"Yeah." O.D.'s boss answered his call quickly.

"George, I just got a text from my dad. Something is happening at home. He won't say anything. It can't be good." O.D. drove toward his next stop out of habit. Should he stop to respond to his dad?

"Go." George didn't hesitate. "What's left on your truck can wait."

On my way.

O.D.'s fingers shook as he pressed SEND.

Mentally he went through the list of notification protocols. Death notifications were made in person. Injuries were confirmed by phone calls, preferably from the soldier. So what could be happening at his house? Thankfully, Dad went home for lunch. Maybe whatever upset Mom hadn't found her alone.

A car ran a stop sign in front of him. O.D. braked just in time.

Find your head, Dee. Needs to be in the same place as your feet right now. His Grandpa's words rang in his brain, bringing calm reassurance. Just get home.

The big brown truck bounced down the bumpy driveway that led past the barn up to their house. Dad stood at the door of his truck with his phone in his hand. Mom was sitting on the porch swing, swaying a little harder than normal as her tennis shoes kicked the painted boards.

A familiar white SUV pulled away from the house as he arrived, their neighbor Hope Caldwell. Hope's mom waved feebly from the passenger side. A strange pang of jealousy popped into his mind. They had more information than him.

"Dad." O.D. stepped down from the truck.

"We still don't know anything." Dad squinted at the porch. "Your mom and Catherine Caldwell are worried about a news story about attacks in the Middle East. No names released yet. They didn't even mention a unit. But there is at least one dead with several injured. Mom is sure your brother was there. I'm debating whether to get Cody out of school."

O.D. glanced toward his mom again. Eyes closed in prayer, she stopped swinging.

"It's your call. It's hard to know what to do right now. I don't know if he'd rather be here fretting with us or just waiting till we have something to tell him." O.D. headed for the porch.

Thankfully, O.D. had decided not to follow John K. to the military. He'd trailed after his big brother so many times. But right now, maybe his place was here at home. It would be nice to feel a little more certain of that.

1

Three Months Later

A cool autumn wind bounced around, threatening to lift O.D.'s cowboy hat off his head. No time to worry about that as he helped Mom down from the passenger side of Dad's truck. She insisted they all ride to the airport together, though it would be crowded with three grown men in the back on the way home.

"Thanks." She hugged him after both her trademark high-tops were on the ground. "I can get out by myself, but you're sweet to help."

"Come on! We're in an unloading zone." Cody ran around from the driver's side, rushing them into the terminal as Dad went to find a more permanent place to park.

O.D. blinked as the clouds rolling overhead made the natural light inside the building flicker. The soft buzz of conversation increased as they approached the bottom of the escalator that brought passengers down from the secured area.

"Hey, it's Cody!" His younger brother was instantly

surrounded by teenaged friends. Several girls held homemade signs with phrases like "Welcome home, John K.," "Our Hero," and "God Bless the USA."

"Oh my." Mom stopped in her tracks. "I hope your dad gets here soon."

"He's on his way." O.D. gently pushed his way through the crowds, trying to locate a good place for Mom to see the top of the escalator.

Light flashed from his right side—a television news crew stood nearby.

"We're live at the Little Rock airport, where a group of soldiers is scheduled to land today to rejoin their families." The reporter ignored the commotion going on behind her. "One soldier, in particular, has captured so many hearts in our state. Here's the mayor of Crossroads, Arkansas, his hometown. Mayor Jones, why have so many River Valley residents showed up to greet this soldier today?"

O.D. turned to listen. The mayor of Crossroads? Really?

"John Kennedy Billings is the oldest son of a prominent businessman in our community. He's been our hero back to the time when he was playing football in high school." The mayor straightened his tie, standing tall in front of the camera.

"I understand there was a question about him ever coming home. Is that right?" The reporter thrust the microphone toward the round-faced man again.

"Yes. He was listed as missing in action for a few weeks. Then, he spent some time in a hospital recovering from injuries sustained in an IED attack."

"Well, we can tell the whole town of Crossroads is happy he is coming home today." A rousing cheer went up from behind her, stopping many suitcase-toting bystanders in their tracks. "We will have video of his arrival for you at six o'clock. Back to you, Joe."

The camera light switched off. The reporter turned to find a spot near the escalator.

O.D. was flabbergasted. What a crazy day. Of course the community was proud of his brother, but wasn't this sort of extreme? John K. would love the attention. Mom crept up to a safe spot in front of Cody's group of friends. O.D. stepped back to look through the glass walls. His dad hopped across a parking lot curb.

"O.D.!" He turned toward the coffee kiosk, a familiar blonde waved. Next to Faith Caldwell, her sister Hope stood quietly, her honey-colored braid falling on her shoulder. She balanced a cinnamon roll in one hand and a large coffee in the other.

"Come sit with us." Faith pulled out a chair.

Walking over, he took off his cowboy hat, placing it in front of him on the table. He was a bit surprised to see them here. Faith's nervous energy contrasted with Hope's stillness.

"Hey, how are y'all?"

Hope didn't look up until she had finished sweetening her coffee.

"We're okay." Faith replied. "But how about you? Are you excited to see John K.? Do you know when his plane arrives?"

"Actually, I've been checking online. It looks like there was a weather delay at DFW. We may be in for a bit of a wait. Hey, Hope."

"Hey." Hope finally acknowledged his presence. "Cody and your mom sure look excited."

"You bet! The returning hero has the whole state in a stir."

She focused on her coffee again.

"We just dropped our grandparents off so they can fly back to Houston." Faith talked for both sisters.

"How's your dad?" O.D. couldn't imagine what his own dad would do in Smiley Caldwell's boots.

"He's okay, I guess." Hope met his eyes. Being quieter than her sister was typical, but he didn't like the pain etched in her eyes.

"Speaking of dads, there's mine. Excuse me, ladies." He smiled at Faith but failed to catch Hope's eye.

O.D. walked through the milling crowds, gently touching his dad's sleeve as he approached.

"So, Dave, I guess you are pretty proud of your hero son?" The mayor faced them, pumping Dad's hand vigorously.

"Of course. And let me introduce you to our other son." Dad reached over the head of a teenaged girl to grab Cody's arm. "Cody, have you met Mayor Jones?"

The other one. Not "the youngest." Not "another of my boys." The other one. O.D. stepped backward. He held his hat in his hands and stood on tiptoe, trying to peer over the crowd. Chants of "USA, USA" washed around him.

"There he is!" Cody pointed, then waved.

John K.'s smiling face lit up the top of the escalator. He strode down the moving stairway, a head taller than the other passengers. He waved at the crowd but locked eyes with their mom, pushing straight for her.

O.D. swallowed back a lump in his throat. Finally, Mom might start sleeping through the night again. Dad moved quickly through the crowd to reach his wife. He enveloped her and his oldest son in a huge hug.

John K. bumped into Cody as he took purposeful steps in O.D.'s direction.

"Hey, Squirt." He pulled O.D. close. "How's it going?"

Squirt. The nickname fit better now than it did when John K. deployed—even Cody towered over O.D.'s five foot nine.

"Welcome, home, bro." O.D. grabbed a bag of chips John K was clutching. There was something distant in the blue eyes of his long-time hero. Not fear but hesitation. Was something holding him back from this happy day?

John K. headed toward the flashing light above the luggage carousel. O.D. followed, as always. Could it truly be this easy for their lives to return to normal?

2

B reathless. That should be a good thing. Like the giddy feeling after a good ride. Or the happy sensation when she'd been surprised on her birthday. But this—this was different. Hope could not take a breath. And breathing would be required to walk across the Crossroads arena tonight.

Why was this hard? Dad led the way, Faith held her hand, and her brother Junior brought up the rear. But one important person was missing, and her absence gripped Hope's stomach, limiting air supply.

Dad took the first steps through the powdery dirt, his boots leaving deep prints in the freshly smoothed surface.

"Come on, Hope." Faith tightened her grip. "Let's go. Mom would want this."

How many times had she heard those words? Of course, Faith was right. Hope had spent all her time making sure things operated just the way Mom would want, ever since her cancer emerged from the shadows to bully its way into their lives.

They rarely walked out to the center of the arena as a

family. Hope remembered when Calvin Junior made his debut here. Dad had carried him that day, since he was not old enough to walk by himself. Other than that, they'd only done this once or twice in the past fifteen years. Faith and Junior were always in the spotlight, while Hope stayed behind the scenes with Mom. Dad called them the wind beneath the rodeo's wings.

Now Mom was gone. The leaves started to fall, the rodeo was in full swing. She could hear the echo of Mom's voice in her head. 'Keep going. One boot in front of the other.'

Overhead lights blinded her. Would Dad ever stop walking? This must be far enough. The crowd gradually stilled, waiting for her Uncle Dub's voice from the announcer's stand.

"Ladies and Gentlemen, welcome to the Caldwell Family Rodeo here in beautiful Crossroads, Arkansas. This little group you see before you is certainly a sight for my sore eyes. Since my dear sister-in-law Catherine ended her battle against cancer by declaring Victory in Jesus, we have missed this branch of the Caldwell Rodeo family. Tonight, I turn the announcing duties back over to my capable brother, Calvin 'Smiley' Caldwell."

The crowd erupted, as always, for Dad. Whoops, hollers, applause.

"Thanks, Dub." Dad's voice through his wireless mic was strong, assuming the vigorous tone he always adopted for the rodeo. "We don't want to delay the excitement. You won't believe the quality of the contestants in tonight's festivities. But my family wants to take just a minute to thank each one of you from the bottom of our hearts."

Hope's eyes focused on her dad's face.

He swallowed hard before continuing. "If we've learned one thing, it's that we believe in the power of prayer. Your pleas to the Heavenly Father have girded us up through the roughest time in our lives. We're back, a little battle-scarred but stronger than ever. We have a new angel watching over us. I can hear her telling us to mount up, to get this show on the road." By the time he finished his speech, he was nearly shouting.

Wild cheers. More whoops, more hollers.

"Do you kids have anything to say?" He moved the mic below his face turning toward them.

Speak? How can you speak when you aren't sure you can breathe? Hope merely shook her head, as did Faith.

Junior brought his own mic. "I agree, Dad. Those prayers have been great. The Caldwell kids are ready to go tonight. And don't forget. In our house abide these three. Faith, Hope, and Junior. And the greatest of these is ..."

The whole crowd helped him finish his familiar jab. "Junior!"

Dad reached for Hope's hand on one side, Faith's on the other. Faith grabbed Junior. Together they sprinted to the entry tunnel. There was no choice but to breathe. Finally, relief. Maybe they could pull off their first night back in the spotlight after all.

Faith darted over to mount Champ in preparation for carrying the flag for the grand entrance. Junior exchanged high fives with several contestants lined up to make their entry.

Dark yet sparkling eyes caught Hope's glance. The brim of an oversized black hat dipped in a subtle nod. She'd never seen O.D. Billings so serious. The moment didn't last, as he met Junior's fist bump, then the two of them exploded into a leaping shoulder smash. That was more like the showoff calf roper.

Hope took her usual spot next to the exit gate, waiting for the moment she would cue the cowboys to walk forward as they were introduced.

Just to her right, at the edge of Hope's peripheral vision, a glint from a well-dressed man's bolo caught her eye. As she motioned to the first cowboy in line, Uncle Dub came down from the announcer's booth to stand next to the stranger. The two shook hands, then walked out of the spotlight. Who was this guy? Her dad would pronounce him a "dignitary." But what was he doing here tonight?

She turned her attention to the old familiar Lee Greenwood song playing over the speakers as the cowboys and cowgirls trudged to their spots in the arena.

Faith nudged Champ's side with her boot as they sped off, the American flag fluttering behind, just as Lee's voice warbled, "And I'll gladly stand up … next to you." The crowd was on their feet, responding with enthusiasm.

A bitter lump worked its way up Hope's throat. Her excitement tinged with a new dread. Life was fragile, so short. She refused to look up toward the announcer's stand because she would not see her Mom leaning over the rail. Bowing her head, she added her petition to the opening prayer her dad led. *Please, God, protect everyone here. Hold our family up for the next few hours. We need You more than ever.*

The crowd intoned "Amen" in unison. She caught a glimpse of O.D. Billings's piercing eyes again. Had he even bowed his head for the prayer? She nodded in his direction when he tipped his hat before leading the procession of riders back to the ramp. Not a famous hero like his older brother, or a daring bull-rider like the youngest, O.D. was by far the most interesting, at least to Hope. But he had only ever thought of her as the skinny little neighbor girl.

Heading for the stairway to the announcer's platform, Hope eyed the same stranger standing with her uncle Dub near the rodeo office. A group of bull riders crossed between them, so she stopped at the foot of the stairs, listening.

"Yeah, I'm glad you're here. My wife and I are more than ready to talk about your offer. But we'll have to wait a day or two to talk to my brother. Emotions are still raw. He doesn't need to hear about any big changes tonight."

Hope couldn't understand what Uncle Dub said after that.

"Sure, I get it," the dignitary patted Uncle Dub's shoulder. "I'll just enjoy the show. Call me. But don't wait too long. Our board will decide soon. I think the Caldwell rodeo would be a great fit for our corporation."

Hope caught her breath. She held her hand over her mouth as she scrambled up the wooden stairs. Had Uncle Dub seen her listening to their conversation? Was he really thinking of trying to sell the family business? What timing. Had he been waiting for her mom to die? This wouldn't have happened before the cancer diagnosis. Wow.

As she reached the top of the stairs, Dad announced the first event of the night. His voice sounded so familiar. Almost normal. She half expected to see her mom at his right elbow, ready to hand him notes or pour another glass of water to keep his throat fresh.

Hope pulled out the folding chair next to her dad, as Mom told her to do. 'Just stay close. Make sure he has everything he needs,' she'd said. 'The best thing that can happen during any rodeo is for nothing unexpected to happen. You will have done your part if no one knows you are there.' Dad turned her way, winked, then focused back on the arena just as she glimpsed the little tear running down his cheek.

The first event of the night went smoothly, as the youngest participants took their ponies through their paces, dodging poles. Junior's banter with Dad filled in the time when poles needed to be reset, or a timid pony balked in the entryway.

Hope spied a question mark her dad had written at the top of the list of calf ropers who would come up next. Her cue to go back downstairs to confirm that the contestants stood at the ready. Patting him on the shoulder, she hurried down the stairs, only touching the banister when she turned the corner at the bottom.

When Mom had been here, Hope hadn't been in the announcer's stand much. She'd mostly stayed at the bottom of the stairs, making sure everyone was in line, waiting for instructions from Mom. 'Hope, run grab me another cup of coffee for your dad.' 'Find out a little about this new bull rider. Who are his parents? Where does he go to school? Something.'

Hope scampered towards the entryway tunnel with her clipboard. Just outside, an informal line of cowboys with horses waited to enter the arena. She talked to each man in turn, checking their name off the list, then giving them a number to indicate the order of their ride.

"O.D. Billings." He pointed at his name on the list. "Number three."

"Yes. Thanks." She smiled. As if he needed to tell her his name.

O.D. pointed at her list again, then gestured with his left thumb to the guy standing next to him. "Jose Ramirez. Four."

She couldn't restrain another smile. "Thanks." She nodded. He nodded back. How could eyes that dark have such a sparkle to them?

Hope made a point not to look O.D.'s way as she walked back to the stairway.

Mom had always tried to tell Hope that there was satisfaction in being behind the scenes. But O.D. didn't seem to be happy with that role. He spent so much time drawing attention to himself with his antics in the arena that Hope doubted anyone comprehended his true character.

Once, Hope imagined O.D. might become more than a next-door neighbor. Dad had invited the Billingses over for one of his famous cook-outs. O.D. had spent a lot of time helping her bring things out from the kitchen. Faith even mentioned that Hope's senior prom was coming up soon. She'd never forget what O.D. had said about that.

'Not my style. Getting all gussied-up to prance around pretending to have fun. Give me a bonfire in the back forty with some crazy cowboys. I'm all good.'

Except for the gussied-up part, isn't that what he did after every ride? He was very good at prancing and pretending. And then he'd had the nerve to show up at her prom with someone else. That still made her shake her head in disbelief.

She took the stairs two at a time, placed her list next to her dad's right elbow, with all the cowboys checked off. Dad shook his empty coffee cup in her direction as Junior told a corny joke over his portable mic. She picked up the cup, turning back to the stairway. Maybe this folding chair next to dad wasn't even needed. She certainly didn't see herself sitting in it for long tonight.

She was almost back down to the dirt floor when the toe of her boot caught a splinter on the stairs, lurching her forward. Strong arms caught her before she did a nose-dive.

"Are you okay?" Faith asked from behind the rescuer.

"Yep." Hope managed only a quick response as she pushed back against a flannel shirt that smelled like fabric softener to find herself staring straight into O.D's smiling face. Why was he showing up at every turn tonight?

O.D. set her securely on her feet. "See y'all at the house later?" Was that last wink necessary? Maybe not, but it was certainly O.D.

"Sure." Faith waved at him as he ran back to mount his horse.

"Hope, who is that guy over there talking to Uncle Dub?"

She pointed as Hope stole a glance at the over-dressed man from earlier.

"I don't know," Hope whispered. "But I think he's bad news. We'll talk about him later. I need to get Dad some coffee." There was no need to upset Faith until after her barrel race.

"O.D. invited us over to their house for a welcome home party for John K." Faith stood on her tiptoes, looking over a crowd that had gathered at the concession stand. "He always was so great-looking. I wonder where he is?"

Hope followed her glance. She didn't see John K. Billings either. There would probably be a crowd of fawning girls around him. Faith hadn't been the only one to have a crush on O.D's older brother before he joined the military.

"You and Junior can go on out to the Billingses'. I'll bring Dad when we get all of tonight's rodeo business put to bed." If that wasn't her mom's actual voice coming out of Hope's mouth, she didn't know what it was.

After waving at the young man counting out change to a customer, she headed back toward the stairs, fresh coffee in tow. She was tempted to see if Uncle Dub was inside the office. What would she do if he was? Should she confront him? She steadied the cup of coffee with both hands. It would be better to just get back up to the announcer's stand, keep things normal as possible.

3

O.D. removed his hat, knelt in the dust, folding his hands in front of him. A small rivulet of sweat rolled down his forehead to the top of his nose. Two, three, stand up. After all, the calf had been the victor this time, so the crowd didn't expect him to point to his Maker to give kudos. It was more than a little embarrassing when his energetic prey wriggled away. But there was a science to getting the little critters wrapped and tied just right. You couldn't ask for a perfect storm every time.

"Well, folks, that was a slippery calf. Junior, you didn't rub him down with lard, did you?" Smiley Caldwell was in rare form again.

"Oh, Daddy. You know I don't do things like that." Junior popped up from his utterly unnecessary barrel. "Especially not to my good friend, O.D. Billings!"

O.D. clicked his tongue, using the special signal his horse responded to, leading him to the exit gate. Next ride would be better. He spotted John K. talking to Dad at the end of the ramp. Dad wore a relaxed look that O.D. hadn't seen in more than a year. The results of O.D.'s calf-roping attempts didn't seem to be on his mind at all.

Mom had been preparing all week for tonight's "back from deployment" party. Even then, no one would notice the middle, shorter sibling. Just a lowly calf roper. Nothing flashy, like younger brother Cody's upcoming bull ride promised to be.

Tara Williams, his old high school chum now a local television reporter, strode up with her cameraman in tow. "Hey, O.D. can we have a word?"

"Sure." He settled his feet in the dust, checked with the cameraman to see where he should focus his eyes.

"Hi folks, it's Tara Williams out here at the Caldwell Family Rodeo. We've got our favorite calf roper, O.D. Billings, who had a not-so-great ride tonight. So, your fans want to know something. What about your name? What does O.D. stand for?" She poked the mic at him.

Mom waved at O.D., but his eyes bypassed her to the cowgirl standing behind. Had Hope been watching his ride? She stared his way right now, anyway.

Better answer Tara's question. "Well, Tara. I'm obviously disappointed tonight. I let that one get away."

"Obviously Disappointed." Tara laughed, "Well. That's an unusual name, for sure. Thanks. And better luck next time." She signaled to the cameraman before they hurried off.

"Clever." Mom spoke up as she approached him. "Should we start calling you Obviously Disappointed instead of Orville Dewayne?"

"Huh?" Oh no. What had Tara asked him? "I thought she said. 'How are you feeling?' Maybe we can reshoot that." Tara's blonde hair bobbed under her cowboy hat as she ran toward the group of bull riders. And Hope was gone too.

"That's my boy. Charming and witty without even trying. I

am so glad to have all three of my sons back together tonight." Mom took his arm to grin at him from eye level. O.D. wished once more that his mom had to look up at him. Oh well, that's the hand he'd been dealt—no profit in wishing to be taller.

"Hey, Squirt." Only John K. could get away with calling him that. "Ready to go grab some arena food? Are they still loading the nachos with jalapeños?"

"Probably, but there's also a food truck outside with some barbecue. If we go now, we might get ahead of the line." O.D. didn't have to think this one over. He was famished.

"Where's the Marshall?" John K. draped his arm around his mom's shoulders.

"Right here!" Cody ran up from somewhere to their right. "But you know I never eat anything before my bull ride. If I do—"

"Whoa, whoa. Spare us the gory details." John K. laughed. "You've got time to walk out to the midway for a minute, right? We'll be back before the barrel racing is over."

O.D. followed the crew through the open barn door of the arena, waving his arm band at the usher who stood there. His brothers were in a great mood. Dad lit up like he must have when each of them was born. Bursting with pride, ready to pass out cigars at the return of the hero soldier. O.D. had stopped trying to make his dad smile like that.

"Come on, Marshall Cody. You can watch while I eat." Dad tousled Cody's hair, pulled him up to the front of the group.

John K. kissed the top of their mom's head, lagging back next to O.D.

"Hey, did y'all hear?" Dad stopped as he passed the ticket booth. "John K. is going to be the new general manager of the dealership when Harold retires next month. The Billings Boys ride again!"

"Hey, great! Way to go, John K.!" Cody high-fived his oldest brother, then hugged his mom. He linked arms with both parents. They were off again.

"Not happening." John K. leaned in close to O.D.'s ear while waving at the three in front.

"What?" O.D. stopped, grabbing his brother's arm.

"I don't plan to be the general manager of anything right now. Save me, little bro!" He slapped O.D.'s back, then ran to catch up with the group.

O.D. trudged toward the food trucks. John K. didn't intend to help their dad at the truck dealership? He shook his head with disbelief. That was all Dad had talked about for eighteen months. *When John K. gets home, we'll do this. When John K. gets home, we'll try that.* Always 'when,' never 'if.' John K. bugging out on their dad would kill him.

O.D. tried to ignore the buzz John K. created outside the food trucks as the whole community recognized him.

"He was missing in action for a couple of months."

"He's so handsome. And that little brother of his. Wow. What a bull-rider."

Just once, O.D. wanted to overhear something about the middle brother, the calf roper.

"Hey, O.D.," Dad called at him from the lemonade line. "If you're standing in line for nachos, get me some with extra peppers. I'll buy you a lemonade."

Well, what do you know? Sometimes, Dave Billings did remember there were three sons in the family.

"Sure." He peeked back to see Cody holding court with a gaggle of giggling girls.

When he reached the spot John K. found at the picnic table, he traded Dad his nachos for the offered lemonade. Might as well settle in for a minute.

The family chattered as they ate until Cody reminded them that he needed to get back to check on his bull before his upcoming ride. O.D. ferried their empty containers to the trash can and moved to the rear of the line again as they returned to the arena.

He stopped just before his parents headed up to the grandstand, spotting a familiar honey-brown braid peeking out from a well-worn baseball cap turned backward.

"Go, go, go!" O.D. was surprised at the volume that came out of Hope's mouth when she encouraged her sister. He moved up to stand near the rail next to her.

Faith and Belle moved as one, leaning oh-so-close to the first barrel, staying upright just long enough to pick up speed on the way to the second, followed by the third. As they turned the final corner to head back, he marveled again at the graceful strength of the oldest Caldwell girl. She was such a natural at this sport.

"She did great." He smiled at Hope, who was checking the time displayed in the center of the arena.

"Yeah. But she came close to knocking that last barrel over. There is such a thing as overconfidence." Hope stood back from the railing to turn toward him.

The last barrel racer swooshed past them. Wow, those girls were fast. But not fast enough. Faith's score would hold. She would be the winner once again.

"Well, I'd better go check on my brother. He drew a mean bull tonight." He touched her shoulder.

"I'll be praying. That's what I always do during the bull riding. I figure it's just a matter of time before Cody talks Junior into starting that too." Hope's eyes focused on her younger brother clowning between events.

"Thanks for the prayers. I hope y'all will drop by tonight. Mom has quite a shindig planned for John K." A strange man stood over the bull pens. His brand-new ten-gallon hat and newly pressed shirt stuck out at the little family rodeo.

"We'll be there. But we may not stay long." Hope spoke over her shoulder as she walked away.

"Come on, Little Dee. Cody's riding first." John K. nudged O.D. before he hurried toward the gates where snorting bulls waited to be led to the loading chutes.

"First? Oh great. Well, best to get it over with." O.D. ran along behind. Any chance his brother might stop calling him 'Little Dee' or 'Squirt'? Probably not. He arrived at the chute just in time to hear Mr. Caldwell's lead-in intro.

"Ladies and gentlemen, now it's time for the most-anticipated event of the evening. The young men you're about to watch have been practicing, watching, analyzing for most of their young lives. But nothing can ever prepare them for this little eight-second ride."

The crowd whispered to each other. A low rumble began as the music grew louder. Cowboys with prodding sticks guided the bulls into the chutes, where young men with either cowboy hats or helmets climbed the metal gates to prepare for their turn to mount the huge animals. Some joked with the other cowboys, some kept their eyes glued to the bulls, trying to get an idea of how they would move when the gates burst open.

"Hey, Dee. Over here." Cody perched on top of a chute, adjusting his riding glove. "I've got Kemosabi tonight."

"Great. You know he hasn't been ridden this season." O.D. tried not to sound nervous, but he once more wished his little brother had taken up a different sport, like lacrosse, or better yet, chess.

He perched on top of a metal gate. The mixture of manure, hay, and sweat filled his nostrils. His leg muscles tightened as the gate rocked with each bump from the angry creature that filled up most of the narrow space below them.

"Looks like a good tight wrap." John K. nodded at Cody as he settled in on the massive animal.

"Okay, ladies and gents." Smiley Caldwell's voice blared through the speakers. "Here is our first contestant, the youngest of the Billings Boys. Cody has some big boots to fill, with the family's favorite soldier returning tonight and calf-roping brother O.D. cheering him on. I think you'll see he's up to the challenge."

The crowd cheered. O.D. allowed John K. to do the last-minute reassuring. Cody visibly relaxed. His baby brother glanced O.D.'s way before nodding to the judge.

"Here comes Cody on Kemosabi!" The raucous rock music exploded as the gate opened. The lumbering giant barreled out.

John K. slapped O.D.'s arm. "He looks great!"

O.D. never could talk while Cody was riding. He stared as the hulking black bull jumped to the left, began to circle, then abruptly turned right.

That sudden unplanned move unseated Cody. He hadn't even made it to three seconds before he hit the ground hard, flat on his back. He stayed down only milliseconds, yet it seemed like hours to O.D. When he finally popped up, O.D. released the breath he had been holding.

Junior Caldwell with Shorty, the veteran bull-fighter, waved in the bull's face, allowing Cody to scramble to the safety of the metal stock pen next to the chute.

O.D. glanced toward his family's usual seats to glimpse the relief in their faces. One more bullet dodged. Of course, he wished Cody could have stayed aboard for the full eight seconds but making it out in one piece was a victory in itself.

"Well, horse hockey." John K. jumped down behind the gate after the bull ran out. "I thought he could ride better than that."

Cody stalked out of the arena with John K. on his heels.

O.D. started to follow but spied Hope talking to Faith under the stairway. He meandered closer.

"But can he do that?" Faith had never been any good at whispering.

"Not without Dad's buy-in." Hope nodded in O.D.'s direction. "But who wants to tell Dad his only brother is scheming behind his back?"

"Sounds serious." O.D. leaned in to listen.

"Have you seen that fancy-dressed dude hanging around?" Hope peered behind her.

"Yeah. I guess it takes all kinds." O.D. recognized concern in her voice.

"We've seen our Uncle Dub talking to him. Think he wants to buy our rodeo." Hope readjusted her baseball cap. "After losing Mom, that would probably just finish Dad off."

"Well, I'm sure it can't happen that easily. If your dad doesn't want to sell, it won't happen." He wished he was confident as he sounded. "We'll talk more at John K.'s party. I'll bet there is some way to stop this."

What right did he have to reassure them? He had enough to worry about with his own family.

"No score for Cody. Hang on tight, y'all. We have another mean bull under another determined cowboy in the chutes." Smiley was in his element. "You ready, Shorty? Junior?"

"We're set, boss." Shorty waved toward the reviewing stand.

"Ready!" Junior popped up out of the barrel in the center of the arena, then ducked back down. The crowd showed their approval with enthusiastic applause.

Yes, this whole experience was worth saving. He would just have to find a way to help the Caldwell sisters put a stop to their uncle's plans.

4

After Hope got the horses settled for the night, the drive to the Billings place did not excite her. Since their land adjoined at the back, it would have been quicker to saddle up to ride over. But here they were in Mom's SUV, on the dark, bumpy road. Dad's performance swagger was gone. His head rested against the passenger window. He had given in to exhaustion.

Funny how even the horses sensed the family's down mood. Champ had been happy to see her. He always enjoyed his brushing. But since Belle was still charged up after her barrel racing night, it took a bit to get the stall-mates calmed down. Hope understood. None of them were quite sure how to act these days.

"Thanks for driving, Punkin." Dad straightened up in his seat. "You know I need this recovery period after every show."

"Sure, Dad." Hope spotted a flickering white tail dart into the woods just past the driver-side ditch. She peeked to the right to be sure the deer's buddy would not follow.

"It was tough without your mom, but we did it." Dad

27

reached over to pat her leg. "Thanks for stepping up. Don't know what we'd do without you."

Hope nodded. Yes, good old reliable Hope. Tonight, she would have enjoyed nothing more than a hot bath before sitting on the back porch in the moonlight until sleep overtook her.

"So Faith and Junior are already at the Billingses'?"

"Yes, sir." Hope's thoughts flickered back to the stranger Uncle Dub talked to at the rodeo. What might be going on with them while the rest of the Caldwells enjoyed this party?

"These Billings folks are good people. Good to have neighbors who care." Dad tilted his hat over his face, sank back into the seat. "Yep. Good people."

He might begin snoring in a minute. There were another five minutes on this dark road before the turn-off to the Billings ranch. Dad would rouse easily. Let him rest.

"Let me rest!" Her mom's shrill cry echoed in Hope's head, as if it had been tonight, instead of more than a month ago.

"You want me to leave?" Hope stood up to leave the bedside.

"No, honey. I'm sorry. I was talking to God." Mom quieted a little. "Hope, what did I do to deserve this? Why is He making me suffer?"

"I don't think you did anything wrong. Should I get you another pill?" Why didn't the medicine make her mom sleep like it was supposed to?

"They won't let me have any more medicine. They don't want me to overdose." Her wry laugh sounded like a Halloween witch. "I'm going to die, but no one wants it to happen on their watch."

"Almost there," Dad's voice brought Hope back to the dark road.

"Yep." She slammed her brakes to veer into the wide gravel driveway. "Sorry, Dad."

"Hey. I should have driven. We have depended on you too much lately." He ran his hand through what was left of his flaxen hair. "We won't stay long, I promise."

Hope checked the rear-view mirror to see if her eyes were red. Not too bad. If only she could keep the memory of those terrible last days with her mom at bay until she was home in her own room.

———

"Hey, there they are." O.D. bounded out through the attached garage to shake Smiley's hand. "Great to hear your voice in the announcer's stand tonight."

"So good to be back, young man. So good." Smiley reached around him for a solid hug. If he was just putting up a front, he was a terrific actor. This guy must be made of steel.

"Hope, glad y'all came." He reached out toward Hope, pulling her closer. "John K. will be happy to see all of you."

"Looks like quite a crowd." Hope pointed toward the assortment of vehicles that lined the driveway. "The whole community of Crossroads is so proud of your brother."

"Thanks. We think he's pretty special too." O.D. held the door to their mud-room open.

"So, are things as bad over there as they look on television?" One of the neighbors had John K. cornered next to the mantle in the family room.

"Well, I don't know what you've been seeing. It's just a primitive country. Folks are trying hard to keep their families alive." John K. slid away toward Smiley, holding his hand out. "Mr. Caldwell, so glad you came. I'm sorry I didn't get to tell Miss Catherine goodbye. She was one of my favorites."

"You were one of hers, son." Smiley clasped John K's hand. "She loved all of you boys like her own."

O.D. couldn't help smiling. Miss Catherine had been one of the few who put up with all three of the Billings boys. Most everybody else honed in on John K. the football star or Cody the bull rider. But Hope's mom loved to talk to all of them. All at once or one at a time, she never tired of hearing about their latest adventures.

Guests hung on John K.'s every word. Mom had the supply of snacks under control. Once more, O.D. was a fifth wheel. Was the wind whipping up outside?

He reached into an ice chest for three root beers.

"Faith, Hope, want to go out to the fire pit?" The girls grabbed the offered bottles, following him out the back door.

Faith stood near the fire while Hope sank into a nearby patio chair.

"Kind of noisy in there." O.D. gestured toward the family room with his thumb.

"Wherever our brothers hang out, it's noisy." Faith laughed, sipping her root beer.

Hope fiddled with her bottlecap. "I'm probably not very good company. It's been a long night."

O.D. glanced back inside. John K. stood in front of the fireplace, not looking any more comfortable than the rest of them. Mom's heart was in the right place, but maybe this party was not a great idea.

"So, Hope. Tell me what Uncle Dub said to that stranger tonight." Faith sat in a wicker chair near her sister.

"O.D. probably doesn't want to hear that." Hope stared into her bottle.

"No. That's okay." O.D had to admit he was a little curious too.

"Well, Uncle Dub said he and Aunt Tina would be willing

to talk about selling, but Dad probably wasn't ready so soon after Mom died." Hope's voice was so quiet, O.D. leaned closer.

"Of course not." Faith stood up. "And he might never be ready."

"We can't let that happen. But I don't know how we can stop it." Hope said.

"The rodeo has a board, right? They would have to approve something like that." O.D. said, moving closer to the girls.

"Sure. But gate receipts are down, and the bills are still piling up. Uncle Dub might be able to convince them pretty easily." Hope stood up to glance out toward their SUV.

"Well, we just have to get attendance up, then." Faith downed the rest of her root beer.

"Tara Williams from KRVA was there tonight." O.D. stood facing the girls. "Maybe we can find out how to get you two a spot on her noon-time program sometime to promote the rodeo."

"You think you could get them to talk about us on television?" Hope's eyes hinted at a sparkle.

"Yeah, they are all about promoting local events." O.D. winked at her.

"We've got to do something. What would Dad do if it weren't for the rodeo?" Faith said.

"It's not just about Dad." Hope moved closer to Faith. "It's a great event for the community. Parents feel safe bringing their kids there. We grew up there. It needs to be around for the next generation too."

"Okay. I will talk to Tara for you. You can repeat what you just said for the world to hear. Folks will come down there in droves. Then your uncle will not be worried about selling it." O.D. wasn't sure it would be that easy, but it sounded good.

"Me?" Hope turned to face him. "No. You are the one that

can do the talking. You're the celebrity in this bunch, Mr. Hot Shot calf roper."

"Yeah!" Faith stood on the other side, flashing her famous blue eyes his way. What a team these two were.

"But just doing a segment on the news about the rodeo won't be enough. There needs to be something in it for the fans." Hope paced at the edge of the patio.

"Like a contest or a drawing?" Faith chimed in.

"Yeah. Maybe if you could get your dad to give away a truck." Hope's voice gained volume with each word.

"A truck?" He stopped looking at the clouds racing past the stars to face the girls. What was he getting into? Would his dad buy into this craziness? "Maybe now that John K. is back to help Dad with the dealership, I might have some extra time. I'll see what I can do." He could drive the Save the Caldwell Rodeo bus for a while, especially if these two pretty neighbor girls were along for the ride.

John K. burst out of the back door, tossing his truck keys up and catching them. "Great party, bro. Ladies, thanks for the real Crossroads welcome!" He sprinted toward Dad's shop, where his vintage pickup was parked.

"Where are you going?" O.D. started after him.

"Last I checked, I only have one daddy. I already told him I was leaving. Gave Mom a peck on the cheek while I was at it. Don't wait up, Squirt." John K. had already reached the cab of the old green GMC and cranked it to life.

"We need to get Dad home." Hope elbowed Faith. "He's liable to fall asleep standing up."

"Yeah. Let's go find Miss Felicia to say goodbye. Thanks so much for inviting us, Dee." Faith dropped her root beer bottle in a nearby trashcan.

"You're welcome. Sorry the guest of honor left in such a hurry." He rolled his empty bottle between his hands.

"Hey, this is probably pretty overwhelming for him." Hope glanced in the direction of the pickup that was kicking up gravel as it left the driveway.

"Yeah, but did he lose all of his social skills while he was gone?" He immediately wished he hadn't said that. The Caldwells didn't need any of his family's drama to add to their own. "So. I'll call Tara tomorrow, then talk to my dad. I know he'll want to help. The Caldwells have always been able to count on the Billings Boys, right?" He launched his empty bottle to the trash can, following with a little fist pump as it clanged against the others.

"Yeah. We really appreciate it. We won't let our whole life go down the tubes." Hope followed Faith back inside the house. "Thanks so much for agreeing to help us."

The girls found their dad, then rounded up Junior. What in the world had he just promised to do? Had Dad ever listened to any of his ideas? Maybe he should ask John K. or Cody to make the proposal. Then the idea would sail through with no problem.

Nope. This was all him. For once, he would take on something important and see it through.

A cool breeze tickled the hair on the back of his neck. Staring after his older brother never benefited him. He headed out to see his horse. When all else failed, he could always talk to Buck.

———

O.D. settled the full sack of assorted biscuit sandwiches in the passenger side of his truck. The aroma filled his nostrils. His stomach growled. As the local television station passed on his right, he thought of the promise he'd made to the Caldwell girls. He pressed the handy voice recognition button on his steering wheel. "Call Tara."

"What's up, buddy?" Tara answered quickly.

"I need a favor." He spent the rest of the drive home filling his friend in on their idea without mentioning the threat of a buyout. Not his part of the story to tell.

"But how can I convince Dad to go for this?" O.D. stopped his truck in his usual spot near the stairs leading to his apartment.

"Remember our communication class in high school? Emphasize what the Billings Boys will get out of this. Improved image in the community, spotlight on family, all that stuff."

"Okay. Thanks for being my sounding board. I'll tell the girls we have a date for their big television debut." O.D. gathered up the sack before opening his truck door.

"Sure. See ya down the road." Tara disconnected.

5

Hope skidded Mom's SUV to a stop near the barn. She didn't regret staying late this evening to catch up on the bookwork at the arena, but she had to wonder if Junior had done his chores. She flipped the light on in the barn to find the two stall-mates all settled for the night. That little brother of hers was not completely useless. As she left the barn, Aunt Tina stepped out of the passenger side of their black Cadillac Escalade. Had Faith expected to host family for dinner tonight? What if this was a business visit? Was Uncle Dub here to talk to Dad about the rodeo?

The sun dipped behind their house, turning jet trails into pink cotton candy. She inhaled a deep breath of the crisp air. If only she could pitch a tent for the night. The moon was rising behind her; it would be cold soon. If she built a good fire, her sleeping bag would keep her warm. No, she'd better go in.

Inside the back door, she hung her shoulder bag on a hook. Her mom had done such a great job on this hall tree. Baskets for each one of them with their initials. A place for everything and everything in its place. She could still hear Mom telling Junior, "*It only works when you use it, son.*"

"Hi, Hope!" Kayla greeted her from in front of the fireplace.

"Hey, Kayla." She walked over to wrap her cousin in a quick hug. "Are y'all here for supper?"

"No. We went to Ross's steakhouse tonight. Dad said he needed to talk to Uncle Smiley about something." She walked toward the kitchen. "Looks like Faith put on quite a spread, though."

"Just a taco bar. Oh, and tamales." Faith ran a dishrag across the granite countertop. "It's still hot, Hope. You can fix whatever you want."

"Hey, Smiley." Dub stood near the front door with a cup of coffee. "Join me on the porch?""

Hope needed to jump in. This would be the "talk" about selling.

"Hi, Uncle Dub. I got the bills caught up tonight at the office. The gate receipts are looking good." How could she stop their conversation?

"Good. We're grateful you're back to take over the office." Dub raised his eyebrows toward Dad, then opened the front door.

A text alert caught her eye—a message from O.D.

Talked to my dad and the TV station about the contest. Can you and Faith meet me for lunch tomorrow?

Sure.

How about 12:30 at Amy Lou's?

Sounds fine. C Ya.

She took two long steps to reach Faith next to the kitchen sink to show her the text. Faith's face reflected Hope's concern about Uncle Dub talking to Dad.

"Change the subject." She whispered, standing directly in front of her sister.

"Hey, Uncle Dub. Could you and Dad come with me to take a quick peek at Champ?" Faith dried her hands on a kitchen towel. She headed to the back door.

Hope nodded. If anyone could change the direction of a conversation, Faith the barrel racer was the best.

"He stumbled this evening as I was working him out. Sort of has me worried about that right front leg." Faith grabbed her jacket, heading out back without waiting for a response.

"I won't be long, honey." Uncle Dub patted Aunt Tina's shoulder.

Mention anything about a horse or one of his prize bulls, and Uncle Dub the stock contractor was right on it. Faith was a pro at turning on a dime.

"Hey, Kayla. Looks like Junior left a tamale or two over here in the kitchen." Hope placed one on her plate. "Want to help me take care of this problem?" For all of her fashion model ways, her cousin could definitely eat. Hope smothered the tamale in chili sauce, sprinkling grated cheese on top.

"Speaking of Junior," Dad opened the back door, "where is that everlasting pain in my side?"

"He said something about a noise in your truck's rear end." A little white lie wouldn't hurt. Maybe Hope was getting the hang of this subject changing.

"Oh no. Dub, you know we can't have Junior tinkering with machinery." Dad put his cowboy hat on his head on his way out the door.

Crisis averted. Hope re-read O.D.'s message. This Billings boy did have a knack for turning up at just the right time.

Hopefully, he'd have a plan for them tomorrow. Her poor brain couldn't handle much more stress.

———

Jangling bells announced O.D.'s grand entrance through the glass door at Amy Lou's Diner. Without his trademark cowboy hat, not to mention those silly shorts he wore for his job, Hope almost didn't recognize him.

"Sorry, ladies." He scooted into the wooden bench across the table from them. "I had to change the order of my deliveries to end up here instead of at the edge of town."

"We haven't been here long." Faith put another lemon wedge in her glass of water.

"Okay, here's a salad with grilled chicken and a chili cheeseburger with rings." O.D.'s Aunt Candace placed the dishes in front of them, reaching for her pad. "You want regular fries or Cajun with that double cheeseburger, Mr. Billings?"

"Cajun today. Thanks, Ann-Ann. Oh, hold the onions." O.D. winked at Faith. "To keep my dragon breath at bay." Candace shook her head before walking away.

"Here, Prince Dragon-slayer, have an onion ring while you wait. You are more like yourself with onion breath." Hope used her fork to hand him one. What a blowhard.

"I thought you'd never ask." After a quick bite, he cleared his throat. "So, how are things in Caldwell land?"

"Kind of good, as long as we all stay out of Dad's way. He's a whirlwind. Mowing, painting, tending to animals. The ranch has never been more spic and span." Hope used her knife to cut a manageable bite of her messy cheeseburger. "But we think it's just a cover. He's struggling most of the time when he's not at the rodeo."

"So, what did your dad say about the contest?" Faith opened a pack of crackers.

"He's all for it, with conditions." O.D. tucked a slice of tomato into his burger.

"Like what?" Hope wiped her mouth with a napkin.

"He said he wants the folks to buy tickets, with the money going to charity, instead of giving a truck away for free. I suggested we trade the winner title for title with whatever they have been driving, so no money changes hands. He can promote our previously-owned lot too." O.D. waved in his aunt's direction. She brought him a large glass of his favorite soda.

"He's okay with giving away a brand-new truck?" Faith laid her fork down.

"Wow! That is so cool!" Hope sat up straighter. O.D. had accomplished a lot in his conversation with his dad.

"He'll pick the one to give away, but it'll be a good one. He's hoping it will get people to come out to look at the others on the lot. We'll sell the chances at the dealership. Do y'all have an idea of a good charity?"

"The local cancer society?" Faith locked sad eyes with Hope. "Or what was that place you and Mom used to volunteer for?"

"Cedar Ridge." Hope's cheeks flushed. Perfect. She remembered the smiles of the kids who were riding a horse for the first time or the older ones who never thought they'd be able to ride again after an accident.

"There you go." O.D. gave Hope a thumbs up. "That's a great place. Folks could buy tickets for the drawing at the dealership or Cedar Ridge, but they have to be at the rodeo on the night of the giveaway." He counted on his fingers. "Helps a great charity, advertises for the Billings Boys, increases attendance at the rodeo."

Hope's mind was reeling. Could they do this? Faith and O.D. waited on her response. "Sure. Let's go for it."

"Okay. Then Tara will put you two on her morning show next Tuesday. We can try to have everything ready for the first entries at your Friday night rodeo." O.D. snagged another onion ring from Hope's plate.

The bells on the front door jangled again. Heads turned to watch the newest customers enter the diner. Hope glanced down as she poked Faith's side. "It's Uncle Dub with that stranger from the other night." Why hadn't they settled into a table in the back? There was no hiding in this booth near the entrance.

"Hi, Uncle Dub." Faith was good at meeting trouble head-on.

"Hello, girls. Billings." Uncle Dub led the way as the stranger tipped his too-clean cowboy hat in their direction. They headed toward the back of the crowded diner.

"Who do you think that guy is?" Faith tried her much too loud stage whisper again.

"Just keep your ears open. This place is already buzzing." Hope sat against the wall, facing sideways.

Candace walked over and placed their ticket on the table.

"It's just hard to get used to having that casino owner in here." She muttered to herself.

"Casino owner?" O.D. asked.

"Yeah. Imagine. Up until a few years ago, you couldn't even buy beer in this county."

O.D. grinned.

"Well, not legally. Then, they passed a law legalizing medical marijuana. Now one to allow gambling. Our grandparents are flipping over in their graves." She shook her head as she walked away.

"So, why would a casino owner want our rodeo?" Faith leaned closer to O.D.

"They have all kinds of entertainment at those places. Concerts, bull riding. Maybe he's planning to build his own arena or just use yours." O.D. pulled out his wallet.

"Well. We can't wait any longer. We have to talk to Dad." Hope used her last onion ring to scoop up the leftover chili on her plate.

"You're going to tell him what Dub is planning?" O.D. leaned to the left, watching the two men all the way to their table.

"No. We don't know what he is planning. I mean, we should tell Dad about your truck giveaway. We need to get him excited. Sounds like a job for you, Faith." Hope turned around in her seat again.

"We'll do it together." Faith scooted toward the edge of the booth. "Dee, do you want to come over tonight to help us talk to him?"

"Oh, no. I'll just stick to my own Dad. Text me. Let me know what he says." He placed some money on the table. "I'll take care of buying your lunch today, partners."

"Partners?" Hope stood up.

"Sounds better than co-conspirators." O.D. walked them to the door.

She searched the back of the diner to find her uncle and the casino owner with their heads together over coffee. Would this idea of theirs do any good?

Hope pulled her denim jacket closer before heading toward her truck. Was this a good time to start a big promotion, just before the coming holidays? They'd have to play up the idea of helping Cedar Ridge. Small-town hearts would flip over cute kids riding horses.

She slid behind the steering wheel to head the SUV down

the main street of Crossroads but decided to turn left instead of going toward the arena. Since this was the off week for the rodeo, there wasn't much happening at the office. She pulled into the gas station. Pumping fuel inspired her to enjoy the bright sunshine and just drive.

Hope realized that the next road turning to the left would take her to the cemetery. She had not been there since right after Mom passed away. The raucous music coming from the radio speakers was out of place, so she switched it off, traveling the rest of the way in silence. She remembered how much her mom had loved this spot, how they used to come here to decorate her great-grandparents' graves.

A cloud blocked the sun for just a moment, then moved away as Hope's SUV entered the gate at the side of the cemetery. She stepped out, inhaling the cool briskness before walking toward the little mound of fresh earth in front of a standing wreath of faded flowers.

The November breeze blew some dry leaves across the toe of her boot. Hope stared at the headstone. Mom had refused to let Dad buy a double marker. "You still have a lot of life ahead. Who knows if you might marry again? Would your new wife want you to be next to me?" They were used to Mom's practical attitude, but how did that decision affect her dad's heart?

The smell of damp leaves and decaying blooms assaulted her nose. Hope closed her eyes. She was back in the guest room that had been turned into a hospice for Mom.

"I'm glad you're here." Mom's voice was unnatural that day. "Hope, I have something very important to ask of you."

"Sure, Mom. Can I get you another pillow, something to eat?" Hope was tired after spending the day helping Dad fix the corral.

"No!" she shouted. Her eyes were wild. "No more ice cream, no more magazines. I have been waiting until you were the only one in the house, because you are the strongest. You will help me."

"What do you want?" Hope's voice shook.

"You know where your dad keeps his guns. Go, get one. A big one."

"Mom!"

"I can't take another minute of this pain. Surely you can understand that. If you bring the gun, hand it to me, I might have enough strength left to pull the trigger. Please, Hope. Please. Go. Get. Dad's. Gun."

Hope backed out of the bedroom. "No, Mom. No!"

"Why not? You have helped me take our old dogs to the vet for that last merciful shot. Even valuable racehorses get put out of their misery. Why will you not help me get this horrible pain over with? Why, oh why?" She wailed then, long and loud.

"Mom. I will bring you some more medicine. There must be something that will help." Hope was afraid to move closer. Her mom was trying so hard to get out of the bed. She might grab Hope if she came close enough.

"You don't love me. Not really. If you did, you would help me go home to see Jesus. No one here loves me as much as they love an old dog or a horse. Oh God, please take me, now." Mom sobbed until she finally became weak from the shouting. Hope still couldn't go any closer.

She should have called Dad away from his rancher's association meeting, but she didn't want him to see her mom like this. She stayed in the living room listening as Mom cried. Gradually, the latest dose of medicine made her sleepy, and she became still. Hope peered into the room before collapsing shakily on the couch, waiting for Faith to come back so she could head to the barn for a long ride.

Hope sat on the cold, damp ground in front of the headstone. Mom was at peace now. But the memory of that terrible day would not leave. Every time she had been at Mom's bedside after that, there had been an unspoken plea, a look of disappointment. Hope had been very good at providing meaningless things to ease her mom's suffering. But she couldn't give her what she wanted most. Not that.

The wind whipped through the cedar trees that surrounded the cemetery. A new dampness settled on Hope's eyelashes. There was no peace in this place. Not for her. She ran to her truck. She didn't care if she ever came back here again.

She waited until the engine ran long enough to warm the air that poured out of the heater vents. A paper napkin from the glove box wiped away random tears. Why couldn't she shake that memory? Everyone else in the family was moving on. Most of them thought she had too. They didn't know she had failed her mother when she needed her most.

God, I am sorry. So sorry I couldn't help Mom. I should have been able to quote from Your Word, pray with her, bring her some measure of peace. I failed. Now, please help me move on. She blinked back tears, then threw the truck into Drive.

6

"Hey look, it's the president!"

O.D. slid into the smoky bar behind John K.

"John Kennedy Billings." The loud guy in the red baseball hat made sure he had everyone's attention. "And his calf-ropin' security detail."

"Hey, guys." The bartender had a drink poured before John K. reached his leaning spot. "What about you?" He turned toward O.D.

"Make it a virgin lemonade, Joe. He's my driver."

O.D. picked up the cold glass, following his brother to a booth near the pool table. The three men went quiet as they approached.

"Johnny." One muttered. "How's it going?"

"Hey, man. Can't complain." John K. sat next to him. "You know my little brother, right?"

"Oh yeah. Not the bull-rider. The other one." This from a linebacker-sized blonde guy on the other side of the booth.

O.D stood next to the table. Yeah, the other one. He didn't

feel he had been invited to sit. "I'll just walk around a little, John K. Be back in a minute."

What was it that turned him off about this place? The smoke? That was a big part of it. The music was loud, but he liked music. The guys who kept bumping his arm, sloshing his lemonade and their own drinks all over everywhere? He just didn't enjoy it like a lot of his friends did. Like his Grandpa Dee said—not all wrong, just unnecessary.

He walked over to the old-fashioned jukebox, flipping through the selections. There were quite a few good tunes here. He dug in his pocket to find some quarters. Maybe some lively music would improve his mood.

Two girls came out of the restroom nearby. One had black streaks of mascara running from her puffy eyes. The other was comforting her. Long, dark hair covered their bare shoulders. Their clothes were too small, even for their tiny bodies.

"It will be okay. I promise," the comforter was saying.

"I don't know how," the younger one said. She made eye contact as O.D. put coins in the jukebox. She shuffled through the crowd to the door, pushing her friend away.

After O.D. finished choosing some songs, he walked toward the booth, where his brother was laughing with his friends.

"Hey, John. Are you about ready to go home?" O.D. stood next to the smoke-filled booth.

"What? Oh yeah. I guess it's past your curfew." The table erupted at John K.'s joke.

He should have expected that. He'd been tagging along after his brother for years. But yes, morning would come early. This was not his idea of fun.

"Hey, just take my truck and go whenever you are ready." John K. tossed the keys to O.D. "Will one of you ne'er-do-wells make sure I get back to the Billings Ponderosa?"

"Hey, I've got your back, bro." Linebacker high-fived John K.

"Okay." O.D. stuffed the keys down in his pocket, making his way through the thinning crowd to the door of the bar. He gave the bartender a five-dollar bill, more than covering the cost of his lemonade.

The cool night air splashed his face as he walked toward the old GMC. Even with temperatures nearing freezing, he could breathe much easier out here.

The truck obediently roared to life. O.D. pulled the lever to turn on the headlamps. Dim dashboard light illuminated the bench seat. He jumped as a shadowy figure leaned against the passenger side door.

"Mmmpph." The shadow stretched and sat upright. O.D. slammed on the brakes.

"What, who?" He couldn't even form a proper question.

The dark-eyed girl he'd seen crying inside scooted closer to him on the bench seat.

"Sorry. I just needed a warm place to sit for a minute." She shivered as she held her bare shoulders with her red hands.

"Don't you have a coat?" O.D. moved closer to the driver's side door.

"No. I think I left it somewhere." She sniffed, then snuggled closer. "Please don't make me get out. I'm so cold." Her eyes closed, she settled under his right arm.

Oh no. What in the world would he do? Who was she? Where did she belong?

"Wake up. Come on." He pushed her away, but she collapsed on the seat. She had either been drinking or was on drugs. He found her shoulder bag in the floorboard. Maybe there was ID in there. Did he have the right to search through her stuff? Maybe he should go back inside. Maybe John K. would help.

"What? A girl? Do you have any idea what to do with a girl?" He could just hear the reaction. What great fun that table full of fools would have with this.

He picked up his cell phone, imagining another conversation.

"Nine-one-one, what is your emergency?"

"Yeah. I found someone in my brother's truck."

"Okay, sir. We need more information. Is this person breathing? Do you need an ambulance?"

He tried poking her once more, but she just nuzzled closer.

"Hey, wake up!"

She roused, staring at him with fear in her eyes.

"Don't hurt me, please." She moved nearer to the passenger door again but didn't get out of the truck. "Please don't leave me out there. It's so cold."

"Here," O.D. removed his camouflaged jacket and placed it around her shoulders. She slipped her arms through the sleeves, sinking back into the seat again and closing her eyes. Then, sitting bolt upright, she opened the door and leaned out. "I don't feel so good."

Oh no. Now what? O.D. waited. He was grateful when she closed the door without getting any of her mess inside John K.'s truck.

"I'll be okay now. I just need to sleep."

"Tell me where you live, and I'll take you home."

"No. You can't do that. My dad is going to be so mad. I don't know what he will do." She was pleading again. "I know you. You are a strong, brave soldier. Just let me sit in your truck and rest. I won't cause any trouble over here." Her eyes closed again.

Of course. She had confused him with his brother. All the more reason John K. should be dealing with this, not him.

The door to the bar busted open, and four guys stumbled out.

"Come on, Mr. President. Let's go find some action somewhere. This place is getting on my nerves." The loudmouth in John K.'s group pushed O.D.'s brother into the back seat of a modified hearse. The others piled in, laughing. Mr. Linebacker took the wheel.

"Hey!" O.D. stepped out of the driver's side of the truck. Just that quick, the hearse took off, slinging gravel from the lot on its way to the highway. Now what?

The girl snored peacefully, her small bag wedged between her knees. Well, so much for trying to ID her. He started the truck, then found his cellphone on the dashboard.

O.D. nudged the sleeping form. She certainly was a snuggler. Wow. What some guys with fewer scruples wouldn't give for an opportunity like this. All he could think of was finding somewhere safe to drop her off.

———

The girl never flinched when he turned off the engine. He stepped out to meet Aunt Candace as she crossed the concrete parking lot. He didn't want to park next to the huge plate glass window. No sense providing dinner or breakfast entertainment for the customers.

"Okay," O.D. removed his hat, holding it in his hands. "It's like this. I went with John K. to one of his favorite hangouts. Don't ask me why. Anyway. He had another ride home. When I went out to leave in his truck, there was a girl in it."

"What? Oh, for cornbread's sake, Dee. So, she made a mistake. No biggie. Easily explained." Candace tapped her foot, pulled her sweater closer around her.

"But. She didn't know I wasn't him. Then, she passed out.

And, and ... she's still in there." He could have rehearsed this explanation a little longer.

"Where?" Aunt Candace jogged to the passenger side of the truck to peer in. "Oh no." She gently opened the door, moving forward to make sure the girl didn't tumble out. "Lissa. Melissa Escobar. Come on, rise and shine, little one."

"You know her?" O.D. stood behind her.

"Yes. Her mom used to work here. Always causing some kind of excitement. She'd be a good kid if she didn't feel the need to try the substance of the week." She pushed the girl over to crawl up into the truck seat. "Let's get back in to talk. The noses pressed against that diner window are getting kind of extreme."

O.D. walked around to climb behind the wheel.

"Lissa. Wake up, honey. Come on." She jostled the girl, trying to make her sit upright. "I think she's okay. She's just had too much of whatever it was. She needs to sleep it off. I'll call her mom and tell her to meet you at the curb. Their house isn't far from here."

"Before she went to sleep, she asked me not to take her home. Said her dad would be really mad." O.D. started the truck.

"Probably true. But he never hits anyone. Just frustrated a little bit with this wild child. Her older brother never caused this much ruckus. Or at least not that I ever heard about." Aunt Candace opened the passenger door, letting a cold, damp breeze blow in. "Here's the address." She glanced at the contacts in her phone, then scribbled something on her order pad. She tore off the page, handing it to him. "Come back for a piece of pie and a cup of coffee. You're a good man, Little Dee."

A huge sigh escaped O.D.'s lips. Ann-Ann and Little Dee. They'd been buddies a long time. She would have made an even better mom than an aunt, but that had never been in the cards. Now, with Uncle Duke gone, she was by herself. He was beyond grateful she had rescued him one more time.

O.D. took another look at the scribbled address. He navigated three or four turns before spotting a porch light, with a lady in a long bathrobe huddled on a front stoop. He jumped out and ran around to open the passenger door.

"Mmmph?" Lissa reached for him, settling on his shoulder. "G'night, sweet prince. Thanks for saving me." Before he could get out of the way, she kissed him, full on the lips. He set her on her feet in front of her mother before he stepped backward, hoping she wouldn't fall.

"Here ... I mean ... She's ... I'm ..." As Aunt Candace would say, oh for cornbread's sake. Just get this girl away from me.

"Thank you, Mr. Billings." The mom reached around Lissa's waist, guiding her toward the porch. "Melissa Elaine, you have caused enough trouble for one night. Let's see if we can get you to bed before your father wakes up."

O.D. drove back to the diner, grateful to be alone in John K.'s truck. What a crazy night. He could use some rest before going to work in the morning. But after all this, he would just stay awake staring at the ceiling if he went home. Maybe he'd take Aunt Candace up on the pie without the coffee.

He slid onto his usual stool at the counter, three down from the cash register. A man in a mechanics shirt with his name on the pocket pulled out his wallet to count the bills. A lady across from him in the booth propped up a sleepy little boy.

"Table six." He handed Aunt Candace two twenty-dollar bills. She nodded as she placed the money next to the register.

"So, coconut meringue, or pecan? Or maybe you're up for some adventure. We have a chocolate caramel pie that I hear is the bomb." She tapped her pencil on her pad.

"No more adventure. Coconut is fine. With a glass of milk

instead of coffee." O.D. leaned forward, watching the cook flip an omelet.

Aunt Candace slid O.D. his pie and a fork before taking two steps to the cash register as the man from table six approached.

"Your ticket has been taken care of, sir." She opened the drawer, placed the twenties in, counting out some change.

"What?" The man stepped back. "Who did that?"

"Just a friendly stranger. Be careful on your journey, may God bless your family." She dropped the change in a can next to the register.

"Well. If you see this stranger, tell them thanks very much." The man smiled, hugging the lady as she walked up carrying the little boy. "Goodnight, ma'am."

Aunt Candace stood in front of O.D. as he scraped the last crumbs of pie crust then drained his milk glass. "My hippie sister and her cowboy husband sure made some good kids."

"Aww shucks, ma'am." O.D. was suddenly very tired. "I think I'll just go on home. Thanks for the pie." He placed his last five-dollar bill next to his plate. If this was the way a typical night went for John K's crowd, he wasn't up to it. He'd just be an old fogey before his time.

7

Hope walked through the kitchen out the back door. Better check on Belle and Champ before supper. The conversation she'd had with Dad about the truck giveaway had gone more easily than expected. A little too easy.

"Sure. Whatever you want to do, girls." Dad was distracted as he headed for his room to change clothes. But then, that was his usual attitude these days. Better let O.D. know. She typed a quick text.

> Our dad gave the go-ahead.
> Can you or someone from the Billings Boys be at a board meeting on Thursday?

Time on Thurs?

> 1:00

K. Should work

Great. Talk to you tomorrow.

Yep.

Long-winded, wasn't he? Hope laughed. She ran the last few yards to the barn. The calendar said it was time to start wearing a coat out here, but the temperatures still took them on constant amusement park rides. Heating up, cooling off, then settling in for long spells of rain.

"Hey, girl." As she reached Belle's stall, she patted the big chestnut nose. "Mind if we take a little ride?" Hope led the horse to the tack room just inside the back door, threw the saddle blanket over her back. Years of this routine made it commonplace. They both played their parts well: Belle remaining calm, Hope adjusting with precision.

Once mounted, Hope started riding in easy circles around the perimeter of the corral. There was no use working up a sweat since the temperatures were bound to drop in just a few hours. Cool, damp air filled Hope's nostrils. A gentle breeze toyed with the loose hair around her face.

As they arrived back at the entry to the barn, she stopped to pat Belle's neck. "Good girl. Thanks for the ride." She swung her left leg over the horse's side and lowered herself to the ground. If only every task she was involved in was this easy, this natural. Instead, the promotion Faith and O.D. were concocting took her into strange territory.

———

Hope took a deep breath as she stepped out of her truck at Cedar Ridge Ranch the next morning. A hint of moisture hung in the air, mixed with the musky smell that followed horses everywhere they went. Hope remembered how much Mom had loved coming here. "Strange that on our day off from the rodeo, we spend our time around more horses, right?" That comment always made Hope laugh.

"Hey, Hope." Randy Jennings waved at her from the office door. "How's the rodeo business?"

"Can I talk to you for a minute?" Hope stepped closer.

"Sure, come on back."

Randy's tiny office was covered with photos of smiling kids on horses. Most included a happy trainer nearby. He loved bragging on all of the positive results of their work here.

"So, I have a crazy idea I want to run by you." She channeled her mom as she explained their idea for raising funds for Cedar Ridge. Mom's presentation would have emphasized larger attendance at the rodeo, more attention for this wonderful facility. A definite win-win.

"Sounds great. What do you need from us?" Randy stood as Hope finished her explanation.

"As soon as our board approves, Faith and O.D. Billings and I will start promoting the contest around town." Hope said

"Of course, we will talk it up too," Randy said. "I really appreciate y'all thinking of us, Hope."

After leaving Cedar Ridge, her truck turned almost automatically into a drive-thru burger place where they usually had her order ready before she finished repeating it. She pulled up closer to the menu board. O.D. jumped out of the driver's side of his brown delivery truck to hit the order button. It probably was hard to reach the button from the steering wheel of that monster.

"Hey!" O.D. spotted her. "Fancy meeting you here!" He waved wildly before jumping back into the driver's seat to move the truck forward.

Hope pushed the button. She recited the familiar lunch order for herself and Dad.

"Yes, ma'am. Drive around, please."

Hope pulled up to the first window with her money in her hand.

"Your order is already paid." The young man handed her the bags.

O.D. honked the horn of his big brown truck as he pulled out into traffic.

———

"Heavenly Father, first of all, thank You so much for bringing Virginia and Bill safely here from Plano. It's a long trip, so we appreciate their continued interest in this little enterprise. This is a tough day for us, with Catherine's chair empty. Help us to honor her, as well as You, with the decisions we make today. You've never steered us wrong. We trust You. Be with us now and forever. Amen."

Smiley made praying sound so natural. Hope's hand shook a bit as she picked up an ink pen. O.D, smiled at her as she opened the notepad in front of her. Maybe his presentation would cheer her up a little.

"Okay. Thanks, Hope, for preparing this agenda." Smiley passed the papers around the table.

Smiley nodded at Faith as she settled into the seat next to him. Hope squirmed in the leather chair. He tried to catch her eye again, but she was focusing on the polished table in front of her.

"O.D. Billings has come from the Billings Boys dealership to explain an idea he's been working on with my girls. I've clued Dub and Tina in, but Ginny and Bill, this may be new to you. I'm always happy when the young people show an interest in our dusty old business. I think you'll like this. O.D.?"

He squeezed behind the podium that was placed a little too

close to a blackboard at the front of the room. Just inside the door, the stranger from the rodeo removed his hat and sat in a folding metal chair. Would Hope's Uncle Dub introduce this guy later? All the more reason to make this pitch for the contest attractive to the board members.

"The rodeo is one of the oldest forms of entertainment." O.D. launched in, glancing at his notes. "Families have been enjoying it together for centuries. The Billings family has been proud to join with the Caldwells in promoting this sport to our community for as long as I can remember." He dropped easily into his after-the-ride interview patter.

"Our best sponsor." Smiley settled back in his chair.

O.D. flipped through the slides of Cedar Ridge. He also showed pictures of the gleaming new truck his dad had selected. His voice strengthened as he reached the end of his speech.

Hope drummed her pen to the Billings Boys theme music as the presentation ended. O.D. almost laughed out loud.

"So, if you approve, the Billings Boys are ready to start promoting this contest. I hope it brings tons of new people to the rodeo. It should help to continue some good work in our community."

A warm sensation filled his heart as he sat down. *Ms. Catherine? Do you approve?*

"So, this won't cost the rodeo anything?" Tina asked. Her husband kept his poker face intact.

"No, ma'am." Hope spoke up. "In fact, we hope it will generate revenue. Since the winner of the truck is selected at the rodeo and you must be present to win, we think everyone who buys a ticket will be there that night. Hopefully, they will like what they see and come back."

"Are we ready to vote?" Smiley turned toward Dub, who nodded.

"All in favor?"

A low rumble of "ayes" echoed throughout the small board room.

"Thanks, O.D. We look forward to this. It should be something the community can get behind." Smiley rolled his chair back up to the table.

"Dub, we have you down next. You have the floor."

The over-dressed stranger silently squeezed out the door to the parking lot.

"Nothing further," Dub grumbled.

Smiley shrugged his shoulders before turning to his brother. "You sure?"

"Nothing at this time." Dub sank back in his chair. His wife stroked his shoulder.

"Okay. O.D., we won't hold you up. The rest of this meeting is pretty routine. The girls will be glad to work with you on this contest idea. Be sure to give our thanks to Dave and Felicia for their unfailing generosity." Smiley shook O.D.'s hand.

"Yes, sir." O.D. placed the little zip drive he had brought into his pocket. He'd enjoyed this almost as much as gathering up a calf's legs with his best half hitch. Tipping his hat in the general direction of Hope and Faith, he opened the metal door that led to the parking lot.

"Great presentation, young man." The fancy stranger stood to his right, smoking a cigarette.

"Thanks. O.D. Billings," He offered his hand to the man.

"Quinton Heston." Not exactly a firm handshake. "Have you got just a minute?"

"Sure." What in the world could this guy want with him?

"I'm new around here. Just trying to get a feel for the community."

Strange, how the man could look right at him but at the same time focus on something else.

"It's a great place. Sometimes the folks are reluctant to leave their comfort zones, but that is to be expected, I guess." O.D. was not qualified to speak for the whole town. But he did have a feel for what the majority of his neighbors were like.

"I can tell that rodeo is an important part of things. Maybe not as much as places farther west, but still big." Heston nodded toward the board room. "Anyway, you did a good job in there. You speak well. I get the idea you could sell ice cubes to Eskimos."

"Thanks." So, he just wanted to compliment O.D. on his speech? What else was going on here? He understood why this guy was a little scary to the girls.

"Well, I think I'll go back inside for a bit. See you around town." Heston moved toward the door of the board room.

"Yep." The old saying about keeping your friends close and your enemies closer popped into O.D.'s head. He settled behind the wheel of his pickup. *No use worrying about it. Just get on with the day.*

8

O.D. chuckled as he read the text on his phone.

What time do we need to be at the television station tomorrow?

If Hope would look back at their texting thread, she would find this answer:

9:00.

Being so nervous about being in front of cameras was not a problem for him. But he understood Hope's anxiety. She spent all her time behind the scenes. Faith was the rodeo queen in the family. Truth be told, though, O.D. had always thought the younger Caldwell girl's homespun good looks were more appealing.

Okay. See you.

This was immediately followed by another text from Hope.

G'night.

He sent a thumbs up in reply.

He finished the last piece of meaty pizza he and John K. had been sharing. He had hoped to talk to his older brother about Dad's plans for the dealership tonight, but when Lissa and her pretty, dark-haired friend posted themselves in the booth next to the boys, all serious conversation had gone out the window. For the last little bit, John K's head had been huddled next to the two girls.

"Why not? That's my question." John K. stood up at the side of the table. "Everything is pretty well dead in this town. The action is happening elsewhere!"

"What's up, John K?" O.D. reached for the ticket. He took a step toward the cash register.

"We're headed to Oklahoma!" John K. pulled the older girl against him as she giggled.

"Tonight? Why?" Surely they were joking. Starting out for the next state at ten o'clock at night?

"Maria and Lissa want to go check out the casinos over there since ours is a few weeks away from opening. No time like the present. Come on, Little Dee. Let's go have some fun." John K. steered the girl in the direction of the exit.

"Wait!" O.D. caught his brother's arm. "Can I talk to you for a minute?"

"Be right, there, girls. Hey, my truck is kinda old. Did you ever drive a three on the tree?" John K. stepped back to stand next to O.D.

"A what?" The girl laughed, running ahead of John K. "Oh, yeah. A standard transmission. No problem. My dad taught me how to drive his old truck. "

Lissa stopped next to O.D. as they passed by.

"Your big brother is a lot more fun than you." She poked

him. "But I think you're cuter." She patted his arm. "Hey, wait, Maria!"

"Are you serious?" O.D. barely controlled his voice, trying not to shout until the girls were out of hearing range. "You're going across state lines with these two girls?"

John K. stepped back, scanning O.D. from his head to his boots. "Amazing. For a minute, I thought that was my daddy standing there. Listen. I am a grown man. I can do what I please. No need for you to feel responsible. If you don't want to go along, you're welcome to get in your own truck and go home to Mama. In fact, you can even tattle on me when you get there. 'John K. did something really bad'. But I am going to have some fun."

"What has gotten into you?" O.D.'s effort to be quiet was a losing battle.

"What's gotten into you?" John K. punctuated the word by poking O.D. in the chest. "You are not my guardian. Here's some cash to pay for the pizza. Now. I'm leaving. See you later," He crammed the money into O.D.'s hand, then turned to rush off, gathering up the girls who were whispering together near the outside door.

O.D. paid their bill and hurried out to his truck. How did the community see this guy as a hero? Running off in the middle of the night on a whim? Was this the leader his dad wanted for the family business?

John K.'s truck jerked out of the parking lot, the older of the two girls at the wheel, with John K. in the middle and Lissa hanging on to the passenger door. O.D. followed for a bit, then abruptly turned the steering wheel onto a dirt road. Crazy. Well, he wasn't going along. After all, the Caldwell girls were counting on him to be at the television studio at nine o'clock.

O.D.'s cheeks flamed in anger. Why did his brother's irresponsible actions bother him so much?

The signposts reminded him that a freeway entrance was getting closer. John K. was supposed to be setting an example for the younger two. What would their parents say about John K.'s plans for tonight? Just what did he have in mind? What if he and those girls started drinking, causing an accident? They couldn't be very far ahead of him. His truck could easily catch up. No need to go home to stew about this. He just needed to find John K. and talk sense into him. With no sign of the old GMC when he reached the freeway, he decided to head west. Surely, he could find them when they stopped the first time.

O.D. turned on the radio as he eased into the sparse traffic on the interstate. Nothing sounded good tonight. Rock and roll? Too crazy. Country? Too sleepy. He turned the music off again as he passed a long tractor-trailer truck. No need to give the local troopers a target for a citation. A new light illuminated near his speedometer. O.D. hit the steering wheel in frustration.

"Are you kidding? A professional truck driver starts off across the state with an empty tank?" His voice echoed in the quiet cab.

He pulled over in the right lane to slow down, allowing a couple of eighteen-wheelers to pass him. The warning light should give him a few miles of grace before the truck would shudder to a halt. Not that he deserved it.

"Thank you, Lord." He uttered his first sincere prayer in a long time when the highway sign announced a gas station at the next exit.

By the time his truck slid up to a gas pump under the brightly lit canopy, a beeping noise had joined the blinking light on his dash. He muttered to himself as he inserted then removed his credit card and began pumping gas. How was he going to find John K., exactly? Sure, he could scan the parking lots for the distinctive truck, but how many casinos were in

Oklahoma? Boy, for someone who bragged about keeping his head where his feet were, he had pretty much left his good sense at home on this trip.

Back on the dark freeway, he wandered back in his mind to all the times he'd followed after his older brother.

When Dad made an assignment, like cleaning the horse stalls, John K. often came up with an excuse, like football practice or getting his running miles in. O.D. had always stepped up, with Cody close behind. Dad would shake his head but say something like, "Makes me no never mind, it just needs doing."

O.D. never accepted John K.'s excuses. It wasn't fair that O.D. had to endlessly pick up his slack while the world glorified the handsome oldest Billings boy. Not fair. O.D. was not about to let him get away with it again. Time to make his brother accept his role in the family.

———

Bright overhead lights illuminated the last, smooth roadway leading to the casino. This place was more John K.'s style. Flashing lights of all colors, billboards showing videos of people having fun. A place where you could leave the worries of the world behind. What happened here stayed here. O.D. guided the truck toward the front of the parking lot and found the old green GMC holding its own beside four-wheel drives and vintage Cadillacs. He parked nearby, jumped out, grabbing his phone and his fleece hoodie before locking the door. The cowboy hat stayed in the seat. No use drawing attention.

He trotted across the parking lot, the Oklahoma wind cutting through him on its way. Inside, flashing lights and jingle-jangling noises bombarded him. His friends on the rodeo circuit, as well as the guys at the delivery company, were always shocked that he'd never been inside a casino.

"Hey," he had always argued, "I can find lots of better ways to spend my money." Cigarette smoke burned his eyes as he scanned the room. So many people of all shapes and sizes, posted before glittering screens or standing in groups around huge tables. Happy shouts as coins dropped, collective sighs as someone missed a target of some kind.

O.D. spotted the girls first, standing next to a poker table, Maria's hand rubbing John K.'s shoulders.

John K. leaned forward. Placing the three cards in his hand face-up on the table, he pushed his stool backward. "I'm out." He turned toward O.D., shaking his head. "So, you decided to join us after all?"

"Nope." O.D. stood with his hands in his pockets, trying to remember at least one of the grand speeches he had been rehearsing on the long drive. "This is the craziest thing I have ever seen you do. We need to go home, John K."

"I hope they are paying you well to be chief babysitter of the family. But hey. Where is Marshall Cody tonight? He might need more looking after than I do."

"Yeah. Your brother told me about your high and mighty attitude." Maria faced him, hands on hips. "What's wrong with letting him have a little fun? He served our country. Don't you think he deserves it?" She tossed her head, causing her long black hair to bounce against her shoulders for emphasis.

"Sure. I guess." He couldn't even defend himself to this girl. "Are you having fun too?"

"And just what do you mean by that? I'm over twenty-one. I can make my own decisions." Her dark eyes flashed. "And, for your information, Lissa and I have our own room to go back to when we're tired of losing money. Don't go making assumptions about something that is none of your business."

"I didn't … " What? He didn't say anything about how many rooms they had. But, well … he had wondered. This was a major disaster. Maybe he just needed to get back on the highway headed east.

"I should just go." O.D. turned to walk away, but John K. grabbed his shoulder.

"I don't get it. Why did you come if you're not going to stay?" John K. stood with his hands on his hips.

"I don't know. I just thought I might talk to you. Get you to see that you need to start acting like an adult."

O.D. checked the time on his phone. Two in the morning and a three-plus hour drive ahead. "I need to go home. Faith and Hope are expecting me to promote their rodeo on TV tomorrow morning."

"Hey. Come over here a minute." John K. nodded toward an alcove near the ATM machine.

O.D. examined the toes of his boots. What a bonehead he was.

"Let me be the big brother for a minute." John K. reached into his pocket. "You don't need to drive back home right away. Go to my room for a bit. Watch TV or take a nap. I'll be up later." He placed a keycard in O.D.'s hand, with a folder identifying the room number. "I agree this was an irresponsible trip. For you, not for me. But Mom would never forgive me if you plowed that pickup into the back of a semi somewhere between here and Crossroads. Night, night, Little Dee." John K. took Maria's hand as they walked toward the poker table, with Lissa trailing behind.

———

"Move over, bed-hog."

O.D.'s eyes snapped open. Where was he? The flickering TV

reminded him that this was not the apartment over his dad's shop.

"Hey." He opened his eyes while John K. removed his boots, jeans, and shirt before pulling back blankets. "What time is it?"

"Do I look like an alarm clock? I thought everybody learned to use their phone for a watch while I was deployed." John K settled into the bed with a sigh.

"Six-o-clock!" O.D. jumped into his boots as he turned the phone back over on the nightstand. "I'll never make it."

"Make it for what? If you had something important this morning, maybe you shouldn't have followed me to Oklahoma." John K. burrowed down into the pillow, closing his eyes.

"Well, anyway. I've got to go. You need to get yourself home too, sometime today." O.D. found his hoodie on the chair and pulled it on over his wrinkled flannel shirt. "I've been thinking. I'll just move back into my old room, you can have the apartment again."

John K. sat upright, switching on the lamp.

"No." After bolting out of bed, he stood to face O.D. "I thought we had that settled. You don't need to change a thing because I'm back home. I may not stay long. You just be Little Dee, I'll be the no-good older brother. Quit trying to make my decisions for me."

"Well. Just give our dad a minute of your time now and then. He has this picture of you in his head that is hard to shake. A picture of a guy who cares about his family." O.D had said too much. John K.'s jaw dropped, then he stomped into the bathroom, slamming the door.

"He's still not answering." Hope smacked her phone facedown on the counter in front of her.

"Hope! My goodness." Faith's whisper was louder than her normal voice.

"Is there anything else I can do?" The very patient lady standing behind her set down the hairbrush next to Hope's phone.

"No. I can't believe how much you've managed in just a few minutes." The image in the mirror was surprising. She'd dressed up for dances at school, Faith had helped her with makeup before, but a whole new person met her gaze today. It was probably the lighting in this cramped room.

"Thanks so much." Faith handed the makeup artist a tip. She touched Hope's shoulder, guiding her to the door. "Quit worrying about O.D. He said he'd be here. He's probably in another makeup room. I can't believe I am the one telling you to chill for a change."

"And he couldn't send a *K* on his phone? The king of texts?"

Hope peeked both ways down the hallway outside the makeup room.

"I was driving." The deep voice came from her left.

She heaved a big sigh as she turned to meet his eyes under the brim of a black hat. Those dark eyes were not quite as bright today.

Hope scanned O.D.'s rumpled exterior. "Did you not go to see the makeup lady?"

"Sorry, they did the best they could. I asked for a razor, but the girl said everyone would like the 'tousled' look." O.D. grinned. "I guess you are not 'everyone.'"

"Did you sleep in that shirt?"

"No, I took it off to sleep. Did quite a bit of driving in it, though. Long story." O.D.'s tone dropped a peg or two.

"Hey, O.D. Glad you're here." Faith called out to them. "Tara is doing her first segment. She said she'll just wave when they are going to commercial so we can come out to sit down."

"Yeah. Let's do this thing. If I say anything dumb, just poke me. I just rolled in from Oklahoma a minute ago." He was obviously trying not to meet Hope's gaze.

"Oklahoma? Why? Did you forget we were doing this today?" Hope tried to keep her voice from growing louder.

"Not for a minute, ma'am." O.D. turned toward her. "I promise I'll fill you in. I'm new to this stay-out-all-night thing, but I think I've pulled it off so far."

Stayed out all night? Faith was trusting this guy with saving their rodeo? Hope's cheeks burned. This was crazy. How could he just roll in after staying out all night, expecting to appear on-camera?

"You two handle this. I'll just watch." She was surprised to hear those words coming out of her mouth, but she stood behind them. Faith and O.D. could make complete fools of themselves, but she would not be involved. Not today.

Tara gestured to them as the show took a commercial break. Faith whispered to Tara as they approached. A young man standing just out of camera range responded to Tara's request, placing two chairs next to her.

"I'll introduce you first, O.D. This is ... which Caldwell?" Tara shook Faith's hand.

"Faith, ma'am." Faith's voice trembled.

"Let's just use first names. I'm Tara. I promise I won't ask you anything that you don't have the answer for. O.D. brought a slide show that we will use to expand on the details. Just give us that rodeo queen smile. Everybody will want to come to your next event. Okay?" She squeezed Faith's hand.

"Hey, on the subject of names, Tara." O.D. was smoothing down the shirt he wore, tucking it in a little better at the beltline. "While you're talking to me, ask me about my initials again. I didn't give you the best answer last time."

"Yeah, that was great. O.D. Got it." Tara adjusted the battery pack that controlled her microphone. Another one hung overhead to pick up what O.D. and Faith would say.

Somewhere, a producer started the countdown: "In five, four, three, two, one."

"Welcome back to River Valley Roundup." Tara started out standing, then stopped in front of her chair to shake hands with O.D.

"You might recognize this gentleman from the Billings Boys' ads that show up on ARV3. He's the middle son, O.D. Today, though, he is here as one of the star performers for the Caldwell Family Rodeo. Calf Roping is your event, right, O.D.?"

"Right, Tara." O.D. slipped easily into interview mode.

"And this young lady next to you. Did you meet her at the rodeo?" Tara smiled, reaching for Faith's hand.

"Sort of. This is Faith Caldwell. She's a champion barrel racer, but she's also a neighbor of mine. We've known each other since we both had to have a boost from our daddies to get up on a horse."

Hope shook her head. Faith wasn't needed in this studio. O.D. was in complete control.

"Welcome, Faith. So, is every member of your family involved in the rodeo?"

"Yes, ma'am, uh, Tara." Faith swallowed, her hands clamped in her lap.

A noise from behind her turned Hope's head. Dad stood with Junior behind a glass partition. Her crazy brother was waving his hat, trying to get Faith to look at him. Not now! She glared at him through the glass.

Faith was smiling and had loosened her grip on her own thumb when Hope turned back toward the set.

"My Uncle Dub and Aunt Tina manage the livestock. My dad is the announcer, and my sister runs the office." Faith's voice was a little louder now. "And my brother Junior. Well. He's the rodeo clown."

"Yes. A pretty good one." Tara laughed. She gave Junior a little 'calm-down' gesture with the hand that was out of camera range.

"And you're neighbors?" Tara turned to O.D.

"Yeah. We all live a ways outside of town, but you can see my house from the main road." O.D. paused, took a breath. "The Caldwells, now, they really live in the country. You have to turn at our place and go down a long dirt road. Around the curve, over the hill. They're way out there." Had he forgotten what he was going to say next? Hope squirmed in her chair. Maybe he could remember if he'd had a little more rest. Oh, what a terrible flop this was going to be.

"O.D. brought some pictures taken at the Caldwell Rodeo. They have a very special event coming up soon." Tara hadn't forgotten her direction. She was a real pro. "Right after we come back from this message." She turned to O.D. and Faith, then glanced out toward Hope. "Everybody okay? Hope, are you sure you won't join us?"

"I'm fine." Hope waved at Tara. She did want this promotion to go well, but she wasn't about to try to rescue her sister and this fool showoff now. They could fend for themselves.

"Okay. I'll have the remote, so if either of you wants to talk about something on the screen, just hold up a 'stop' sign with your hand. We just have a few more minutes. We want to get the details of this contest covered so that everyone will want to enter. Ready?" She smiled, squeezing Faith's hand again before the producer began his countdown.

Hope had to admit the slide presentation was well done. O.D. and Faith managed to highlight the important things about the contest. There were also some great shots of the kids at Cedar Ridge. She relaxed in the folding chair as Tara finished the slide show.

"That pretty well wraps it up. We hope all of you will come to the Caldwell Rodeo, buy a chance for a great new truck, and support the Cedar Ridge Ranch. One of you will be arriving in your regular vehicle, then driving home in a brand-new truck from the Billings Boys! O.D., we just have one more question. What do the initials O.D. stand for, really?"

"Well, Tara, Optimistic Dread pretty well sums it up. I know that sounds like an oxymoron. I am happy we are helping a great cause, but what if the winner drives up to the rodeo in their grandpa's Oldsmobile clunker? My dad might regret this whole title for title trade idea."

"Optimistic Dread? Well, as my grandmother would say, you are a caution." Tara laughed, facing the camera. "That does it for River Valley Roundup. Thanks for watching. Be kind to each other. We'll talk again soon!"

"Thanks, y'all." Tara stood to hug Faith. "Great segment. You two are the cutest. I think everyone will want to come out to watch the rodeo. The truck giveaway is just an added bonus." She shook O.D.'s hand, then waved at Hope before she left the studio.

"Well!" Dad met them as they walked toward the door of the station. "We have a couple of TV stars on our hands. Great job, you two!"

"I am glad it's over. O.D., you did so good. I hardly got two words out." Faith patted his shoulder.

"Hey, look at Hope!" Junior stepped back to hold the door for her. "I guess you just came for the free make-over. Why didn't you talk?"

"Faith and O.D. had it under control." She stopped to find her sunglasses as they came out onto the street. O.D. bumped into her from behind.

"Not that you needed a makeover, but you do look nice." He spoke directly into her ear as she regained her footing.

"Thanks." It was surprising he could see well enough to notice after being up all night. She made a point to look straight ahead, grateful when he moved a little to her right.

"Well, nothing resembling breakfast happened at the Caldwell ranch today. It's still too early for lunch." Dad stopped halfway down the sidewalk, turning to face all of them.

"That's why they invented brunch!" Junior bumped O.D. off the curb.

"Right as usual, my boy. What say we head to the local pancake house?" Dad opened both driver's side doors of his truck.

"O.D., are you coming?" Faith caught up with them.

"Sorry. I have Saturday deliveries to make." He moved closer to Hope. "There's one guy who orders frozen mice for his pet snake. If they're on my truck today, I sure don't want the little squeakers thawing out."

"Oh, my gracious." Faith slapped his shoulder. "What did Tara say? 'You are a caution!'"

Hope slid past the two of them to climb into the backseat of Dad's truck. Frozen mice. Where did he come up with this stuff? He had a line ready for every occasion. Maybe there was nothing real about this guy.

———

"Long day?" Aunt Candace arranged silverware on the napkin in front of O.D.

"Yeah. Longer than any I've had in a while." O.D. weighed the choices for dinner in his mind. He was too late for supper at home, but his appetite was not the greatest at the moment. He was getting the formality of a meal over with before he went home to see if John K. had ever come back from his big adventure. "Just give me your special, I guess."

"Great choice." Aunt Candace turned toward the cook behind her. "Chicken spaghetti for one."

An empty coffee mug appeared near O.D.'s right hand. The man who placed it there spoke to Aunt Candace. "Can I get a refill, please?"

O.D. turned to face the casino owner he'd met at the Caldwell rodeo board meeting.

"Great job on your TV appearance at lunchtime today." Heston nodded at Candace as she poured his coffee.

"Yeah." O.D. wasn't sure how to react. This guy certainly had no clue that he was widely viewed as public enemy number one.

"You're a natural at promotion. Are you thinking of being

75

an entertainer of some kind when you're through roping calves?" Heston emptied a container of cream into his cup.

"Me?" That was a laugher. "No. I'm a truck driver. The Caldwells asked me to help with this contest idea. I've never had any trouble talking."

"You have a talent for marketing. I'm actually looking for some help in that area." He turned to face O.D.

"What kind of help?" O.D. salted his plate of spaghetti.

"When the casino gets rolling, we will need to attract the locals. Tourists are great, but we have been much more successful with regulars who live near our facilities. We could use a spokesperson they already know and trust." Heston was focused intently on O.D.'s face.

"Really?" Was this guy offering him a job? "Me?"

"Yeah. I'd like to talk to you more about what we have in mind. It would be a step up from driving a delivery truck."

O.D. met Heston's eyes. What a crazy thought. He'd only been inside a casino once, and that had not turned out well. His mind was having trouble processing this.

"It's something I've never considered. Can I get back to you?" He set his fork down, reaching for his glass of water.

"Sure. Here's my business card. You can shoot me a text, we'll talk more. Our opening day is still a few weeks off, but we need to start getting the word out, so we'll fill this slot pretty fast." Heston picked up his check before walking toward the cash register. "We'd love to make you part of the DownRiver family."

"Thanks. I'll let you know." O.D. followed Heston with his eyes as made his way through the crowded diner, stopping to greet customers on the way out. The DownRiver family? Could he think of a casino as a family activity? He thought back to the atmosphere he'd found his brother in last night. Family had been the last thing on anyone's mind.

He finished his meal quickly, hardly even noticing the flavor of one of Amy Lou's signature dishes. He'd flirted with the idea of the professional calf roping circuit. But PR man for a casino? Sounded strange, even inside his head. But, if Dad wanted John K. to work with him at the dealership, and not O.D., maybe he should give his own future some more thought. There was no guarantee of making a living on the pro rodeo circuit, and he did love to talk. A PR job was not totally out of the question. Right?

10

"Sorry, boy." O.D. brushed the horse's coat as he led him back to his stall for the night. "No time for a ride tonight. Anyway, there's no moon. I wouldn't want you to stumble on the trail."

He didn't have a deadline, but he owed Heston an answer. His parents wouldn't be much help. Casinos were not their cup of tea, for sure. Maybe Grandpa Dee would have some insight. He'd certainly seen the world. First in the military, then as a private security contractor. As long as he was having a good day, he could probably offer O.D. some advice.

"Good idea, Buck. I will go see Grandpa Dee tomorrow." He patted the buckskin's nose then turned out the overhead light, leaving just a dim one near the walkway. "Good night, buddy."

———

O.D. was amazed at how alert his grandfather was today. Days like this made him wonder if Grandpa Dee actually needed to be in this facility. Other days, he couldn't button his shirt.

"Now, this looks like a good supper." O.D. tucked Grandpa Dee's napkin into the top of his shirt. "Barbecue chicken, corn, broccoli, yeast rolls. Not half bad."

"You have lowered your standards way too much." Grandpa picked up a fork.

"Ha! Well, you always said to find some good in everything. Right?" O.D. scrolled through the pictures on his phone, trying to find his mom's mural.

"Hey," O.D. found the picture, waiting for Grandpa Dee to take a sip of his coffee. "Want to see your daughter's latest creation? Our barn is attracting a lot of attention this week."

"That girl. Well, I guess it's good she's painting her own barn these days. Is she still using a spray can?" He leaned over to peer at the screen. "Probably looks better in person."

"See, there's John K. standing at the top of the hill in his army fatigues. Everybody is lining the roads with flags to welcome him home." O.D. expanded the picture to show Grandpa the details of Mom's latest work.

"She's good. We had trouble finding enough flat surfaces for her to practice on when she was a kid. Any building she thought was abandoned was a fair target for her. Sometimes, the owners were okay with it, but the law said trespassing was trespassing." Grandpa wiped his chin with a napkin. "Hey, at least she didn't burn the old places down, right?"

O.D. smiled. "Yep. Could have been worse."

"You're a good kid. So glad you're back from the war." Grandpa Dee wiped his mouth and turned his attention back to the chicken.

There it was. He had confused O.D. for John K. Again. O.D. couldn't hold back a big sigh. The main thing was that Grandpa recognized him as one of the family, right?

"So many go off to war but never come back." Grandpa Dee scanned the dining room.

"Yes, sir. You always said those are the real heroes."

"Right. Me, I had it easy. Not quite a desk job, but just fixing up the airplanes. I wasn't ever within a thousand miles of the real action. Don't get me wrong, I'm not complaining." Grandpa soaked up the barbecue sauce with his roll. "But just be sure that I don't get in front of a combat vet when they are handing out benefits."

"Yes, sir. I'll remember."

Grandpa Dee pointed his fork at a man who was shuffling toward their table.

"Sit here, Jimmy."

The man stopped, stumbled, then moved toward them.

"Never came back." Grandpa whispered to O.D. then turned toward the man. "Here, let my grandson pull out your chair. Have a seat."

O.D. listened sadly as Grandpa Dee tried to engage his friend in conversation. There was never really a good time to bring up his job dilemma. He patted Grandpa on the shoulder as he stood up to step away from the dining table. "You have a great evening, Grandpa Dee."

"You, too, Little Dee." His grandpa toasted him with his coffee cup. "See ya 'round."

Well. Maybe he did know which grandson had come to visit. At least for now. O.D. smiled at Grandpa's friend Jimmy. He headed out by entering the code of the day on the keypad to unlock the front door.

The wind picked up as he drove past the Billings Boys truck dealership on his way home. Salesmen leaned against shiny pickup hoods. Not a lot of business today. John K.'s old green GMC was parked next to the service entrance, with a canvas tarp covering a full load. Camping gear? He sighed as he pulled his truck into a spot next to it.

"Come on, Dad." John K. was about three steps ahead of

Dad as they emerged from the service department entrance. "I'm a big boy. I'll be fine. Please just let me have some space."

"Sure, son." Dad jogged to catch up. They reached the old pickup at about the same time. O.D. didn't even open his door. He could hear everything from here.

"If you don't get it, go talk to Grandpa Dee. He understands where I'm coming from. I just don't fit into anybody's plans right now, okay?" John K. slammed the door. He stopped before backing all the way out and waved his left hand in O.D.'s direction. The old truck lurched as it continued its backward route. The tires screeched as it moved forward again, leaving the parking lot with a vengeance.

11

"I'm home!"

Hope smiled. She would have known Junior was coming in by the slap of the back door and the ruckus he always caused by dropping his loose change in the jar in the mudroom.

"Well, the Hogs almost did it." He would only be disappointed at the outcome of the latest football game for as long as it took to find a snack in the kitchen.

"Yeah." Junior walked through the kitchen, sinking into the couch.

"What's up?" She used the remote to turn down the volume on the cooking show she was watching.

"Everybody at the Billings place is kind of messed up today." Junior reached down to pull his boots off.

"Messed up? How?" Faith placed the veggies she was pulling out of the refrigerator on the kitchen island.

"John K. just up and left at halftime." Junior stood up to stand between them.

"Well, we've all been known to do that. Nothing much

happening at halftime anyway." Cooking pots clattered as Faith found the one she wanted.

"No. He really left. I guess he'd been packing up his truck during the first half. He just came in to tell his mom he was leaving." Junior paced between the kitchen and the living room. "When she asked him where he was going, he said to the dealership to see his dad, then he wasn't sure."

Faith stopped her cooking preparations in mid-chop.

"He didn't say when he was coming back?" Hope could imagine how upset Mrs. Felicia would be over this.

"Nope. Just hugged his mom, shook Cody's hand, and ran out the door." Junior stopped with his hands in his back pockets.

"When O.D. got home, he just came in, pecked his mom on the cheek, and said he was going to bed. Wasn't even five o'clock."

Junior took a bite of an apple he picked up from the counter. "Cody just sat there staring at the TV for the rest of the game. He didn't even get riled when the refs made that terrible call and the Razorbacks lost. I asked him to bring me home before his dad got there. It's just too weird."

Silence engulfed the Caldwell kitchen. Faith picked up a cookbook next to the stove. Hope walked over to stir the roux her sister had started on one of the burners.

"So, gumbo for supper?" This was something she could help with. Someone had to jump-start the cooking, or they wouldn't eat tonight.

"Yeah." Faith placed the cookbook back on the counter and handed Hope a box of chicken broth.

"Hey gang," Dad slammed the back door and sat on the bench in the mudroom to take off his boots. "Wow. I can hear the crickets on the back forty from here. I listened to the end of the football game on the radio." He paused, standing in his stocking feet. "But we're sort of used to snatching defeat from the jaws of victory, right? What else is happening here?"

"Junior told us John K. left home." Hope stirred the broth into the pot.

"What? Deployed again? But that takes a while. He should have a few weeks at home." Dad chomped down on an apple.

"No. He just left. Packed his truck up and pulled out in a cloud of dust." Junior waved his apple core above his head.

"I can imagine how bad his mom feels." Faith was chopping celery and onions.

Hope stepped back from stirring to let the pot simmer. This is when their mom would be on the phone with Felicia, probably headed out the door to drive over to the Billings place. Funny how the two of them could solve all of their problems with a thirty-minute conversation.

"Well. As much as we want to help, the Billings bunch has to sort this out on their own. They know us well enough to call if we can do anything." Dad headed for his bedroom. "How long till supper, Faith Elaine?"

"About thirty, I guess. I'm putting the cornbread in the oven now." Faith wrangled the giant skillet to the oven, plopping some shortening in before placing it inside to warm up.

"If you've got this, I think I'll walk out to the barn for a few." Hope hugged her sister's shoulders.

"Yeah, thanks for the help. I should be good now." Faith smiled and squeezed Hope's hand.

A sneaky wind from the north prompted Hope to zip her fleece-lined jacket as she walked toward the barn. Dad would already have the horses in for the night, but she jogged out to visit anyway. The mist hitting her cheeks held a hint of sharpness. She wondered if they were in for an ice storm.

Inside the barn, Belle and Champ were bumping each other in the stall.

"There, now." She reached to touch Belle's flank. "Settle down. You don't want to go outside right now. It's getting nasty."

Champ nuzzled her hand, hoping for a treat. "No, boy. I just came out to say hello. You two will be fine."

She picked up a brush and worked Belle's chestnut coat to a shine. What was going on at the Billingses' house? Why would John K. leave after just getting home? It must be hard to have a younger brother trying to watch out for him after being on his own in the army for so long. But she could understand O.D.'s concern. After all, the whole family had been so worried, especially for the few weeks he was listed as missing in action. Maybe she had been sort of rough on O.D. this morning. He must have a lot on his mind.

She pulled her phone out.

Everything okay at your house?

No answer.

———

O.D. listened to the tip-tap of icy drops hitting the window of his loft bedroom. November was such a strange month. The fall colors were just reaching their peak, but outside, the trees could be covered with a shimmering coat of ice. Between the drops, he could hear a more metallic sound. Sleet hitting the metal roof of the barn? No. This was a definite clang. Almost as if ...

He rolled over to check the time on his cell phone. Three-thirty. There was a text from Hope from earlier. No need to answer now.

Why was Mom painting at this time of night? He'd known her to get up early, but this was extreme. It wasn't the right weather for paint to cure.

His feet hit the floor next to his bed. He stumbled over to the side of the room that faced the barn. The vapor light magnified the icy droplets falling from the sky. She was down there in a raincoat using a long-handled roller to spread white primer over the side of the barn. Should he go down and try to bring her inside? She worked with long, strong strokes. He realized that the whole objective was to cover the picture she had created just over a week ago. No need to interrupt. There would certainly be no convincing her to stop. He pulled a ladder-back chair over from the dining area, wrapped himself in a blanket from the bed, and sat watching while the sleet became fiercer.

"Mom, stop. It's okay!" She couldn't hear him, but he just couldn't stand this. She returned to the rolling pan and increased her speed, covering the last bit of color on the barn before dropping the roller and running toward the kitchen door.

Didn't John K. know what he was doing to his mom? Or did he care about any of them anymore? Was he camping tonight? They had endured nights like this in a tent before. But those times, it had been the example of the scoutmasters that made them stay. If the old guys could stand it, so could the scouts. Just a glorified game of chicken.

Maybe his brother was sleeping in his truck. But the heater in that old rattletrap didn't do much unless you got up to over 45 miles an hour. People talked about turning into your father, but he was actually morphing into a mother hen.

The house would be stirring soon. Mom would get up to fix

a huge breakfast without mentioning her painting project. Dad and Cody would be dressed for church when they came to the table. They probably found comfort with those good folks at Southside. But he just wasn't up for that today. Where was God in this situation anyway? Sitting back, watching as the Billings family slowly crumbled? Some big help He was.

Everything OK at your house?

Hope's text glared up from his phone. Okay? Not hardly.

Nope.

She was fishing for more, but that's all he wanted to say right now. Summed up the situation perfectly. The Caldwell house would be preparing for worship this morning too. They'd all been invited to Smiley's Cowboy Church many times, but his mom had always been more comfortable in a traditional setting, and their dad said being together as a family was the most important thing. So, they spruced up to sit with their hands in their laps at Mom's preferred location. Sometimes the message reached his ears, but most of his time was spent watching the hands on the clock, fiddling with his tight collar or trying to stretch his toes into the dress shoes that never got broken in before he outgrew them.

Call me if you want to talk.

He was a little surprised the text came back so quickly.

Or meet me at our service today. Y'all are always welcome.

He resisted sending another "Nope." Invited out of

sympathy. No, he didn't need that. He was just fine up here in his little loft. He checked his pantry and found the makings of a peanut butter sandwich. That would be the perfect breakfast today.

Placing the bread on a paper towel, he covered both slices with a smooth layer of peanut butter. Aunt Candace's peach jam dolloped into place, he closed the sandwich and carried it to the window. Lights blinked on and off in different parts of the house. No one would come to see about him. He'd missed church before. They would get along fine without him. He sometimes wondered if even God remembered that Dave and Felicia had three sons, not just two.

He should answer Hope's text.

No thanks. Talk to you soon.

12

B uck trudged along up the hill between the Billings and Caldwell places.

"I know, boy. It's kind of chilly. But there's no ice on the ground yet. Moving keeps us warm." O.D. reined him gently around an old stump in the path. "I promise I won't keep you out long."

Tiny ice pellets pierced his cheeks.

"John K. is a grown man," O.D. said out loud, prompting a snort from Buck. "If he wants to camp out in this weather, it's his decision."

The sun peeked through the clouds as he reached the top of the hill. He stopped near the front porch of his Grandpa and Grandma's old house.

"The place looks kind of sad, Buck Man." He dismounted and stepped up on the weathered boards. It was past time for a workday up here. "Time to stop waiting on Cody or John K. to help. Looks like it's up to me and you."

Tying Buck to a tree, he walked around to the back of the little house toward the Caldwells' houses. Dub's place, with the pens full of rodeo stock, and Smiley's with mostly pastures left open for grazing a few cattle and their two horses. It was good to have neighbors that weren't interested in selling to some big land developer. Was that about to change with Ms. Catherine gone?

The clouds cleared, and he actually felt some warmth on his face. November still couldn't make up its mind. He sympathized. He had hoped that coming to his old thinking spot would clear his head about Heston's job offer. No chance. All he could think about was how John K. was messing up everyone's plans. If his brother would just take his place with Dad at the dealership, life could return to normal. Whatever that was these days.

Buck showed his impatience with a toss of his mane as O.D. returned to the front of the house. "Sorry, fella. We're headed to the barn, I promise. Hey, when we get back, remind me to give Hope a call. "

Maybe talking to a human would be better than this nowhere conversation with his horse.

———

Cleanup was easy after their quick lunch. Hope retreated to her bedroom, sitting cross-legged on the quilt her Grandma Caldwell had made from red and blue bandanas. Using some images from O.D's presentation, her several social media posts ended with: "Don't forget, if you want to be part of the action, entry fees are due tomorrow at noon. Let's get ready to rodeo!" The last phrase always brought a smile as she thought of Junior using his wrestling announcer voice.

Sleet pounded on her windowpane. Would anyone come out in this weather? At least it was an indoor, heated arena now. She remembered hearing her dad and Uncle Dub talk about the first days of the rodeo, when it had been outdoors, then with a roof over the stands but not the arena. They'd come a long way.

She couldn't help thinking about O.D.'s older brother. Where was John K. sheltering in this lousy weather?

Hey!

O.D.'s text startled her.

Want to go for a ride?

In this weather?

Really? Was he certifiable? Didn't most guys just call when they needed to talk to a friend?

I'm not getting Belle or Champ out in the sleet.

No! I meant in my truck.

Hope checked the forecast on her phone. Sleet and heavy rain. Chance of thunderstorms. In November. But nothing severe coming up on radar.

Sure.

She was no smarter than he was.

———

"Thanks for coming along." O.D. reached over to slam the passenger door as Hope slid in. "The inside of my room was getting depressing. Could make a guy go off the deep end."

"And heading out for a ride in the sleet says perfectly sane for sure." Hope pulled her knit cap down around her ears.

"Yeah, I think so, don't you?" O.D. laughed. What was it about this girl that could change his mood on a dime?

"So, no word from John K.?" She always cut straight to the chase. Another reason he admired her.

"Nope. Not answering texts from anybody. To be honest, that's sort of why I wanted you to come along. I plan to drive by some of his usual haunts. His truck is pretty easy to spot, but in this weather, an extra pair of eyes will help."

His windshield wipers struggled against the ice forming in front of him. Hopefully, this stuff would not stick to the roads.

He drove into the parking lot of the pizza place, nearly deserted at this time on a Sunday evening. No old green truck here.

"I just needed to feel like I was doing something. I thought about going to see Grandpa Dee, but he really likes his Sunday evenings after all the church people leave. He can watch football or nap. He calls it no hustle-bustle day."

"I think hustle-bustle keeps me from thinking too much." Hope settled back in her seat, adjusting the heater vents to blow towards her.

"Yeah. Me too." O.D. caught a glimpse of the loose hair around her face ruffling in the warm breeze as she rubbed her hands together.

"So. If you find him, what do you plan to say?" She didn't face him, just kept looking out the window.

No beating around anybody's bush for this girl.

"That he is tearing his family apart. If he doesn't care, I want him to know that I do." With his jaw set, O.D. drove down the next road checking the back yards for John K.'s truck. "Dad has been dreaming for years of turning Billings Boys over to him. It's all he talked about while John K. was deployed. Now that he's back, he doesn't even give Dad the time of day. Just disgusting."

"Did he act like he wanted to be involved when he was younger?" She was turned sideways in the seat, facing him now.

"I don't think he had much choice, to be honest. Dad took over after my grandpa got sick and moved with my uncle to Montana. Now he feels like it's time to pass things along to his oldest son."

"Why not you?" She tightened her scarf around her neck. He needed to get that heater checked soon.

"Me? I think Dad forgets I'm here most of the time. Especially since I moved out to the barn apartment." She didn't know the half of it. "When he's not wondering where John K. is, he's worried about whether Cody will survive his next bull ride."

"I guess you just don't demand as much attention as the others. That's not always a bad thing." She had a point there. He didn't want anyone worrying about him. Not really.

He spotted a familiar compact car at Amy Lou's. He'd seen Maria driving it around town. She might know where John K. was.

"Want to see if Aunt Candace can find us a piece of pie and a Coke?"

"Sure. Maybe it's a little warmer in there." Hope buttoned her jacket as the truck stopped.

"Well, look here. The two most prominent families in the river valley have sent their brightest offspring to honor our diner." Aunt Candace placed silverware in front of each of them.

"Well, you're feeling your oats this afternoon." O.D. smiled. The weather outside never affected her mood at all.

"Gotta do something to dispel this gloom. I'm not a meteorologist, but I don't think sleet and snow before Thanksgiving is a good way to start the winter. Hi, Hope."

"Hi, Ms.Candace."

"Got any pie today?" O.D. tried to look behind her to the glass case that displayed their specialty desserts.

"Coconut with meringue so tall you'll need a ladder to finish it. Chocolate, apple, and pecan to get you ready for Thursday. Just sold the last pumpkin."

"You had me at coconut." Hope pulled her fork out of the folded napkin.

"Gotta go with chocolate. With a Coke for me. Hope?" O.D. sat back against the vinyl booth.

"Sweet tea will be fine."

"You got it." Aunt Candace tapped her order pad with her pencil.

He nodded at his aunt's trademark wink. A glance around the room found Lissa and her boyfriend Billy with Maria in the back corner.

"Sorry we haven't had any luck finding John K." Hope sipped her tea when Aunt Candace set it down.

"I didn't think we would. I'm sure he probably drove a long way yesterday afternoon. I guess he needed a break." O.D. tapped his fork on the table.

"I feel sorriest for your mom." Hope wadded up the napkin next to her plate.

"Yeah, it's tough on her."

As Billy paid their check, he almost wished the threesome would just pass by without stopping on their way out the door.

"Hey!" Maria stopped next to their table. "Where's that no-good brother of yours? He stood me up last night!"

"I really don't know." O.D. scooted away from her.

"Yeah. Whatever. If he wanted to dump me, he could at least have the guts to call or send me a text. Just tell him never mind. I get the message." Maria huffed out, setting the bell above the glass door jangling.

"He's not worth it." Lissa patted Maria's shoulder, heading for the door.

Billy waved at O.D. as he followed Lissa out.

"So, that was John K.'s girlfriend?" Hope turned to look behind her.

"I guess she thought so." O.D. pulled two twenties out of his billfold.

"Here you go, sweetie." Aunt Candace set the creamy pie with the towering meringue in front of Hope. "Enjoy."

"Don't worry about your brother." She patted O.D.'s hand. "He'll be back. I think we all just overwhelmed him."

"I hope you're right." O.D. handed her the money. "Table twelve, okay?"

"Sure, precious." She winked again.

"What was that for?"

Oops. He didn't normally pay for anyone else when he wasn't alone.

"Oh. Table twelve is the one behind you a little ways. Don't turn around. Mom is eating pie, Dad has coffee. Kids are sharing a burger and fries. They probably could use some help." Outside the front window, Maria led the threesome to her car.

"So you just paid for their meal?" He could tell she was dying to turn around to look.

"Yeah. I don't have many expenses living at home. I guess I should be saving to get a place of my own, but I figure I can put my money to good use this way." He got a forkful of chocolate pie, but somehow he wasn't feeling it this evening.

"Oh."

Strange reaction. 'Oh.' Not 'That's nice.' or 'You might need that money later.' Just 'Oh.'

The television behind the counter flashed a familiar logo.

"Turn that up, please, Ann-Ann."

Candace used the remote in her apron pocket to bring up the volume.

Hope's eyes lit up as scenes of the rodeo and Cedar Ridge Ranch replaced the normal trucks in the Billings Boys' commercial. The spot concluded with a plug for the contest.

"That was great!" She washed down a bite of pie crust with some sweet tea.

"Yeah, our ad agency does a good job. I told them to be sure to emphasize Cedar Ridge too. I hoped y'all would like it." Wow. This girl could eat. She had already almost finished the pie.

"This is actually happening. I need to make entry forms. I also need a way to keep up with the money. I'll get that done tomorrow." She graced him with one of her rare smiles. "I'm glad you and Faith pushed me into this thing. I think it will bring us a lot of attention. I'm sorry for the way I acted at Tara's show yesterday." She concentrated on her lap.

"No problem. I guess I was acting like a jerk. I was tired after following John K. all the way to Oklahoma. I couldn't get him to leave the casino, so I crashed in his room and overslept. I barely made it back in time for that interview." This was the first time he'd explained to her. She must think he was a total idiot.

"And you haven't learned. Still out trying to find him." She met his eyes with a sad smile.

"Well. At least I had enough sense not to go by myself this time. I promise I'll just go on home after I drop you off. I think it thundered a while ago. The weather is about to get nastier."

"Thunder? With sleet?" Hope did turn around now to look out the front window of the diner.

The young father from table twelve got his surprise at the cash register. That never got old. He picked up the ticket for their pie, waiting until the little group walked out, chattering happily.

"Yep. Grandpa Dee says thunder-sleet is always followed by snow. We'd better get you home before your Daddy comes after me with a shotgun." He slid out of the booth, stepping back to allow Hope to precede him.

This girl was a pretty good sport to come along on an insane mission like this. Evidently Aunt Candace approved too. Her wink after he paid their check was accompanied by a full-on smirk.

O.D. held the passenger door of his truck as Hope pulled herself up to the seat.

"Before my grandpa died, he said it was tough when he came back from the army." Hope peered under the front of his hat, trying to look him in the eye again. "He said he couldn't talk to anyone about anything unless they had been in the military. He said we just didn't get it."

"Yeah. My Grandpa Dee said almost the same thing." She had a way of knowing what was in his head. "I need to give John K. some space. I guess we're all having trouble adjusting to him being back."

"I get that." Hope didn't look away. "Worry keeps us busy. But I guess it doesn't do much good."

"Are you always so sensible?" O.D. walked around to the driver's side. He took the first deep breath he remembered in a long time as he slid into the driver's seat.

"I don't know why I can't let John K. do his own thing." He finally broke the silence, as they got closer to her house. "It's just that Dad has been waiting all this time for his oldest son to come home so he can think about retiring. I guess we all bought into that idea. Now it's hard to let it go."

"Yep." Hope checked her seatbelt, pulling it tighter. "We're having a hard time finding normal at our house too."

"Hey, I just realized it's not sleeting anymore." O.D. flipped his headlights to bright as the truck bumped off the pavement towards Hope's house. "I think I even see the moon now."

The moonlight behind her caught tendrils of Hope's hair that had come loose from her braid, creating a halo in the darkness of his truck cab.

She had talked him down from his frantic search for John K. But what would she think about the decision he was making now? Would she see him taking a job at the casino as taking the enemy's side in her fight to keep the Caldwell rodeo? Of course she would.

"No thunder sleet tonight." Hope leaned forward as the truck came to a stop in the Caldwells' yard. "Hey, thanks for the ride and the pie. I hope y'all hear from John K. soon."

Hope opened her door. The cab's dome light blinked on, along with a beeping alarm. So much for a quiet, romantic moment.

"Thanks for coming along. I guess we'll have to adjust to him not being here again." He smiled at her as she stepped down from the truck seat. "Sleep tight. See you soon." He should have walked around to open her door. What a doofus.

13

The phone on Hope's desk buzzed as soon as she replaced the receiver. Why was it so hard for folks to trust their earlier entries for tomorrow night's rodeo?

"Yes, Mrs. Howell, we have both of your girls registered for mutton busting. Everything is fine. Yes ma'am. Of course, I know you have a lot to be done before Thanksgiving morning. Thank you. We miss my mom too." She was tired of hearing those empty platitudes.

She closed her eyes and saw O.D.'s face in the cab of his truck last night. He'd been so preoccupied with finding John K., but she thought he had been glad to have her help. They'd known each other for a long time, but suddenly things were very different.

"Good morning, Miss Caldwell." Faith stood in the doorway with a box of donuts. "Do you have my name on your list of barrel racers this week?"

"Oh, stop." Hope wadded up a piece of scratch paper and fired it in her sister's direction. "I hope I get all of these phone messages handled before the end of the day. The emails are pretty easy. Just a reply with the standard confirmation. But phone calls require conversation."

"Do tell." Faith laughed. "That's a brilliant observation. That's why I'm here. I've been thinking I could help with the entry forms for the contest. I've designed some stuff like that before."

From the other office, Faith exclaimed in frustration as some graphic or another didn't behave as she thought it should.

"There!" Faith stood in the doorway, her face flushed.

"We've got content on Facebook and Twitter. Check it out." She picked up Hope's phone from the desk. "I scheduled a Facebook live broadcast for the beginning of the rodeo. You may have to get it started for Dad."

The little bell over the outside door jangled, and O.D.'s voice boomed into the room. "Pizza delivery!"

"Oh, I forgot to tell you I ordered pizza." Faith trudged toward the other office, still focused on the phone in her hand.

"Do you have a new job?" Hope saved the bull-riding page of the spreadsheet.

"No. I just sort of intercepted Faith's order." O.D. held the boxes high, looking for a clear space to set them down.

"Our breakroom table is back here." Hope led the way through the office Faith was using, past Uncle Dub's closed door.

"I've never been in the inner sanctum of the Caldwell operation before." O.D. placed the two boxes on the table. "Large meat lover with extra cheese, and a small veggie."

O.D. sat in front of one of the boxes. "Mind if I have a piece?"

"Help yourself." No, she truly didn't mind. It was feeling more and more natural to have this guy around.

Faith came in, setting her phone next to the pile of paper

plates on the table. "We're getting lots of interest on our contest posts, O.D."

"Cool. Dad says we've had a few people come to look at the truck today."

"I hope some people come tomorrow night." Hope retrieved a greasy, meaty slice of pizza for her plate, adding some parmesan cheese from a bottle they kept in the office fridge. "Entries are down because of the short turn-around."

"It may take a while for word to get around. Folks are saving a little money for the Black Friday and Cyber Monday sales too. But they may come check us out this week, then enter next time." O.D. checked his phone before getting another bite of pizza. "Hmm. That's strange."

"What?" Hope could wait to look at her phone till later. Pizza was so much better before it got completely cold.

"Our marketing guy at Billings Boys sent a text telling me that the ad rates have gone up a whole bunch at the TV stations today."

"And?" Faith leaned back with her veggie pizza.

"We may have to find some different time slots for our ads, at least until we recheck our advertising budget. Not a lot of folks are thinking about buying a new truck at 11:30 at night or during midday soap operas." O.D. turned his phone face down.

"No one is thinking about going to the rodeo then, either." Faith picked her phone up. "I am just learning about this advertising stuff. Hope, will this mess up our ads for the rodeo?"

"Wow, what a bunch of negative Nellies." O.D. grabbed another piece of pizza.

Hope stood up to find a cup for her canned soda. He just didn't get it. His family's business would continue with or without this contest. But what would they do if Uncle Dub was successful with his scheme? Dad didn't have anything to fall back on. Neither did she. Rodeo was their life. Suddenly, even the pizza had no flavor. She walked back into the other office, leaving O.D. and Faith to chatter about time slots.

"Hey." O.D. stopped by her desk on his way out the front door. "Don't worry too much about this contest. Folks around town love your rodeo. It will all work out, I promise." He glanced at his phone again and took a step back.

"John K.?" Hope shouldn't ask, but he did have a strange look on his face.

"No. Nobody's heard from him. I guess he really wants a break from us." O.D. sat down in the old vinyl chair next to her desk. "Actually, this is from Tara, down at the TV station."

"Oh. Well, none of my business." How often did he talk to this Tara?

"Yeah. I never get texts from her. It's kind of strange. I'll just read it to you."

He didn't owe her an explanation, but he started reading before she could stop him.

"Just checking on your mom. The mural is gone."

"What happened to the mural?" Hope walked to the trash can with her empty paper plate.

"She covered it up with white paint. I didn't know anyone but our family would notice." O.D. laid his phone down on Hope's desk.

"Of course they would. Lots of people like your mom's murals. What are you going to say to Tara?" He didn't usually have any trouble thinking of clever comebacks.

"I'm not sure. I think Mom decided we were sharing a little too much about our family. No one but you guys knows that John K. left." O.D. stood up.

"Well, then just say, 'She's fine. Thanks for asking.'"

"Sure. Simple. I always overthink things." O.D. picked up his phone to finish his text then set it down to gather the trash from their lunch. He winked at Hope before walking out the door. "Thanks for being the one who has it all together around here. For real."

Hope stared at the door after he left. Was she finally seeing the real O.D. Billings? No fancy talk or bravado? She remembered his generous gesture at the diner when he paid for a stranger's meal. He had trusted her to go along as he searched for his big brother. That was quite a change from his typical devil-may-care attitude.

O.D.'s phone was still on her desk, with a message flashing.

"Hey!" She tried to catch him, but he was out of earshot. As she picked up the phone, the text caught her eye.

Any thoughts about the PR job?

What? What job? Well, none of her business. But she couldn't resist glancing at the sender. Heston? The casino owner?

"Hey," Faith took the phone from her hand. "I'll take it to him." She ran out the door, leaving Hope trying to catch her breath. Her face heated. She shook her head in disbelief. This couldn't be happening.

14

O.D pulled out his phone to check the messages. Heston's was still unanswered.

Had he thought about the P.R. job? Sure, he'd thought about it. But while eating lunch with Hope and her sister seemed natural, nothing about the casino job felt that way. Should he be turning down a chance to take his first grown-up job?

He gave Buck his head as they climbed the hill behind the barn. Vapor lights were beginning to snap on around the ranch, but there was enough light to see the familiar trees and boulders that had been their landmarks for as long as he could remember.

Buck stopped at the crest of the hill, and O.D. dismounted, walking to the front porch of the old house. He peered down the hill to where the orange flag on top of the survey post marked the line between the Billings and Caldwell properties. It might be a good idea to buy a little bit more from them. O.D. was more determined than ever to stake his claim here on the top of the hill. But maybe it would make more sense to remodel the old house than build a new one.

The money from that casino job would certainly help.

Buck made restless noises as darkness fell in earnest.

"Yep, you're right as always." He turned and mounted again. "Let's go get some supper, boy."

On the ride back to the house, he kept seeing Hope's face in the dim light of the cab of his truck last night. He could picture her up there, sitting on the porch with him, looking down on her family's land. Hope was so natural, so grounded. Good for the land, the future house, and for him.

She'd never given him a second thought. But then, he hadn't taken the time to ask about her dreams, either. A little strange thinking of her in this new way.

Mom had kept the chili hot for him, so he grabbed a piece of cornbread and settled at the kitchen island. They had gotten used to John K. not being here for supper when he was deployed, but tonight, his absence hung over them thicker than the leftover smell of garlic in the kitchen.

Why didn't he at least text someone to let them know he was okay? The question of the day.

He had his own text to send. He picked up the phone to reply to Heston. Was a text proper in this situation? He'd never turned down a job before. *Just get your head where your feet are, O.D. Or, in this case, where your fingers are.*

> Thanks for thinking of me, but I don't feel your job is a good fit for me.

That should say it. It wasn't a good fit. Not now. Probably not ever. He took a deep breath. Hitting "Send" had never felt so good.

"Tonight's early late news is brought to you by

DownRiver Casino." The commercial before the 9:00 broadcast jolted his dad, who picked up the remote to turn up the volume.

"Huh? It's supposed to be the 'Billings Boys Early Late News." Dad stood up.

"Yeah. What happened?" Cody stood up too.

O.D.'s phone alerted him to a text from their marketing manager at the dealership.

Tell your Dad I will call the station in the morning. They booted us from our slot.

"Dad, Clark says he will take care of this tomorrow." O.D. was shocked. The dealership had sponsored the 9:00 news for years. Maybe their commercials would still air during the broadcast somewhere.

"Harold said they were going up on their ad rates. I gave him a top figure to spend for the month." Dad was pacing. "I just didn't know everything would change so fast."

"It will all work out." O.D. hoped he sounded confident.

He texted the marketing manager at the dealership back.

We'll talk tomorrow.

———

"So, this is where we enter the contest?" O.D. stopped in front of Hope's white-paper-covered table on his way to the concession stand.

"Yeah." Hope answered without meeting his eyes. What did he care? He'd probably be a casino employee by the time they held the drawing. She handed Faith an entry form, walking away without glancing back at O.D.

"Hey! Hope, wait up." He caught up quickly, just before she turned to go back up to the announcer's stand.

"What's up?" She controlled her voice. No need to make a scene out here in front of rodeo patrons.

"I thought you might want to know, there will be some new Billings Boys ads airing on another TV station starting tomorrow night just before the late news. For some reason, KRVA's ad rates suddenly went up." He peered at her from under his black hat.

"Okay. I guess they will they mention the contest?" Why was he telling her about their ads?

"Yeah, I asked our marketing guy to include a little scroll across the ad. Should work pretty well." O.D.'s voice dropped, like he couldn't think of what to say to her. Did he ever plan to tell her about this new job?

"I've got to go help Dad get ready for the first event." She turned to go up the stairway toward the announcer's stand.

"Okay. See you later?" He reached out toward her, but she had already bounced up the first few steps.

"Yeah." She pressed her lips together, then continued up the stairs. She was certainly in no mood for any more of O.D.'s big-talking cowboy routine. She'd just concentrate on the rodeo tonight.

"Welcome Ladies and Gents to the Caldwell Family Rodeo!" Dad's cheerful voice boomed from the speakers as she stood behind him. "We know you have a jillion things to do to get ready for your turkey dinner in a couple of days, so we're glad you are here. Mama, if you came with Dad and the kids tonight, you can still go home to make your pies after they go to bed. For now, let's all enjoy some rodeo."

Dad winked at Hope while the crowd applauded. She glanced at the lineup of events.

"Everybody down there ready?" He covered the

microphone with his hand, waiting for her nod. "Now, ladies and gents. Here's one of my favorite events for our junior riders. It sounds simple. Get on your pony, head for the first barrel over here on the right. Or you can start on the left if that works better. Just let us know."

"Wait a minute, Daddy. Which way do we go, right or left?" Junior entered the arena below them on a pony so short that his boots were almost dragging the ground.

"Oh no. I shouldn't have said this was for junior riders. Sorry, folks."

Hope smiled. Her dad and brother loved coming up with these little routines to entertain the crowd.

"Go right, Junior." Her dad pointed. "Okay. So. At the first barrel, pick up a flag."

Junior's pony balked. He gently kicked its flanks. After making a random circle, they managed to get to the barrel.

"Got it. Now what?" Junior turned to face the announcer's stand.

"Okay, now, you ride to the next barrel and go around behind it."

"The one in the middle?" Junior turned the pony's head to face the barrels.

"Right. I mean, correct." Dad responded, nodding.

Junior and the pony headed to the middle of the arena. "Okay, Daddy. But what do I do with this flag?"

"Take it to the other barrel, over here to my left."

Junior and the pony made a quick dash to the barrel. Attempting to jab the flag in, it bounced off with a clang.

"Oh, no. Can I try again?" Junior asked.

"Nope, sorry. That's a no score. So, after that, folks, we may all need an intermission." The crowd laughed. "I tell you what. Let's give these kids that have been practicing a chance. They may do better than my namesake here. Ladies and gents, let's hear it for the riders in our pony flag contest!"

Hope tried to pay attention as the youngest contestants showed their abilities in the arena below her. She remembered her pony days. It meant so much to hear the approval of the crowd after giving her all.

She leaned over the right side of the stand to see if she could spot the next contestant in line. A familiar black cowboy hat caught her eye. Who was O.D. talking to on the other side of the entrance lane?

She caught her breath as she recognized the overdressed man leaning toward O.D. as Quinton Heston. Couldn't they have one performance here without being reminded that this man wanted the whole thing to end? Her cheeks flamed. For all O.D.'s talk of the importance of family and tradition, this conversation showed his true colors. She wished the two of them would just leave so that she wouldn't have to think about either one until tonight's rodeo was over.

———

"Hey, keep moving, Old Dude," Junior called to O.D. "Don't want to stiffen up before your big event!"

"What's up, Junior?" Well, at least one of the Caldwells was still speaking to him.

"Yeah, if Tara asks you what the initials stand for tonight, you can tell her Old Dude. Ha! I kill me."

Yes, Smiley was the king of corny jokes, and Junior was the clown prince. O.D. shook his head, turning to give an exaggerated bow in Junior's direction before mounting Buck to head for the arena entrance. As the current leader in points for the season, he would be the last of tonight's riders.

Buck spluttered impatiently. This horse was always ready to go. O.D. secured his pigging string in his mouth. Ready.

Behind the barrier, Buck was all about composure. The calf ran into the arena, the rope dropped. They were off. O.D. honed in on the flipping tail of the Angus calf while the looping rope over his head grew larger with each twist of his wrist. Buck was focused on the black calf, too, with his head down out of the way of O.D.'s spinning lariat. The calf slowed slightly. O.D. let the loop fly over its head, tightening quickly to jerk the calf to a stop.

He. jumped down and landed with his pigging string ready. After throwing the calf to the ground, he dropped with one knee in the bawling calf's side. Buck backed up slowly, keeping the rope taut, allowing O.D. to half hitch the three feet in one smooth motion before he jumped up, flinging both hands in the air.

"Hey!" Smiley shouted. "12.6. Best time tonight! Looks like O.D. wins another one!"

O.D. eased Buck forward and waited to make sure the calf stayed tied. Then, he removed his hat, dropped to one knee, pointed skyward, two, three, four, pointed to the crowd. Cheers and applause erupted from the stands. Yes, not a bad way to spend an evening.

Mounted securely again, O.D. rode Buck out of the arena as the crowd cheered.

"And that, ladies and gents, is how it's done." Smiley's patter calmed the audience. "I want to take two quick seconds to thank the Billings Boys for their unwavering support of this rodeo. You know our families are back-fence neighbors. We're always here for each other." O.D. waved in the general direction of the announcer. Was Hope standing up there watching?

The lights blinded him, but as he lowered his gaze, he

spotted Heston standing near the gate. This guy couldn't take "no" for an answer. The salary he had mentioned earlier tonight was amazing, but the latest advertising changes reminded O.D. that he wanted nothing to do with the casino business. There was a big difference between being a good businessman and being a sleazeball.

"Don't forget, tonight is the presentation of the annual Thanks for Hanging On Award." Smiley continued smoothly as the next event started. "Davis Billings started this years ago to recognize the bull rider who lasts the longest on a bull the week before Thanksgiving. If more than one rides for the full eight, we'll draw a name from the hat. Only contestant who can't win that award is Cody Billings, the youngest of the Billings Boys. Stick around for that in two shakes of a filly's tail."

"Hey, O.D." Tara Williams was waiting as O.D. exited behind the chutes into the misty rain falling outside the arena. "If you've got a minute, we'll get your reaction to your ride. We can get this on nightside at ten."

"Sure." He stopped with Buck's reins in his hand. The horse would not go anywhere, but at least it made him appear to be in control.

"This is the winner of the calf roping competition at the Caldwell Family Rodeo tonight, O.D. Billings." Tara held the microphone near O.D. while facing the camera. "Our viewers are still wondering what the O.D. stands for." She turned to face him, moving the mic to pick up his response.

"OverDrive. Tonight, it was all about the horse, not me. Buck was in OverDrive."

"OverDrive? Oh mercy." Tara laughed. "I guess we will never get a straight answer to that question, will we? Seriously. That was a great ride. Calf roping is not the most glamorous event. You make it exciting for the audience here in Crossroads."

"We're fortunate to have this family rodeo." O.D. jumped on his chance to promote the drawing coming up. "And there is a lot of excitement building around the contest that started this week."

"Yes. So, I hear your dad is giving away a truck?" Tara pointed. The cameraman turned to get a shot of the shiny pickup parked outside the arena, in the perfect spot to reflect the neon lights.

"Right! Entries cost fifty dollars, which goes to the Cedar Ridge Ranch. That's a cause that touches all our hearts." O.D. took off his hat and held it in his hand. "Folks can buy as many chances as they want, here at the rodeo or the Billings Boys dealership."

"When will the truck be given away?" Tara prompted him.

"Well, a little bit before Christmas, five entries will be drawn. We will call those folks to be sure they are coming to the rodeo. That night, one set of keys will start the truck. The lucky winner will trade whatever she drove to the rodeo for our brand-new truck."

"You're so sure the winner will be a female?" Tara laughed.

"Oh, that's always how it goes, right? Dad may get to drive it, but we all know Mom gets the newest and best vehicle in the family." O.D. placed his hat back on his head, giving the camera his best smile.

"Well, that sounds great. We'll look forward to that." Tara turned back toward the camera. "It's a great night at the rodeo, with barrel racing and bull riding still to come. The Caldwell Family Rodeo will be back to their every other Thursday schedule after Thanksgiving. Come out and support our favorite sport!"

Tara shook O.D.'s hand as the cameraman's light switched off. "Thanks. You're a great interview."

"No problem. We appreciate the shout-out for the contest." O.D. reached in for a quick hug.

"You bet." Tara rushed off.

After securing Buck outside their trailer, he walked back toward the arena. Hope was coming out of the concession stand with a cup of coffee but hurried away before he had a chance to catch her.

"Great ride, O.D." One of his fellow delivery drivers passed by, offering his hand. He shook it absently while trying to follow the bouncing honey-colored braid.

"Hey, thanks, man. I guess Buck and I just clicked tonight." The driver walked away. O.D. stopped. Yes, sometimes things worked out, but could he get to the bottom of the icy treatment he was getting from Hope?

The thought was not complete in his brain before a whiff of honeysuckle perfume told him she was standing nearby.

"Hey, I could use a favor." Wait, was she actually speaking to him?

"Sure, what do you need?" She backed up before he could take her hand.

"I'd kind of like to be upstairs with Dad, but I need somebody to direct traffic out here while the barrel racing is going on. For some reason, people keep blocking this alleyway. I don't want anybody to get slowed down during their entry."

O.D. placed himself in the middle of the opening. With his hands parallel, he moved them forwards and backwards in his best imitation of an airport runway guide. "Will this work?"

Hope almost smiled before running up the stairway.

O.D. smirked. The snow queen was thawing a bit.

15

O.D. took over barricade duty as each barrel racer prepared for her ride. The alleyway leading out of the arena was a tempting place for audience members. On the path between the concession stand and the restrooms, it was also a favorite spot to peek in to see what was happening during events. But since the girls used it for a good running start with their excited mounts, it was important to keep the pathway clear.

Faith nodded at him as she and Belle waited outside the tunnel.

"Did Hope tell you that our favorite businessman is here watching tonight?" She allowed Belle to pace for a moment as Smiley did a short advertisement for a sponsor.

"Yeah. But don't worry about him. Just do your usual best. You've got this." The idea of the rodeo being sold was weighing heavily on both girls. His own mind was pulled away by John K.'s absence. "Just keep your head where your feet are and go!" His grandpa's words spilled out easily. They always helped during his calf roping run. Hopefully, Faith would be able to focus as well.

Smiley finished his announcement, concluding with his daughter's introduction. "Here she comes, Faith Elaine Caldwell."

Faith stormed through the alleyway aboard Belle. Her eyes were straight ahead as she used her riding crop lightly to increase the horse's speed. Her head turned a tiny bit as they emerged into the arena. Heston must have moved closer to the entryway. What a pest this guy was.

It took very little encouragement from Faith as Belle circled the barrel on the right seamlessly. Picking up speed, the pair headed straight across the arena to the barrel on the left. Did Faith look up again? She was much too concerned about that extra spectator in the stands. Horse and rider circled the barrel a little wider than usual, speeding toward the other end. The cheering crowd was suddenly silent as a resounding clang rang out and the barrel flopped to its side.

Faith snapped her crop on Belle's flank to bring the horse home, but the damage was done. Smiley's announcement held a tinge of disbelief. "That's a no-score for the Caldwell princess tonight. There's always next time. Let's encourage her with a round of applause."

O.D. dared not meet Faith's eyes as she passed through the tunnel. Alone time would be the order of the next few minutes in the barn.

He stayed at his post for the rest of the barrel racing but couldn't shake the feeling that something about tonight was a little off.

"Hey, big bro!" Cody's voice reached him from behind.

"Ready for your ride?" O.D. turned to greet his brother.

"Yeah. Both of 'em. I got Cupcake first, then Bad Boy for the second ride." Cody leaned over the barricade to watch the last barrel racer speed through after her ride. "Mmm, mmm. That Sherilyn is a real looker."

"And she actually had a better time than Faith." O.D. waved at a man across the alleyway from them. He began to move the heavy metal barricade that had helped to block the audience from crossing here on their way to the concession stand.

"Yeah. There must be a disturbance in the force tonight! Miss Caldwell has been knocked off her high horse." Cody leaned on the barricade.

"Hey!" Junior Caldwell stood behind Cody in full clown makeup. "So, Faith showed she's human tonight. Big deal. You'd best just keep your mind on your own business, hot shot."

"You got it, clown-face! See you at the chutes, Dee." Cody snapped Junior's suspenders before running out of the tunnel toward the barn. Junior hiked his floppy pants up and took off after him.

"Yeah. See ya." O.D. shook his head. He wondered if they would always act ten years younger than their actual ages. Wow, he was even starting to think like an old man.

Smiley announced a short break. There was a rush to the concession stands as the arena went into reset mode in preparation for the event everyone anticipated. O.D. spotted the other three bull-riders by their tell-tale helmets and leather gloves. First Junior, then Cody, came back into the arena, their childish shenanigans ended. Junior found his colorful barrel in its usual spot and rolled it out onto the freshly smoothed arena floor.

Cody examined the ropes he was carrying and pulled on his leather gloves. Without a word, he glanced out of the entryway one last time before moving to stand behind the bull-riding chutes. They both hoped John K. would arrive just in time to help with Cody's last-minute checks.

———

Hope tapped a pencil on an empty chair as the music started for the bull-riding competition. She peered down to the spot where the casino owner had been standing during Faith's barrel race. She was happy to see that he'd returned to a seat. Maybe his presence hadn't been the cause of Faith and Belle's poor showing tonight, but something had messed up their rhythm.

Leaning over to get a look at the bull chutes, she spotted O.D. pacing, with Cody doing the same thing at a distance. The little bit of Tara's interview she'd overheard played back in her mind. O.D. had not been asked about their contest, but he brought it up anyway. Was there a chance he understood how important it was to keep the rodeo going? Or was he still just showing off for the cameras? What had he said to the casino owner about his job offer? Maybe she should give the dark-eyed cowboy the benefit of the doubt for a while. Maybe.

"Okay. Everybody settled with fresh popcorn and lemonade?" Smiley began to set the mood for bull-riding. "This is the event you've all been waiting for. Tonight's bull-riding is special because it's the annual Billings Boys 'Thanks for Hanging On' contest. Even if nobody stays aboard their bull for the full eight seconds, somebody is going home five hundred dollars richer. My backup timeclock, Hope Catherine Caldwell, is with me to make sure we get everything just right. Ready, Punkin?"

Hope nodded. Her heart raced as it always did during this event. She couldn't imagine sitting on the back of one of these monsters, let alone trying to hang on when it was angry at the world.

In the chute to Hope's right, Cody Billings sat astride a dark gray beast with a prominent hump on his back. She focused on the top of O.D.'s cowboy hat as he nodded and pointed, helping his brother prepare for his ride.

Cody stretched to a standing position, then sat down again, tightening his grip on the rope and wrapping it around his right hand. The raucous music rumbled, increasing in volume. Dad was in his famous half-standing position, watching for the moment when Cody waved off everyone who was helping, then nodded to the man who was opening the gate.

"Here he is. Marshall Cody Billings aboard Cupcake!" Dad straightened to his full height as Cody and the bull leaped out of the gate. The crowd was cheering, hollering "go, go!" The huge bull twisted and leaped, trying to shake the hundred-and-fifty-pound teenager from its back. Just past the six second mark, he succeeded. Cody flopped off, landing on his feet with a disgusted look.

"That's a no-score. But six seconds on that bull is nothing to sneeze at." Dad sat down, picking up his notes for the next rider's name. "Remember, folks, the Thanks for Hanging On prize cannot be awarded to Cody, or anyone else with the last name Billings or Caldwell."

"So, I can't win either, Daddy?" Junior popped up from his barrel.

"That's right, Junior. This award's for non-family members only." Dad turned his attention to the chutes, where the next cowboy was preparing with his bull.

"And not John K. or O.D." Her clowning brother popped up again.

"Right."

These two had such a talent for filling time. Hope could only stand back and listen in amazement.

"And not Faith, or Hope, or Kayla Grace either." Junior's list of the rest of the family was repeated from inside the barrel.

"No, if your sisters or your cousin suddenly take up bull-riding they cannot win this prize tonight." The music started again. Dad stood taller as the next rider completed his preparations. "But this guy could do it. Let's see how Chase Whitfield and Gator do. Here they come, folks!"

Dad pushed the music lever up as the gate opened. The next bull and rider bounced into the arena. This young man was older than Cody but didn't have his natural ability. It only took Gator a little over five seconds to relieve himself of his pesky burden.

"Okay, folks. There's your time to beat. Five point two-five seconds. Jimmy Harrison is next. He thinks he's just the man for the job."

Hope caught a glimpse of O.D. standing next to Cody with a riding helmet in his hand. She had heard this argument many times. The bull-rider wanted to wear his cowboy hat; a family member or friend suggested the helmet. Many were trying to legislate the helmet as a protective device, but so far, it was optional. The rider still had the final say about his gear. Sometimes personal preference, even superstition, won out over caution.

"Hey, Dad." Junior popped up from his barrel.

"What, Junior?" Dad talked without looking at his clowning son. His eyes remained fixed on the officials helping the bull-rider get ready.

"Have I got a minute to run out to the restroom?" Junior started climbing out of the barrel.

"No!" Dad faked a stern rebuke. "You should have taken care of that way before now."

Junior ducked back into the barrel, rising to peek over the rim, prompting laughter from the audience before hiding again.

"Astronauts wear Depends. Guess I should do that too." Junior grumbled from inside the barrel.

Dad increased the volume of the music. The gate burst open, sending the latest cowboy on a furious bull into the spotlight. This time, the lanky young man was prepared for every twist and turn and plunging leap the animal handed out. The crowd noise grew louder as the timer approached eight seconds.

"There you go, Jimmy!" Dad congratulated the cowboy after the buzzer signaled a successful ride. "That, my friends, is how it's done!"

Shorty and Junior teamed up to rush the bull out of the arena. The cowboy picked up his hat from the dusty floor, waving it before running out to the cheers of the crowd.

"Yes, sir. This makes things interesting. All of the riders have another ride coming up, but Jimmy may just stick with this one. He gets eighty-eight points, with a very good shot at the Thanks for Hanging on Prize from the Billings Boys. If no one else makes it for eight seconds, that was a five-hundred-dollar ride right there."

The crowd was completely involved now, clapping in rhythm to the music as the next contestant prepared for his ride. Hope looked down the stairs again. Cody Billings stood by himself, wearing his cowboy hat. O.D. must have given up on the helmet idea. He was back behind the gate, helping other contestants. She understood the brotherly concern. After all, her own foolish sibling was out there for every single ride, intentionally getting in the way of a vicious animal. It was a good thing that bull-riding was the last event of the evening.

By the time this was over, they would all have used every ounce of energy they had left.

The next bull rider bore a nickname that should have been lucky, but David "Tuff" Kingston lasted less than three seconds. Dad sent Hope down to get a go or no-go from each of the cowboys on their second ride.

Cody and Chase were standing together as Tuff dragged his gear off the arena floor.

"Ready for the second ride?" Hope shouted in their general direction and received a thumbs up from all three guys. The cowboy who had lasted eight seconds stood a few feet away.

"Nope. I'm not taking any chances." Jimmy Harrison adjusted his hat, leaning back on the stock gate. "Maybe none of these other fools will make it to eight."

"Gotcha." Hope ran to tell Uncle Dub that they would only need three bulls this time, then headed up the stairs.

"Just three more rides, Hopie," Faith called to her just before she reached the platform.

"Yep. Is it wrong to be glad this night is almost over?"

"Not a bit. We've got a meal to plan when we get home." Faith flashed her a thumbs-up.

Planning a meal didn't seem as important as eating one right now. Hope found herself thinking of chicken and waffles at Amy Lou's diner. O.D. was pacing back and forth at the stock gate. He certainly didn't look like the over-confident showoff at this moment. From looking at him right now, you would think he was the one about to ride a bull, not his little brother.

"Ready?" Dad was watching for her as she reached the top of the stairs to sit next to him.

"Yep. Just like we thought, Jimmy's leaving well enough alone. It will be Chase, Tuff, and then Cody."

Dad nodded and cranked up the song that told the crowd

the final round was about to start. After just a few bars, he gradually pulled the sound lever down.

"Okay, folks. Our cowboys have put this off long enough. Time for the finale of tonight's rodeo. The final bull-rides. At this point, Jimmy Harrison is in sole possession of the Billings Boys Thanks for Hanging On prize. But he doesn't need to spend it too quickly. Chase Whitfield and Tuff Kingston still have a chance. Even though that $500 check will not have his name on it, Cody Billings is determined not to leave this arena without eight seconds on a bull tonight. Everybody ready?" Dad turned the music back up, standing up to peer down to the chutes. The crowd clapped and cheered. Several stood up, unable to contain their excitement.

The dusty ballet played out just below Hope's vantage point. The first two cowboys must have had chicken and waffles calling their names, just like she did. Neither had their minds where they should be for this important ride. Chase was down after four seconds on Sweetie-Pie. Tuff lasted just five on Rib-Eye.

Cody was already balanced on top of the chute when the huge black bull, Bad Boy, banged in and set the metal gates wobbling. Hope glanced to the right, where she spotted Cody and O.D.'s parents in their usual spot. Felicia's eyes were already closed.

"This is it!" Smiley turned the volume down. "Ladies and gents, before Cody bursts out for his last ride, I want to recognize two more very brave men in this arena. Shorty Jenkins and Calvin Caldwell junior. They may dress like clowns, but their role is vital to the safety of our riders. Let's have a big hand for our bull-fighters, Shorty and Junior!"

Hope waved at her little brother, who at the moment didn't show any traces of a smile. This was serious business for sure. She didn't envy his position in that barrel right now.

The next ten seconds were a blur. Cody and Big Boy bounded out of the gate. Hope felt like she was watching a movie. The bull leaped and twisted high in the air. Cody was ready for every move, his free arm serving to balance him perfectly. The clock climbed ever closer, and with one last triumphant bounce, it buzzed to signal eight seconds. Cody prepared to dismount. Something was wrong. The bull turned back toward the right just as Cody started his leap. He was launched into the air, sending his hat flying. His lanky body twisted awkwardly, with his feet launched toward the arena lights. He came down with a thud, squarely on the top of his head.

The rest of his body flopped to the arena floor.

16

Strong arms held O.D. back. *Move, Cody. Please move.*

"Wait, Dee." The voice in his right ear pinned him as Shorty frantically waved at the bounding bull.

Focused on the tall man's flailing arms, Bad Boy took a step backward, directly on top of Junior's right leg. Hope's brother went down abruptly as the bull passed Shorty, headed for the exit gate. When the pair of arms on O.D.'s left side moved to help close the gate, he leaped forward.

"Cody!" His little brother's eyes looked up, blinking. Cody's tongue came out to moisten his lips. *Thank you, God. He's alive.*

"Dee, I stayed on."

"Yeah, Bubba. You did. Now, lie still. Don't try to move." O.D. knelt in the dust, his hand on his brother's chest. Amazing how good a heartbeat could feel when it pounded against your hand.

"Hey. Did I lose my hands somewhere?" Cody's eyes moved back and forth, searching.

"Your hands? No, they are still there." Paralysis. If he

couldn't feel his hands, the legs were definitely not working. "Just be still."

"Do me a favor, O.D." The paramedics were just a step away now. O.D. waved at them as he focused on his brother's eyes.

"Give Mom two big thumbs up for me. She needs to know I'm okay."

O.D. turned toward the Billings box in the stands with both of his thumbs held high. The crowd cheered wildly, but Mom would have to blink back tears to see the signal.

Okay. For now. He stepped back as the paramedics asked Cody questions, touched different areas of his body. At least a dozen cowboys had assembled in a circle around them, facing outward to provide a shield of privacy. Looking out for a moment, O.D. spotted Shorty helping Junior limp toward the exit gate.

The ambulance crew worked quickly, strapping Cody to the spinal board to load him on the bulky four-wheel vehicle that would carry him out.

"You comin', Dee?" Cody's voice was suddenly years younger as they got him settled.

"I'll be along. Just do what they tell you. Mom and Dad are waiting just off the floor." O.D. trudged behind the slow-moving utility vehicle as Smiley chattered quietly to the audience. Or was he leading them in prayer?

Right now, it was all about his little brother. O.D. concentrated on keeping his head where his feet were. But he wished his head and his feet were anywhere but here.

"Hey." Dad caught his arm as Mom leaned in to look directly into Cody's eyes. "I need a favor. I want to go with your mom to the hospital. She's going to have trouble holding it together after your little brother gets out of her sight."

"Of course. I'll come too." O.D. nodded.

"No. I need you to stay to handle that presentation for the Billings Boys. The trophy is out here on the contest table. I signed the check just before Cody's ride." He pushed a folded check into O.D.'s hand. "I'm counting on you, son."

"Sure, Dad."

'I'm counting on you.' Had those words ever come out of his dad's mouth? Directed toward the middle son, the ordinary calf roper? Not the heroic soldier or the dare-devil bull-rider. O.D. swallowed hard and took a step back as the ambulance crew moved Cody from the four-wheeler into the back of the ambulance. Dad gave Mom a quick kiss before she climbed up to sit next to the gurney.

"See you soon." Dad waved as he trotted toward the parking lot. The ambulance driver waited to be sure his whole crew was aboard before leaving the back of the arena for the nearby highway. The siren whined, then wailed as they picked up speed. O.D.'s head was here where his feet were, but his heart was riding in the back of that vehicle as it sped away.

"You think he's okay?" Hope's voice next to him was softer than her touch on his right sleeve.

"Yeah." He truly did. "He's scared, but he's still Cody."

He could hear the music playing, the crowd clapping along. Smiley had succeeded in making sure the show was continuing inside.

"Faith is waiting for me. We're taking Junior in my truck. No need to wait for another ambulance." Hope had not moved from his side.

"What about Junior? Is he okay?" He turned to look into her face at the trail of tears on her cheek.

"He is in a lot of pain. Doc wants them to do X-rays right away. His ankle may be broken." Fear replaced the usual calm in her face.

"Hey. It's gonna be okay." He hugged her close, her arms

encircling his waist. Right now, he needed comforting as much as she did. She gave him a good squeeze before she stepped back.

"Are you sure?" Her eyes searched his face as she reached for his hand.

"Really." He crouched slightly to look into her eyes, touching her cheek with his finger.

She squeezed his other hand. "Dad sent me to see about the trophy presentation. Here's your portable mic." She clipped the microphone to his shirt collar. "He'll turn it on for you when it's time. Hey, Dad will want to come to the hospital as soon as the rodeo is over. Could you bring him?"

"I'm on it. Take care of your little brother. I'll be along soon." He smiled and squeezed her shoulder. "Move along, now."

"Thanks." There was a pleading look in her eyes. He'd never gotten the sense from her that she needed help dealing with anything. But the last few minutes may have changed everything for everyone.

"Ladies and gents, we will once again pull together as a rodeo family to wish Cody Billings well. The doctors at Crossroads hospital will do their best, with God's guidance, to get our brave bull-rider healed. But now, we have business to attend to."

O.D. waved at the reviewing stand, holding the gleaming bull-and-rider trophy in the crook of his left arm as he walked onto the arena floor. Jimmy Harrison rocked from one boot to the other just inside the entry tunnel.

"In our community, the Billings Boys is more than a truck dealership." Smiley kicked into advertising mode. "They are a big part of the community spirit that makes Crossroads the best place to live. In Arkansas, and for that matter, anywhere in the big-old USA. Tonight, the middle son of the third generation of Billings Boys is here to continue a tradition started by his Grandpa Billings. The Thanks for Hanging On prize! Take it Away, Little Dee!"

Little Dee? Oh well. O.D waved as the crowd applauded.

"Thanks, Smiley. First, I want to thank all of you who are still hanging on in the stands. We are still waiting on word from the hospital about my little brother Cody. Thanks for supporting us with your prayers and for all the years of trusting the Billings Boys with your transportation needs. It's more than that, really. That truck or car you drive is the closest thing without a heartbeat to a cowboy's trusted horse. You depend on it for the work you do, the fun you have, to get your family from place to place safely. At Billings Boys, we love being there for you. Come see us when you can."

Where had that spiel come from? He wasn't sure. But the small audience that remained seemed to enjoy it. *Now, let's get this trophy presented.*

"Jimmy Harrison, come get your trophy, young man!" O.D. held the gleaming award high above his head.

Jimmy walked out, hat in hand, with a smile that stretched from one ear to the other and wrapped around his head.

"Jimmy, on behalf of my Dad, John Davis Billings, and the rest of the Billings Boys family, here's your trophy with a check for $500.00. Thanks for Hanging On." O.D. handed Jimmy the trophy, then reached into his pocket for the folded check. When Jimmy had both in hand, O.D. took off his lapel mic to give it to the cowboy.

"Thanks, O.D." Jimmy had placed his hat back on his head so his hands would be free.

"I want to say thanks to the Billings Boys. My family hasn't bought a truck anywhere else for as long as I can remember. O.D, Cody and your family mean an awful lot to all of us. We're all praying for you." Jimmy held the mic toward O.D.

O.D. waved him off, swallowing a lump in his throat. The crowd was cheering wildly. Smiley stood, applauding with the rest of them. For once, he didn't acknowledge the applause, didn't wave his hat. This was not about him. They were cheering for Cody.

He realized he'd forgotten to promote the contest for Cedar Ridge, but that was secondary right now. He needed to get to the hospital. Taking the mic from Jimmy, he placed it in his pocket. Nothing more to say. Time to see what condition his family was in.

He stood at the bottom of the stairway, waiting for Hope's dad. The rodeo crowd was filing out, many whispering as they passed. Bits and pieces of conversations reached him.

"So sad."

"Just terrible."

"I don't think I could ever come back to a rodeo if I were them."

Did they not see him standing there? Maybe they didn't know who he was. Just so much unnecessary chatter. He shifted from one foot to the other, heart sinking to his boots.

17

Hope sat on the edge of the plastic chair in the hospital waiting room, sipping the hot cup of coffee the volunteer had poured for her. She replied to Uncle Dub.

Thanks for taking Champ and Belle back to the barn.

Anytime. When you see O.D. tell him that Shorty is staying at the arena with his horse until he gets back.

Sure. Tell Shorty thanks.

She walked toward the glass doors that led to the parking lot. Junior's injury was minor compared to Cody's, but she was still glad her dad was on his way.

"It'll be okay." She remembered the kindness in O.D.'s eyes when he told her this. Did he believe that? Maybe Junior would recover without any long-term problems, but what about O.D.'s own brother? Cody was in for a long journey.

A familiar set of headlights turned into the parking lot.

O.D.'s truck slid into the first available parking space. Her dad walked around the front of the pickup to pat O.D. on the shoulder. O.D. sprinted to the hospital entrance.

"How's Cody?" O.D. surveyed the cramped space.

"Your mom and dad are both with him. No one says anything to the rest of us." She had never seen this desperation in his face before. "Hey." She held his arm, forced him to look at her face for a moment. "God has got this."

"Yeah." He took a short breath and squeezed her hand. "Thanks."

"How's Junior?" Dad walked up behind O.D.

"They're sure either his right leg or his ankle is broken. They are doing an X-ray. There wasn't room for both of us in the treatment room, so Faith and I are taking turns." She held her coffee cup toward her dad, but he shook his head.

"I'll go spell Faith. Come on, son. Let's go see if they'll let you find your mom and dad."

All the spark drained from O.D. as he followed Dad through the double doors leading back to the examining rooms. Alone in the waiting room, she watched the TV screen in the corner.

"Tonight, a scary situation at the Caldwell Family Rodeo," Tara Williams stood outside their empty ticket booth for her story. "Sixteen-year-old Cody Billings was seriously injured as he dismounted the bull he was riding." Hope forced herself to watch the clip they showed of Cody strapped on the back of the utility vehicle leaving the arena floor. "The RV3 family joins area rodeo fans in praying for this young man and his family."

Pray. In all the confusion, had Hope done that yet? She closed her eyes to send up a quick thank you. This accident could have been so much worse.

Tara was still talking on the TV screen. "Before leaving to go check on his little brother, O.D. Billings presented the coveted Thanks for Hanging On trophy with a $500 check to

Jimmy Harrison." O.D.'s speech about the dealership being more than a place to buy a truck was impressive. He certainly had stage presence. Maybe he could get some of that bravado back when he went to see his mom and dad at Cody's bedside —she hoped so. They could all use a little cheering up right now.

The automatic door leading in from the exam rooms swooshed open. Faith walked through, heading over to Hope for a hug. "Your little brother is starving. He sent me out to the vending machine." She stood in front of the machine, stretching and smoothing the dollar bill in her hand.

"Are you sure that's okay?" Hope stood next to her, stomach growling at the sight of honey buns and chocolate candy bars.

"Yes. No surgery tonight. The doctor said the swelling has to come down for a few days. So eating is fine." She inserted the bill, waiting for the icing-covered pastry to drop with a satisfying plop.

"So, we can take him home?" Hope released a huge sigh. "That's good news."

"Yeah. The doctor is filling Dad in about what to do for the next few days. But it's not that easy." Faith stared at the soda machine to their right.

"Why?" Hope suddenly remembered Belle and Champ. They needed to be settled for the night soon.

"Junior won't leave the hospital until he sees Cody." Faith faced her sister, tears welling up in her weary eyes. "They are getting him settled in a room upstairs, so I guess we can visit if it's okay with Dave and Felicia."

"Yeah." Hope swallowed a lump in her throat. Her mind went back to Mom, hooked up to so many tubes and monitors, looking so tiny in the hospital bed.

Mom's whole objective each time she was required to stay

here was to get home as quickly as possible. Eventually, even their house was not home for her. Never satisfied to rest, always demanding she be allowed to go Home.

"Cody's in for a long road back. He'll probably be here a while." Faith's mind seemed headed down the same dark path.

"Yeah." Hope was back to one-word answers. She was sure they were expected to visit. But she was not looking forward to this. "What else does our brother want to eat?" Hope found a handful of change in her pocket. Junior reacted to stress by eating.

"He said, 'A honey bun, and ...' I told him I would find something else." Faith retrieved the first item from the bottom of the machine.

"Hand me your change. I'll get him some jalapeno cheese thingies." Hope inserted coins, waiting to be sure they registered before making a choice. "I'll take this stuff back. See you in a minute."

Faith was already checking for messages on her phone. She waved at Hope as the automatic doors opened to go back toward the examining rooms. A chorus of beeps covering whispered conversations welcomed her as she passed people leaning against the walls next to closed doors. So many stories, so much trauma here tonight. She had inherited her mother's hatred for the Emergency Room.

"There she is." Smiley was helping Junior get seated in a wheelchair when she walked into the green-tiled room packed with equipment.

"Whatcha got there?" Junior reached toward her. "I'm starving."

"I don't think you deserve a good boy treat tonight." Hope put the food behind her back. "What's the first rule for a rodeo clown?"

"Distract but stay away." Junior dropped his hands to his

lap. "All I could think about was Cody. And Bad Boy was acting so strange tonight. I hope they were able to settle him down after he left the arena."

Hope handed him his treats. Worried about the bull. This baby brother of hers would never cease to amaze.

"Okay, Mr. Caldwell. You're free to go." The male nurse walked in, standing next to the wheelchair. "It's my job to get you safely to the lobby tonight. Think you can stay out of the way of raging animals for a few days until the surgeon gets your repair work done?"

"Piece of cake. My sisters have a big Thanksgiving meal planned. I'll be too full to waddle anyway." Junior wiped his cheesy fingers on his left pants leg. "Look what they did to my jeans, Hope."

Evidently, the paramedics had cut off one pants leg to get access and reduce the chance for swelling. "They're the bomb." She poked his shoulder.

Junior reached for the nurse's hand and gave it a firm shake. "Let's get out of here."

"I told your mother we should have left well enough alone after God gave us two princesses." Dad followed them with the plastic bag that contained Junior's boots and hat. "But you need a boy, she said. Huh."

Hope's stomach quivered as they passed through the door that led out to the waiting room. Maybe Junior had forgotten about visiting Cody tonight.

"Okay, chief. Thanks again." Junior shook the nurse's hand again as they reached the bank of elevators near the hospital exit.

"No problem. Go home and try to get comfortable." The young man patted Junior's shoulder. "Dad," he turned toward Smiley. "The X-rays will be shared with the surgeon. Did someone show you how to get on the hospital's portal to get updates on the surgery schedule?"

"I've got that covered." Faith walked up with her phone in her hand. "I'll show you when we get home, Dad."

"Is he gone?" Junior tried to turn around in his wheelchair, but with his right leg propped up in front of him, he couldn't manage. "How are we gonna find Cody?"

Hope's heart sank. There would be enough going on in that hospital room tonight without an invasion of neighbors.

"Shouldn't we just get him home, Dad?" Hope hung back to catch his denim sleeve.

"Probably. But to be honest, I'm not sure we will all fit in the truck. We have to keep your brother's leg propped up, so he will take the whole back seat. I may have to call Shorty to beg for a ride." He handed Hope the bag holding Junior's boots, reaching into his pocket for his phone.

"Daddy." All the bravado was gone from Junior's voice now. "I promise we won't stay long. Please?"

"Okay. We'll all sleep better once we know he's going to be okay." He took the bag back from Hope, then followed Faith and Junior into the elevator.

"Wait. We don't know his room number." Hope texted O.D., hoping he would respond.

622

The response came instantly. Maybe a showoff, but he was a good communicator.

She stepped into the elevator and pressed six. Her throat was dry as an empty riverbed. The queasy feeling returned in her belly. Sitting in the emergency room had been hard, filled with memories of the times Mom had come here in terrible pain before they had made the decision to call in hospice. But the rooms upstairs would be worse. She had no desire to see Cody hooked up to all those machines, totally helpless.

No one spoke as they traveled up. The doors slid open on the sixth floor. Junior pointed silently after reading the sign directing them to Cody's room number.

"Here to see the Billings family?" A nurse met them near the desk.

"Yes, ma'am." Hope cleared her throat to become the spokesperson for the group.

"Please remember the other patients are sleeping." The nurse directed them down the hall, where O.D. and his father leaned on the wall in the softly lit corridor. Her stomach lurched. This would be a good time to turn around, get back on the elevator.

Faith stopped pushing and hung back with Hope, prompting Dad to take over propelling Junior toward the room.

"This is hard." Faith whispered as she caught Hope's arm.

"I know. They probably don't need a lot of company tonight." Hope stopped walking.

"Dad is in preacher mode, and Junior ..." Faith started down the hall.

"That could very easily be our brother in that hospital room." Hope squeezed her sister's hand.

"Come on." Faith resumed her pace without letting go of Hope's hand.

"Dave, Little Dee." Dad greeted their neighbors.

"Quite a night." Mr. Billings shook Dad's hand, then Junior's. "Thanks for distracting Bad Boy, son."

"Yeah. Too bad I couldn't keep my leg out of his way, but hey, it's what I do!" Junior craned his neck, trying to peer through the small opening to the hospital room.

They all stood there for a long second until O.D. finally

spoke up. "The doctor says they want Cody to rest, so most of us will have to clear out soon."

"Is he in a lot of pain?" Hope couldn't help asking. The medicine they brought her mom never helped quickly enough.

"Well, he said a while ago that it hurts, but he thinks that's a good sign." O.D. locked eyes with Hope. Did she see fear?

"The doc wants me to rest, too, but I just had to check on my buddy." Junior was getting impatient. Hope was afraid he would try to stand up.

Another nurse opened the door to the room. "Y'all can all visit at once for just a minute, then let's give Cody some quiet time."

Dad pushed Junior through the door, Faith close behind. O.D.'s dad followed.

"You okay?" She whispered to O.D. as they entered the room last.

"I guess I have to be." O.D. stared at the floor.

"Cody, look who's here." Davis Billings stood over his youngest son's face, talking a little too loudly. "Well, I guess that neck brace will keep you from seeing them. It's the Caldwells. All of them. O.D. came back in too."

"Thanks for coming, guys." Hope was glad to hear Cody's voice, even though it sounded weak.

"Hey, buddy." Junior maneuvered his wheelchair to the bedside to squeeze Cody's hand. Cody's fingers moved slightly as if trying to return the gesture.

Felicia Billings raised her hand to her lips, jabbing Davis with her elbow.

Davis nodded, hugging her close.

"Hey, sorry Bad Boy was so rude to you tonight." Junior squeezed Cody's hand again.

"Not his fault. I think I made the whole ride, right?" Cody focused on Junior without moving his head.

"Yeah, yeah. You got an 86 for that 8 seconds. But Bad Boy turned back just as you were sliding off. Nothing you could do about it." Junior pulled himself up taller, managing to look into Cody's eyes. "Hey, you need some sleep. I will be back whenever I can get somebody to drive me over here. My gas pedal foot is bunged up, but we're both gonna be fine. You hear?"

"Yeah." Cody licked his lips. His mom stuck a straw into a can of cola. She waited behind Junior as he rolled his chair out of the way.

"I think we could use a prayer before everybody leaves." Felicia held the straw as Cody took a sip. "O.D.? Could you lead us?"

O.D. glanced at Hope, the now-familiar panic all over his face. "Well, we have a real preacher in the room. Smiley, how 'bout you dial up the Lord for us?"

"I'd be honored." Smiley reached his hands out on either side. As the circle formed around the hospital room, O.D. locked fingers with Hope.

"Abba Father, we are linked together tonight in concern for this young man who is so dear to all of us. We know that the doctors are going to be busy finding out just what's up with Cody's injury. You already know all about it. We rest in the promise that You are with Cody every step of the way. Be with Davis and Felicia, John K. and O.D. as they do everything they can to help. Be with the rest of us as well, as we do our level best to support them. You are all-powerful, all-knowing, all-seeing. We trust Your perfect plan. Thank You for sending Your son to save us. It's in His precious name we pray, Amen."

Hope turned toward O.D. His eyes were wide open, his grip on her hand remained strong. Dad had included John K. as if he were right here in the room with them. O.D. had a tremendous burden to bear. For all his big talk, this superhero couldn't summon any of his powers at the moment.

"Cody, I'm gonna leave you with Mom and Dad tonight. I need to go get Buck home from the arena. I'll see you in the morning." O.D. dropped her hand, patting the blankets on Cody's legs.

Felicia stood to give O.D. a hug, and Davis opened the hospital room door to usher the Caldwells out into the hallway.

"I think my cellphone is dead." Dad glanced at his phone as they got outside the door. "Faith, can I borrow yours to call Shorty? With Junior spread across the whole back seat of the truck, there will only be room for two in the front. If O.D. will take me back to the arena, Shorty can give me a lift home."

"Well, how about this." O.D. stood next to her dad. "How about you go ahead and go home with Faith and Junior. Hope could come to the arena to help me with Buck. Then I'll bring her home."

"Yeah. I probably need to make sure the office got locked anyway." Hope nodded at O.D. "And Shorty lives in the other direction. No need to keep him out any longer than necessary."

"Okay." Dad shook O.D.'s hand. "What would we all do without the two most level heads in this group? Just be careful with my youngest daughter, young man."

"You can count on me, sir." O.D. couldn't have sounded more serious.

Junior's chin almost touched his chest. "Hey," Hope tapped the top of his head. "You behave."

"Yeah." His half-hearted smile reminded her of the face he'd worn as a kid when he'd begged her not to tell their mom about one of his foolish stunts.

"See y'all soon." She leaned into Dad for a hug. They would all sleep well tonight.

O.D. opened each glass door on the way to his truck, following behind her.

"Thanks." She broke the heavy silence as she climbed into his truck.

"Thanks for coming with me. I had all of that hospital room I could take for the night." His dark eyes held about half of their usual sparkle.

"For real. I guess your mom and dad will both stay tonight." She couldn't imagine either of them wanting to leave Cody's side.

"Yeah. Funny." O.D. shook his head.

"Funny?" Hope reached for his hand.

"Sometimes I wondered if they remembered they had three kids. Not just the superhero older one and the daredevil youngest. Now, they're down to depending on the nobody middle son." He checked to be sure her right boot was inside the truck before he slammed the door.

As he slid into the driver's seat, she remembered all the times he had tried to stand out. So much grandstanding after a successful calf roping ride. The real O.D. was hidden somewhere underneath the bluster. That steady, smoldering fire that powered him added a glint of excitement to his deep brown eyes. Probably what the casino owner picked up on too —O.D. could be quite an asset to them.

They rode without speaking for a minute or two. When he started speaking, he addressed the windshield. "You were at the airport the day John K. came home."

"Half the town was there." What a day that had been.

"Yeah. It was something, all right. Just before my war hero brother came down the escalator, the mayor walked up to shake my dad's hand. He said something like, 'You must be very proud of your son.' Dad said, 'Oh yes. So thankful he answered the call to serve. Let me introduce you to my other son, Cody.' I was standing right beside him. It's like he forgot who I was." O.D. was quiet again.

"Your dad takes you for granted because you are always there. It happens in the best of families." Hope could vouch for the loneliness just outside the spotlight.

"I guess. But I'm wondering if I should just move along, find my own place somewhere."

"Like at DownRiver Casino?" Now she'd done it. He'd know she read his text message. It wasn't fair bringing this up with Cody's situation, but it was too late now.

"Huh?" O.D. turned to look her way.

"There was a message from Heston on your phone."

"And you thought I was jumping over to the enemy camp." O.D. shook his head.

"Well, I guess it would pay better than driving a delivery truck." Hope tried to keep her voice calm.

"About twice as much. Heston is persistent. Even talked to me some more at the rodeo tonight." O.D. reached for her hand. "But I can't get excited about that place. Certainly not excited enough to try to convince people to spend their hard-earned money there."

"So, you turned him down?" She should have known. But it was good to hear him say it.

"Yep. Not my style." O.D. squeezed her hand before turning his attention to the road again.

Only a few lights remained at the Caldwell arena when they pulled up next to the stock barn. O.D. stopped his truck, stepping out to greet Shorty, who waited with Buck.

Hope stepped out of the passenger side of the truck toward the entrance to the office. After punching in a code on the security panel, she stepped inside to switch on the lights. This final check each night had been so important to Mom. All money locked up, no stray papers on the desk.

A small stack of contest entry forms had been placed in the middle of her desk. Three entries at $50.00 each. Well, it was a start. Not a rousing start, but something. The little metal lockbox with the entry money was safe in the top drawer of her file cabinet, with the key in its spot under her tape dispenser.

She walked past the desk Mom and Dad had shared. The light on Dad's old-school landline was blinking. No one ever got much response from him with email. He'd always told her to check his messages.

"Mr. Caldwell, Quinton Heston from DownRiver Entertainment. Give me a call when you can. I'd like to get you and your brother together to talk about an idea I had. My numb—"

Hope deleted the message.

18

O.D glanced over at Hope, who was leaning on the passenger-side door of his truck. Maybe she was just feeling the weight of tonight's rodeo. The world in front of his windshield was in the same heavy mood. A saturating mist shrouded the little town. The farther he drove, the harder it was to spot familiar landmarks. November in Arkansas was always strange, but this one was more menacing than usual.

He concentrated on driving. It was a good thing he had the task of returning Buck to the barn and Hope to her house. On nights like this, the temptation was strong to just drive away into the night. No destination until he ran out of gas. He'd often wondered if anyone would notice.

"Is it me, or is it extra dark tonight?" Hope's voice intruded in his thoughts. Or had she even spoken aloud?

"I was thinking the same thing." He remembered what he had shared earlier about his dad not noticing him. Might not have been necessary to tell her. She always read his thoughts anyway.

"I hope Faith and Dad have Junior settled. I think they gave him some medicine that will help him sleep. That will be good for all of us." She sat up straighter, turned toward him.

"Yeah. I hope Cody rests tonight too. Seems like his whole objective is to stay alert, but until they can see what damage has been done, he needs to stay still." O.D. blinked, trying to dispel the picture of his baby brother hooked up to those machines.

"Hospitals have no sense of time. I don't know how anybody rests." She sank into the seat again.

"I guess your memories of hospitals are still pretty fresh." O.D. adjusted the warm air hitting his windshield. There was a fine line between clearing and fogging.

"People talk about being afraid of hospitals. I don't think that's it for me. I just feel so useless. Like there's nothing I can do to help." She pulled her collar up around her neck.

"But you were the one in your family who stayed with your mom when she was there?" He risked a glance in her direction.

"She asked for me. Dad and Junior needed to keep the ranch going. Faith tended to the house. My job was to fetch the nurses when they didn't answer the call button fast enough." Her voice was so quiet.

"Sorry to bring up bad memories." Maybe he should turn on the radio.

"No, that's okay." Hope touched his hand as he reached to find some music. "I haven't talked about it enough. I've been trying so hard just to keep the easy stuff taken care of."

"Easy stuff?"

"The routine. Handling entries at the rodeo, making sure Dad has what he needs to make his announcements, keeping the bills paid. Easy. Predictable." Her voice regained some strength.

"You're pretty good at all of that stuff. I don't think it's very easy." That was an understatement. Details drove him crazy sometimes.

"But I'm no good at helping when the chips are down. When Mom was so sick, nothing I did for her was good enough. No matter how I tried, she always said I wasn't doing it fast enough or not the way the nurses had shown me. Nothing helped her pain. I was the one who always failed her."

O.D. stared ahead. What could he say to change the subject? If only she'd let him play some music.

"Hey. None of us are any good at fixing big things like that. At least not by ourselves. Cut yourself some slack." He slowed down as he neared the shortcut to her house.

"Thanks. You're right. Your family has a lot more to deal with than mine, if we can just keep the rodeo from getting sold out from under us. Thanks for your help with that, by the way." She took a deep breath, blew it out.

Tiny, glowing eyeballs pierced the fog on the right side of the road. Deer. He slowed to watch carefully.

"There's the other one." Hope pointed behind the first deer to his buddy, following close behind.

"Thanks. Glad they both stayed put." Without a word between them, she had picked up on the danger.

He turned into the gravel driveway that led to her house and didn't want to let her out. Driving in the fog was not his favorite thing to do, but somehow, this trip home from the arena cleared his mind. She was the perfect person to be sitting in his truck, no matter the weather.

He settled the truck into Park, turning her way. Her hair was still in its French braid, but tiny tendrils surrounded her face. There was a softness in her eyes as she hesitated before reaching for the door handle.

"Okay, then. If you or your folks need anything, you have

our numbers. Really." She peered under his hat, meeting his glance.

"I know. It's good to have friends. I just don't have any idea what we'll need right now. Sort of hard, this not-knowing." He swallowed hard.

His house would be so empty when he got home. Even though he was used to staying in his room over the shop, the loneliness was already stifling.

"I can run errands for you, bring you stuff. I know how hard staying in the hospital can be." She didn't move for the door, so O.D. scooted a little closer to her.

"Do you mind if I pray? Dad was in full preacher mode tonight, but I think we could use one last chat before we go to sleep." Her voice held a pleading note.

A chat with God? His mom had asked him to do that at the hospital. But he just didn't seem to be able to start that conversation these days. More power to those who could.

"Sure." He placed his hat on the dash behind the steering wheel, bringing his other hand to cover hers.

"Heavenly Father, we need you tonight. Things are in a mess. Stay with Junior, ease his pain so he can sleep. Please watch over Cody in the hospital as Dave and Felicia stay close by. Help the doctors figure a way to help him. You know we want his body to be fully healed, but please help us remember that Your plan for him is perfect. Be with Dee and Buck. Keep them safe as they go home. Just thanks, God, for always being there listening. Amen."

O.D. hadn't closed his eyes. He'd been fascinated by her lips moving, the pressure of her hands tucked into his. She was so comfortable having this conversation with someone she'd never met. Could he ever get to the point where he could talk to God like this? For now, he was content to watch and listen as Hope prayed. Her eyes opened. The spell was broken. She smiled weakly, then abruptly reached for the passenger door handle.

"I guess I'd better go in."

He nodded, afraid his voice would crack if he tried to talk.

"Thanks for the ride. See you soon." She slid out, closing the door.

Driving toward his house, he realized he couldn't stay there. He'd unload Buck to head back into town. That big empty ranch would be too much for him to handle alone tonight.

———

"We have coconut meringue pie left." Aunt Candace brought O.D. his customary cup of coffee with one cream, one sugar to the booth in the back of the diner. "How's Cody?"

"Mom texted me a minute ago. Cody and Dad are both asleep. She's going to head out to the waiting room to find a recliner or a couch. They won't know much until the docs can review all the pictures they took." He surveyed the diner, glad that Aunt Candace was on overnight duty tonight. Not many other people were here on a Tuesday.

"No pie. I am in the mood for breakfast. How about a fully loaded omelet with hash-browns?" O.D. sank back into the vinyl cushion. Might as well fuel up for the day. He probably wouldn't sleep before it was time to make his first delivery.

"As you wish, My Champion." He smiled as she performed an exaggerated curtsy before placing his order. That nickname was leftover from his one and only high school triumph in bull-riding. He'd gladly switched to calf roping after that.

The door to the lady's room closed with a bang. A slim figure in a too-large camo jacket slinked past his table. His jacket. Oh no. It was Lissa. She sat at a table near the counter, glanced his direction, fiddling with her silverware for a moment before standing up again.

Please don't. Too late, she was walking his way.

"Just coming back from the casino?" She slid into the booth across from him.

"No. The hospital." Surely, she'd heard about Cody.

"Oh yeah. That's right. Your brother had a wreck on a bull. Hope he's okay."

"Can I get you anything?" Aunt Candace spoke to the girl but gave O.D. a quick questioning glance.

He nodded in response. He could handle this.

"No. I just need to talk to Mr. Billings a minute. I guess you can bring me a glass of water."

Really? Who came to the diner for a glass of water?

"Order what you like. I'll pay tonight." O.D. pushed a menu toward the girl.

"Okay. Bring me the double waffle supreme, with a side of corned beef hash and extra blueberry syrup." She placed the menu back in its spot behind the napkin holder.

"Yes, ma'am." Aunt Candace scribbled on her pad, shaking her head as she walked away.

"Hungrier than you thought?" He couldn't hold back a smile.

"Yeah. I guess." She was quiet for a long second as she began to shred the napkin she held in her hand.

O.D. had the strange feeling he should just give Aunt Candace some money and leave.

"So, your mom and dad must be pretty torn up." She moved the shreds of paper into a neat pile.

"Yeah. It's kind of scary." Did she just want to talk about his brother?

"Well, maybe it will cheer them up when they find out they're going to be grandparents." She leaned toward him.

After looking to each side, she sat back and took a deep breath.

"What?" What did she say?

"Yeah. That will be some good news. By next summer, there may be a brand-new Billings boy in town. Or maybe a girl. That would be something new. A Billings girl." She pulled his camo jacket around her, resting her hands on her stomach.

"You?" O.D. couldn't come up with more than a word or two at a time. "You and John K.?"

"Why not? You think I'm not good enough for him?"

Aunt Candace brought two heaping plates of food, locking eyes as she placed his plate in front of him.

"Need anything else?" She must have realized he couldn't speak, so she directed her question at Lissa.

"No. This looks just great." Lissa pulled a new napkin out of the chrome dispenser and moved the pile of shreds to the side before covering the thick stack of waffles with syrup.

"Are you sure?" O.D. couldn't imagine eating right now.

"Of course." Lissa put a huge, dripping bite in her mouth.

"Does he know?" Was this why his brother had dropped out of sight?

"I was just about to tell him when he took off. Now, nobody but Maria knows how to talk to him." She carved another bite, refilling her mouth.

"Maria knows where he is?" O.D. sat up straighter. Of course. He should have been talking to Maria about John K.

"Well, not really. They text, but he says he doesn't want to see her, or anybody else. So, he won't tell her where he is." Lissa sat back against the vinyl seat, swallowing a long sip of water. "I can't ask her to tell John K. that he's the daddy. She loves that scumbag. It would kill her."

O.D. thought back to the night he had found Lissa in John K's truck. She'd been scared, desperate. Certainly not the same girl with the bottomless appetite that was sitting across from him now. What craziness.

Instead of launching back into her plate of waffles, she grew quiet.

He picked up his coffee. What would he tell his parents? This didn't sound in character for his superhero brother. But then, John K. had changed a lot since coming back from the Middle East.

"I just don't know what I'm going to do." Lissa pulled another napkin out of the dispenser to dab at her eyes. "I have to tell my parents, I guess."

"You haven't told your parents?" O.D. couldn't believe this. She was acting so strangely—ravenous one minute, emotional the next.

"No. My dad will absolutely freak, especially if he's been drinking when I tell him. I have to wait for the right time." A shadow crossed her face. "I can't ask Mom to keep a secret until I have a plan. I need to be ready to move out."

"Move out? Really? You think they'll kick you out?" O.D. couldn't imagine that in his family. But they were all boys at his house. He sat stunned for a moment. So, what would happen when her problem was obvious to everyone? "Have you been to a doctor?"

"Not the right one. I went to a free clinic. They told me that it's not too late for an abortion." She said the last word so softly, he almost didn't hear. "But I won't do that. It's not this baby's fault I messed up."

O.D. pulled out his wallet. It would take around thirty dollars for their supersized meals. That left three more twenty-dollar bills between him and payday.

"Here." He pulled out the money, pushing it toward her. "Go to a good doctor. Get enrolled in whatever programs they offer to stay healthy. We'll work on the next step when the time comes."

Lissa tucked the bills in her—his—jacket pocket.

"I wasn't asking for money. I just ... I hoped maybe you could talk to your brother. He needs to know. But I appreciate your help." She tackled the plate of waffles again.

O.D. pushed his plate aside. If he tried to eat anything now, there would not be a happy ending. "Sorry. Believe me. I will tell him if I get the chance."

Should he ask her not to tell anyone else? Again, not his decision.

"Okay. Well, thanks for breakfast. I will let you know what the doctor says." Lissa pushed past the empty tables to the front plate glass door. He couldn't help thinking about how alone she must feel.

Grandpa Dee's favorite bible story, David and Goliath, popped into his head. He used to tell O.D. that David was just a kid with a slingshot that day. He never intended to be a brave warrior. His job was to bring his brothers lunch.

He always enjoyed that story. Since he'd started life as a preemie, he never got as tall as most of the other guys, including his brothers. Living in the shadow of giants. Yep, that summed it up.

The moral of that story was that nobody has to do life alone. Grandpa Dee said God would always have our back.

He got more out of listening to those stories than sitting in a church pew.

If only Grandpa's old story about David and the giant were true. He and Lissa could both use a good rock or two in their slingshots right about now.

19

Hope sat at the kitchen island with a cup of hot chocolate and a honeybun. She'd be bringing her brother an identical breakfast as soon as he woke up.

She adjusted the volume on the little television in the kitchen to keep it quiet enough not to disturb Junior, who had settled in the double recliner portion of the sectional last night instead of his own bed. Faith said that would probably be better anyway since he could keep his injured foot elevated.

"Good morning, River Valley. Your first look at the day's happenings is brought to you by DownRiver casino." It was still hard to get used to these ads. So evil just a few years ago, talk of a casino was commonplace now, even welcomed as a source of jobs for the community. She took a tiny chocolaty sip, turning the volume down even more as a commercial started.

"Just in time for the Holidays—an exciting new contest at DownRiver. Win not one, but two new vehicles! A sturdy four-door truck for Dad and a smart little SUV for Mom to haul the kids around in. Best of all, you can enter totally free of charge!

Just drop in anytime to fill out an entry form. We're open twenty-four seven, even on Thanksgiving and Christmas!"

What? They were giving away a truck too? With a car along with it? Who would even remember the pitiful little contest at the Caldwell rodeo that costs fifty dollars to enter? She turned the television off. What a mess.

"Good morning, Punkin. Looks like your brother's medicine is working." Dad placed a pod of his favorite coffee in the machine before positioning a Caldwell Family rodeo mug below the spout.

"Yep. I guess we'll hear from the doctor today about next steps. I'm glad Faith hasn't gone back to school yet. It will be a chore just hauling him around until he can drive again." Hope picked up a piece of her honey bun with a fork. Sweet breakfasts were great, but too messy.

"You text me when you hear something, okay? I'm going to make a lap around the ranch before I head to the office. Uncle Dub wants us to get our heads together about the stock before the next show." He found his favorite travel mug in the cabinet, resetting the coffee maker to get his 'to-go' brew going.

"You want me to fix you some eggs and bacon?" Hope stood up. They were all adjusting to not having a full breakfast on the table every morning since Mom was gone.

"No, honey. Don't worry. The drive-through will see me coming. They have my order ready almost before I hit the order button." Dad sipped on his mug as he waited for the travel cup to fill.

"I'll eat his eggs and bacon." Junior's comment came from the sectional in the living room.

"Yes. I'll bet you will." Hope laughed. "If you can stay awake long enough."

"I have never slept through a meal yet. You can bring my honeybun and hot chocolate first. I have to eat something with my first dose of meds." Junior picked up the remote control, tuning to the same news program Hope had been watching.

Hope shook her head. Oh boy. This brother of hers was going to enjoy being waited on.

What would Uncle Dub have to say to Dad? Would he be talking about selling the rodeo again? Maybe it really would be just the usual livestock update. She couldn't control every conversation those two had.

"What? The casino is giving away a truck too?" Junior turned up the volume as the commercial repeated.

"Well. I guess it's a popular idea. If our contest raises some money for Cedar Ridge, we'll count it a success. We have lots of generous fans, you know." Dad grabbed his coffee, shrugged into his Sherpa coat, and propped his 'everyday' cowboy hat on his head.

"See y'all later. Junior, please behave yourself. Try to be content. Your sisters were not put on this earth to serve you."

"Are you sure about that? I think it just might be their ultimate purpose." Hope detected an edge of pain in his voice. She started lining up slices of bacon in the iron skillet after setting the burner to medium-high.

"You just do your part and stay out of the way of angry bulls." Hope threw a potholder at Junior.

"I was behind the bull. He didn't mean to step on me." Junior had lost the bravado in his voice. "I wonder how Cody is today?"

Faith walked over to sit on the sectional next to Junior. "He's resting, like you should be. You need some help making a bathroom run before your eggs are ready?"

The siblings made the long trip down the hall to the bathroom. Faith really would make a good nurse someday. Mom had not appreciated her help nearly enough.

"Hope Catherine," She could hear her mom's feeble voice

coming from the master bedroom just off the family room. "My goodness. What is taking so long?"

Why was it so hard to remember the good times? There had been plenty of those over the years. But this house echoed with disappointment instead.

So many people had offered comfort by saying, "It must have been a blessing for your mom to die at home." Was it? It wasn't a blessing for Hope. If only she enjoyed the sense of peace they all imagined. Her life had not been peaceful. Would it ever be?

In the cubbyholes near the back door, she found her warm, hooded jacket. Even in this dreary weather, a ride on Champ sounded better than hanging around waiting for time to go to work. She reached into the *H* basket to retrieve her heavy gloves and knitted hat.

"Where are you going?" Faith and Junior had returned to the family room.

"Just out to tend the horses. Maybe go for a ride. You got this?"

"Yeah. This will be fine." Junior raised his hand over his head.

"Okay. See y'all in a few."

The cool mist refreshed her cheeks as she stepped out onto the patio. The brightening sky reminded her that the sun was still out there. Maybe the breeze that tickled the strands of hair on her forehead would muster enough strength to push some of the clouds on their way. No matter, Champ would appreciate the exercise.

"Morning, sweet boy." She began her calming chatter as soon as she spotted the horse standing in his stall. "Want to go for a ride? Let's get you some breakfast first." She stepped out, fastening a rope across the opening of the stall, leaving the half-door open.

"There's our sweet Belle." She went through the same process at the filly's stall, patting the chestnut nose, rubbing the horse's neck.

The horses huffed and snorted as they moved back in their stalls, allowing room for Hope to place a bowl of feed below their noses.

Hope finished the final check of Champ's harnesses and the cinch under his belly.

"Okay, let's go." She mounted in one smooth motion, encouraging Champ to leave the small corral at the back of the barn. The mist became heavier, so they wouldn't stay out long. No use getting either of them too cold and damp. The sun was emerging over the top of the hill that separated the Caldwell property from the Billingses' land. Champ followed the familiar path around cedar trees and past some good-sized boulders.

As Hope and her horse settled into a plodding routine, she listened as the birds started their morning concerto. Trills from the tops of the trees led to prolonged practice sessions by the local mockingbirds. In the distance, a dog barked, greeting whoever was bringing his breakfast. Champ navigated the pathway with no problem. She leaned forward, even standing a little in her stirrups as they reached the top of the hill.

Sunlight warmed her cheeks. Maybe the fog would burn off after all. Champ stopped next to the abandoned house that watched over the Billinges' place. This had been the meeting place for both families of siblings for as long as she could remember. She had always wondered why Felicia changed the subject when the boys talked of restoration.

She swung herself out of the saddle, allowing Champ to search for a new treat to graze on. The sunlight brightened the clapboards that had faded from white to a dingy gray. The porch roof sagged, but the structure that stretched across the front was still inviting. Hope could imagine rocking chairs looking out over the valley, a family enjoying the breeze that swept across the top of the hill. If this place were on the Caldwell side of the property, she might talk to her dad to see if it could be salvaged.

She walked out to pick up Champ's reins, surveying the quiet ranch below. O.D.'s truck was already gone. His horse, Buck, stood in the pasture, enjoying the increasing warmth of the sun. She remembered how quiet, how tender, O.D. had been last night. Nothing like the bragging showoff image he projected to everyone else.

From this vantage point, she could just barely see the whitewashed wall on the side of the old barn near the highway. Had Felicia been contemplating another mural when Cody's accident changed everything?

Champ snorted impatiently. Hope mounted up to head back to the Caldwell side of the hill. Sitting on that porch was tempting, but the real world was waiting below.

20

O.D. found the remote control at the side of Cody's hospital bed. He switched away from the infomercial that had shown up while he dozed off. Wasn't there an old western movie channel anymore? He stopped on a familiar image of Andy Taylor smiling at Barney in the Mayberry courthouse. Easy to pick up on that since he had all the episodes memorized.

Beeps from the IV pole startled him, but he didn't jump up the way he had the first few times. The nurses could hear it too. One would come in momentarily to reset the dripping solution. As long as the more important monitors stayed steady, all was well.

He rolled to his left hip to readjust his stockinged feet in the plastic chair. How had his parents spent so many hours here before his little brother's surgery? He was glad he'd convinced them to go home to leave him on duty for a bit. There was no real rest for anyone in a hospital room.

"How's it going in here?" The friendly nurse with hair the

color of red Kool-aid buzzed past him, quickly satisfying the alert on the IV.

"He hasn't been this quiet for this long ever in his life." O.D. sat up. "Thanks for taking such good care of the little scoundrel."

"Little?" She looked at the screen showing Cody's vital signs. "I do believe he's taller than you, big brother."

"Yeah, well. There is that." One more reminder that he was the shrimp in the family.

"You know, they pay us to do this around the clock. Y'all gave us a list of visitors allowed post-surgery, so if anyone outside of that list shows up, we'll give you a call. You really don't have to sit here all day." She tucked the white sheet around Cody's feet again after taking a look at his toes.

"I know. I guess I'll go find some lunch. Be back shortly." O.D. slid into his boots.

"You're a world champion big brother." She patted his knee as she hurried toward the door.

He checked Cody's face again. Was it regaining color? That gray pallor he wore before they took him back to the operating room had been the scariest thing O.D. could remember. Maybe worse than the skin color was the silence.

He'd loved watching his little brother sleep since he was a baby, but rarely had he slept this soundly for this long. Always squirming, smiling, even chuckling during some kind of happy dream. This stillness was so hard to get used to. It might be helping the healing process, but it was just so out of character for Marshall Cody Billings.

"Okay, dude." O.D. patted his brother's shoulder. "They're running me out. I guess I'll go see what's happening in beautiful downtown Crossroads. Can I bring you a milkshake?" Oh, to hear the canned response they'd picked up from Grandpa Dee as kids. 'Don't shake it too hard.'

He found his baseball cap on the table that held the phone and turned away. On the TV screen, the Taylor family relaxed on the porch as Andy serenaded them with his guitar.

"Be back in a minute." He headed for the hallway, stretching his arms over his head. Sitting so long was getting to him.

Outside in the hospital parking lot, the sun was peeking through the clouds, but the November nip was still in the air. The lunch rush was over. He was the only person walking toward a vehicle right now. He checked his text messages. Completely quiet on this last day before Thanksgiving. Everyone had big preparations to make while the Billings family's life was on hold at the mercy of blinking alerts and hospital shift changes.

Lissa's strange announcement replayed in his head. He had not found the right time to mention it to his parents. Besides, that kind of thing was certainly something John K. should announce. If he only knew how to find him, O.D. would be glad to give him the chance.

O.D. sat in his pickup, at a complete loss for where to go or what to do. He turned on the ignition, easing the driver's side window down to let in some fresh air. On the service road, traffic moved at a more normal pace. It was, after all, a busy weekday in Crossroads. The truck instinctively headed for the Billings Boys dealership.

He stopped in his customary spot behind the service department. Busy routines proceeded all around him. Service techs with their clipboards greeted customers, directing them to the waiting area. Mechanics scurried around pickups and sedans, intent on their inspections. Out back, the smokers waved at him as they took their quick break at the designated distance from everything flammable.

Why was John K. so opposed to working here? To O.D., it

had always been an extension of home. The employees were like part of the family.

He walked behind the counter in the customer's waiting area to fix himself a cup of coffee. The smell of freshly baked chocolate chip cookies teased his salivary glands, reminding him he hadn't stopped for lunch. Customers milled about, with the television in the waiting area tuned to the weather channel. Getting to their destinations before the turkey was carved was foremost on the minds of most who were waiting on the faux leather couches and red plastic chairs.

Shouting echoed from the front of the building.

"What the—?"

"Oh, man. Look at that!"

"Somebody call 9-1-1!"

He ran outside the huge sliding doors in the service bays to see what all the shouting was about. The shouts were louder as he headed through the parking lot, approaching the service road in front of the dealership. The unmistakable shrieks of a horse in distress joined the human voices. Behind a steaming, mangled pickup truck, a dusty white horse trailer was on its side. Bumps and thumps from inside drew him closer.

Customers gathered, coffee in hand, at the entrance to the dealership. O.D. followed a burly young man dressed in scrubs who was headed for the driver's side door of the truck. Others were attempting to reach the driver of the SUV that had obviously been turning in front of the pickup, causing the crash that now blocked all access to the Billings Boys main driveway.

Good Samaritans surrounded the doors of the two vehicles, so O.D. headed for the horse trailer, keeping an eye out for leaking gasoline. *Please. We don't need a fire.* Just two long paces away, he saw a familiar slim figure in blue jeans and boots climb up to the side window, pushing back the sliding glass.

"Hope." This was not her family's rig. She must have been driving behind the wreck.

"Try to keep everyone quieter." Hope peered down into the dark trailer.

O.D. passed her message along to some men standing nearby, his finger to his lips, librarian-style.

"Shhh, easy, buddy." She reached her arm through the window. "He's tethered in the front, but the lead is long enough. He won't choke himself, I don't think." O.D. could barely hear her voice.

"Are his legs wrapped?" O.D. worried that the horse could break a bone in his struggle to stand.

"Yes." She waved at O.D., then leaned back into the small opening. "Easy, fella. It's gonna be okay." She emerged from the window to lock eyes with O.D. "We need a way to get his lead untied so he can stand up."

"Got it!" O.D. sprinted back toward the Billings Brother's lot, heading straight for the department that spruced up the new cars for delivery. He pushed the glass door open and found the long tool they used when keys got locked inside a car. Dodging bystanders, he ran back to the trailer, where Hope was stretched flat, her head and both arms inside the window.

He clambered up next to her. "Here, maybe this will help." He showed her the tool he held. She wordlessly scooted over, pulling one of her arms out of the window.

Oh, man. She'd been beautiful that night in his pickup with her hair down. But now, with her eyes lit with purpose and passion ... *Shake it off. This horse needs help.*

O.D. poked his head through the window next to Hope's left arm. If only she could keep the horse calm for just a minute. He spotted the lead rope, loosely knotted at the front of the trailer. At least this owner knew how to load a horse safely. Rolling to his side, he maneuvered the long, skinny metal tool down and forward, hooking the rope. He closed his eyes, moving the tool gently forward and then back, A small clink echoed as an extra halter fell to the trailer floor. He rolled back over, peering down to verify the lead rope was loose.

"There ya go." Before he could finish his announcement, the horse stood with his feet on the bottom side of the trailer, blowing out a satisfying snort.

"I think I'm stuck." Hope's face was so near. Her hazel eyes shone in the dim light. He chased off a crazy urge to kiss her. *Not now, Romeo.*

"I got ya." He straightened up, scooted back a little, hoisting her through the window by her leather belt.

A cheer went up from the back of the trailer as the owner broke away from the paramedics. His horse stood patiently inside. Hope's face lit up in a victorious smile.

"Great job." He whispered.

"Couldn't have done it without you, MacGyver." Her eyes searched his.

How long could he sit here like this? Maybe forever.

"You two okay up there?" A policeman yelled from the ground behind them,

"Yep." More than okay.

"Yes, thanks!" Hope moved over to the wheel side of the trailer to jump down. O.D. followed, landing behind her.

"Well, what do you know?" Tara Williams scurried toward them, her photographer running along behind. "Can we get a comment from our favorite calf roper?" She didn't wait for his nod before signaling the cameraman to start recording.

"For some reason, I am not surprised to find that the hero of this horse rescue is one of the Billings Boys. Middle son O.D. Billings. How are you feeling now that this crazy crash is getting cleaned up?" She shoved a microphone toward his face.

"Well, Tara, I feel like an Overgrown Delinquent with this lock-buster thing in my hand."

"Overgrown Delinquent" Tara laughed. "My stars! I will find out what your real, full name is if it's the last thing I do!"

"Here's the real hero." He pulled Hope over in front of the camera. "Have you ever met a real live horse whisperer?"

"Seriously?" Tara took a step back. "It's Hope, right? Hope Caldwell of the Caldwell family rodeo. So, do you know these people and their horse?"

"No, ma'am. I was on my way to work." Hope shifted from one foot to the other.

"And you are the one that got the horse safely out of the trailer?"

"It was a team effort." Hope spoke softly into the microphone. "The horse wanted out so badly that he would have tried to come through the window if I didn't stuff myself into it."

"Well, congratulations, you two. Looks like you are both superheroes today." She waved at the photographer, who turned off his camera.

"Thanks, y'all. I need to go see if I can get a statement from the driver. Impressive job. Really." Tara hugged Hope and waved at O.D. on her way to find the driver.

"Thanks for your help." Hope brushed dust off her blue jeans.

"I guess this guy picked a pretty good place to flip his horse trailer. Lucky you were so close when it happened." O.D. guided her toward the roadside as the police began to clear away the extra spectators. "You want to come inside? They have coffee and chocolate chip cookies ready."

"Thanks, but I have a lot to do before dinner tomorrow." She took off her baseball cap to smooth back the tendrils of honey-colored hair that had escaped from her braid.

"At least you will have a dinner. We're still at the hospital."
O.D. shrugged. Funny how they always steered the
conversation back to their families.

"Come over to our place. There will be way too much food."

"I'm supposed to go get Grandpa Dee to take him to visit
Cody tomorrow. We'll eat whatever the hospital has, I guess."
He could see someone running toward him with a telephone in
their hand. Was his brother okay?

"Well, I'm glad you helped today." Hope moved closer and
leaned in to brush his cheek with a kiss. She scampered past
the police line toward her truck.

Stunned, O.D. was frozen for a moment until a service
technician tapped his shoulder.

"Mr. Billings. It's your dad." The guy handed him the
phone.

"You were on TV. You okay over there?" O.D. expelled a
sigh. No news about Cody.

"Yeah, Dad."

"The driver of the truck and the car all right too?"

O.D. backed up a few steps to get a better look at the
accident scene.

"They are loading the driver of the car into the ambulance.
The truck driver is walking his horse around while they
upright what's left of his rig." O.D.'s stomach growled. That
lunch was long past due.

"Take him inside, offer to get him a loaner, make him feel
at home."

O.D. laughed. Davis Billings's mind was always on the
dealership. "Sure, Dad. We'll take good care of him."

"Cody okay when you left?" Dad's voice was softer. Mom
must have come near.

"Still sleeping like a baby. The nurse said I needed a
break."

"Maybe she needed a break from you. You probably smell to high heaven after spending the night there."

"Nah." But after crawling around on top of the horse trailer ...

"Well, come on home, take a shower. You're not driving today, are you?"

"No, I took the day off. Yeah, I'm on my way home." After he drove through the nearest burger joint.

"Okay. I think your mom has stayed away long enough. We'll take over the baby brother watching. Oh. O.D." His dad paused.

"Yeah?"

"Thanks for running by the dealership. Looks like you were right where the Lord wanted you today."

The phone went dead. He handed it back to the tech who was trying to help the wrecker driver get things hooked up.

Right where the Lord wanted him to be. Yeah. Maybe so.

———

Hope closed her eyes as she leaned her head back on the headrest of her truck. She blew out a breath she didn't know she'd been holding. What just happened? How did O.D. instinctively know what she was thinking as they worked to free that beautiful animal from its torture chamber?

A horn honked behind her, snapping her eyes open. A policeman directed her into the right lane, navigating around the tow truck, the television crews, past the wreckage of the pickup and horse trailer. The owner comforted his horse as the paramedics climbed back into their vehicle.

Thank you, Father. You are very good at guarding and keeping us from harm. Stay with this man and his horse till they get safely home. Amen.

She should be breaking down in tears of relieved stress from the ordeal she'd just been through, but instead she was smiling? O.D. had a pretty doggoned great superhero persona when he was just being himself.

Dad met her at the door when she got to the rodeo office.

"Hey, it's the hero of the day! Great job rescuing that horse, Punkin." He hugged her tightly. She smiled at Uncle Dub, coming out of the conference room.

"I just had to let him know he was safe." She took a sideways step toward her desk. "And O.D. showed up to help too."

"Yeah, The TV made a big deal out of both of you." Dad turned the volume down on the set that hung just inside the door.

"Everything turned out okay." Hope picked up some mail from her desk. "What's happening around here?"

"Same old stuff." Uncle Dub walked closer to the television as the now-familiar casino ad aired again.

"Don't forget to register for our huge giveaway. Win a new truck and a great new car. All free, the week before Christmas. DownRiver Casino makes your dreams come true!"

Dad didn't seem to notice. Everyone went to their respective posts in the office to check emails. Hope took a deep breath. Her hands shook a little as she stacked the bills she had received in the mail to begin the payment process. Being a horse-rescuing hero wouldn't mean much if they didn't have a rodeo in the family anymore.

A text from Faith popped up on her phone with a picture.

Think we can make something like this happen tomorrow?

Pumpkins and gourds of all sizes filled a long linen-covered table. Yes, this was definitely something their mom would approve of. The natural look and fall colors would remind them all of her.

> Sure. What do we need?

Some pretty gourds. Rolls from the grocery store. I'm not going to try Grandma's yeast rolls.

Hope smiled. Faith's last attempt at that famous recipe had been memorable, but not for the right reasons.

> Sure.

She remembered O.D. saying his family would not be having Thanksgiving because Cody was in the hospital. Hadn't she seen something at the grocery store about a fully prepared dinner they would deliver?

No reason to beat around the bush. She texted him too.

> Hey

> Would this help with your family's Thanksgiving dinner?
> They deliver.

She sent a link from the store's deli.

> Need to order by NOON today.

She hadn't even stopped to wonder what O.D. might be doing right now.

Great idea!

Thanks!

Talk to you soon.

His rapid-fire responses were immediate. That went well. Now, she needed to finish the rodeo's bank statement so she could get Faith's shopping done. She smiled as she pulled the paperwork out of her "in-basket." This holiday wouldn't be like any other, but maybe it would be bearable.

21

O.D. stopped to allow the automatic door to swing open before he pushed his Grandpa's wheelchair through the front door of the assisted living center.

"Feelin' kind of icy out here this morning." Grandpa Dee pulled his knit cap down around his ears. "I don't get outside much these days."

"You want to go back inside?" O.D. stopped pushing.

"No! Let's just get to your big old warm truck." Grandpa reached down with both hands to move the chair himself.

"Yes, sir." O.D. took over the pushing, glad he'd left his truck locked and running. Good thing Grandpa Dee wasn't a great big guy. Together they could still manage to get him up into the truck seat, but that transition might not work much longer.

As he closed Grandpa's door, he wondered how soon they could get Cody into one of their vehicles, if ever. What kind of modifications would be needed?

"You think the Thanksgiving feast at the hospital will be

better than what they serve here?" Grandpa Dee settled into his seat, snapping his seatbelt.

"Probably about the same." O.D. laughed. "But Mom spent yesterday preparing Grandma's cornbread dressing recipe. Aunt Candace will have a pie."

"Or two." Grandpa Dee laughed. "When she's not pushing food across the counter toward a customer, she's at home cooking. Your Grandma raised two gems, for sure."

"You helped." O.D. stopped in the traffic at the major intersection in the town of Crossroads. It was a little busier out here than he expected for a holiday.

"Not nearly enough. Military life is a tremendous burden on the parent left at home." Grandpa Dee stared into the distance for the next few blocks.

O.D. had never asked about the end of Grandma's life. He remembered Dad running interference to keep the boys away from Mom for a few days as people buzzed around their house and the little house on top of the hill.

None of the adults had wanted to go inside the little house with the beautiful view after that day. The three brothers had taken charge of moving furniture out when Grandpa Dee came to live with them for a time, then went to the care facility.

"It's a lot quieter here than it was yesterday." O.D. slowed down a little as they passed the dealership.

"Yeah. My grandson was all the buzz at supper last night. Looks like you did a great job with your horse rescue." Grandpa pulled his warm gloves up on his wrists.

"It was really all Hope Caldwell. Talk about a real horse whisperer. You should have seen how calm she was. All while she was upside down with her top half stuffed into the window of a trailer." He smiled at the memory.

"Sounds like she's a pretty good Little Dee whisperer to me." Grandpa chuckled.

"You know, I'm beginning to agree." He returned the laugh. If there was one thing he could trust, it was that his Grandpa would keep his confidence. If, in fact, he remembered this conversation an hour from now.

"Well, this is it. Your destination for a gourmet Thanksgiving dinner. Please wait for the vehicle to come to a complete stop before exiting."

"Always the comedian." Grandpa gave him a surprisingly firm poke in the shoulder.

O.D. parked, ran around to the passenger door. It constantly amazed him how well his grandpa accepted change. The moves from the house on top of the hill, to their house, to the nursing facility were too easy. Giving up driving, then using a wheelchair, he had just pushed ahead with a smile.

"I think I can climb down." Grandpa was already moving when O.D. opened the door. "The legs still work, they just don't hold the rest of me up too well." He settled himself in the wheelchair, pulling his cap down tight around his ears. "Let's go!"

O.D. navigated the hallways and elevators to Cody's floor. Just a couple of days out from surgery, he hoped the excitement of the family descending on Cody would not be too much.

"How we gonna fit in that hospital room?" Grandpa Dee stuffed his gloves in his coat pocket.

"They're bringing Cody to a little conference room down the hall. The nurse said she'd take him back to his room if his vitals don't look right." O.D. waved at a familiar face behind the nurse's station.

"You've got it all figured out, don't you, son. You're a born manager." Grandpa waved at the same nurse, following with a wink for good measure.

O.D. pushed the chair toward the conference room. Him, a manager? No, he was just the driver.

"Hey, boss." Clark, the marketing manager from Billings Boys, emerged from the room just as O.D. and his grandpa arrived. "Good afternoon, Mr. Tolliver. All set up, O.D. You should be able to visit to your heart's content."

"Visit?" Grandpa Dee pulled his cap off to smooth what was left of his hair.

"We're gonna do a FaceTime with Gramps and Granny Billings all the way from Montana." O.D. shook Clark's hand. "Thanks to this technical wizard."

"Not a wizard, just a nerd. Y'all have a great day. My mom is waiting dinner on me, so I'd better run." Clark jogged into the hallway.

"Thanks again, Clark. You're the best." He backed Grandpa Dee's wheelchair next to a table covered with a checkered cloth holding three covered dishes. "I'll go see if the rest of the family's ready. You'll be okay?"

Grandpa stretched as he took a deep breath. "Yep. Me and this dressing are already becoming very close. Smells just like your grandma's for sure."

"Okay. Be right back." O.D. counted chairs. This place should work just fine. First time he'd been in charge of a Thanksgiving dinner. At least it didn't require him to cook.

He stepped into the hallway, almost bumping into his mom, who carried an armload of artificial autumn leaves.

"Hi, sweetie. Got Grandpa Dee settled?" She stopped short, waiting for the hug that Dee delivered. "Your Dad is coming with Cody and the nurse. I'm going in to fix up the tables."

"Sounds good. Kind of an unusual Thanksgiving, huh?" He spoke softly. It wouldn't take a lot to make her tear up today.

"But so much to be thankful for." She smiled. "Thanks for getting this all set up for us. Now, go see if Daddy needs anything. I'll see you in a minute." She bustled off, displaying her usual measure of energy.

O.D. glanced out the fifth-floor window again as he walked toward Cody's room. Was it too much to hope that John K. would decide to show up? Was any disagreement worth all of the turmoil he was causing? There was just no figuring out what was happening in his older brother's head. He checked his text messages again. The thread between them was still very one-sided. John K. had read them, but there was no response. O.D. had kept him informed of Cody's room number, the time for the dinner, the arrangements to FaceTime the western grandparents. Oh well.

"Are you sure he will be okay?" O.D.'s dad followed behind the nurse that pushed Cody's wheelchair.

"Yes, Mr. Billings. The doctor said this dinner was perfectly fine. It will be good for him to see something besides those four hospital room walls." She winked at O.D.

"So far, it doesn't look very different." Cody's voice sounded sort of weak, but O.D. was glad to see him in a semi-upright position. Even with the nurse and the IV pole tagging along close behind.

"Hey, big bro!" Cody lifted his right hand to shake O.D.'s as they passed. "Dinner ready?"

"So far, we only have cornbread dressing. I'm headed down to get the rest of it." He pushed the down button on the elevator. Hope's idea about a complete turkey dinner delivered anywhere in the area was the perfect solution for this messed-up celebration. Now, if the delivery driver would show up in the lobby.

"Hey!" Aunt Candace spoke up just before he plowed into her. "I know you could mow me down without a backward glance, but you wouldn't want to ruin the pies!"

"Not for any amount of money!" He decided against a one-handed hug. "Need help?"

"No, just point me to the banquet room." She glanced both directions in the hallway.

"Down there to the left. Mom and Dad and Cody are already there with Grandpa Dee." O.D. stepped onto the elevator, holding the door open for Aunt Candace. Was all this chaos worth it? With the doors closed, he leaned against the metal railing inside the elevator car. Yeah. The fourth Thursday of November without the chaos would have been even harder to handle.

O.D.'s phone pinged in his pocket. Probably the food delivery driver. Hopefully, this transaction could be taken care of without disrupting the rest of the visitors to the hospital.

In the lobby, a young man with a white windbreaker and a chef's hat held a stack of aluminum plates.

"Mr. Billings?" The driver balanced the food on a ledge near the elevator. "I guess this is yours."

"Yeah. Thanks for bringing it. I am starting to question the sanity of trying to have a Thanksgiving dinner in a hospital room." He handed the guy a wad of cash. "That should cover it. Have a great holiday."

"You do the same!" The driver ran out the mechanical doors in front of the hospital. O.D. pushed the up button with his elbow. Sanity? Why even pretend.

Another ping came from his pocket. Whoever that was would have to wait. The hospital staff would not appreciate a turkey, mashed potato, and gravy mess on their elevator floor.

"What floor?" A kind-looking older lady reached for the buttons inside.

"Five. Thanks."

"Smells wonderful." She smiled, but a tiny tear slid down her cheek.

"We're in a conference room up there. Might as well join us." O.D. pulled the pans a little closer to his blue-jean jacket.

"Oh, thanks, dear. My hubby's on liquids before his surgery. I ate a sandwich at home. But y'all enjoy."

When the door opened on the fourth floor, she stepped off. They did have a lot to be thankful for. He balanced the pans all the way to the conference room, where Aunt Candace and Mom took them from him, placing them on the decorated serving tables.

Mom busied herself removing lids, adding serving spoons. She stepped back, nodding at Aunt Candace.

"Okay, Dave. You can offer a blessing, then we'll start filling our plates." Aunt Candace placed a dipper in the gravy dish.

The family formed a circle of sorts. O.D. stood between Cody and Grandpa Dee, crouching to reach their outstretched hands.

"Heavenly Father, we are overcome with joy to be gathered here for dinner with our precious Cody. Thanks so much for bringing him through this trial so far. We know that You will continue to be here with him and with us. Thanks for all Your fantastic gifts. Especially Father, for this family. Such as it is." Dad cleared his throat. Was he going to say more? Maybe something about John K?

Grandpa Dee broke the silence. "Amen."

O.D. helped Grandpa Dee move up to a table. He was glad to see Mom coming over to make sure Cody could navigate with the silverware the hospital had provided.

"Son, do you know how to get the FaceTime thing going?" Dad brought him a cell phone.

"Sure." O.D. set his own plate down in a spot across from Grandpa. He made the connection, Gramps and Granny's faces smiled from the television screen.

"Witchcraft." Grandpa whistled through his teeth.

"Hey, Marshall Cody!" Granny piped up all the way from Western Montana.

"Hi, Granny! Happy Thanksgiving." The room hushed for Cody's weak voice.

"Are you okay to eat all of that food?" Grandpa Billings leaned closer to the screen.

"I might share with the others. Maybe." Cody's voice was growing stronger. O.D. detected some of the old swagger.

"Well, I'm really glad to see your face, son. You had us worried." Grandpa Billings reached for Granny's hand.

"Yeah. Sorry about that. But it's like John K. told me, I just need to keep trying to find my feet. Once I can make them co-operate, I will be up and around again. I already found my fingers and hands. I wiggled my toes for him this morning, so he says if I can just keep track of my feet, I will be fine!"

Mom dropped her fork to the floor.

"John K. was here?" Dad walked to the door.

"Yeah. While the rest of you were still at home sleeping. He'll be back." Cody picked up a fork full of cornbread dressing.

"Well, good. Your soldier brother has a lot of wisdom." Grandpa Billings said from the television screen. "We're proud of all of you boys."

O.D. walked to the table to serve himself some pie. Had John K. actually been here, or was Cody just so used to having advice from him that he was working their brother into his hallucinations?

He pulled out his phone to see the message he had ignored. Not his brother. Hope.

Rode up to the little house. Call if you see this in the next minute or so.

"I'll be right back." He set the pie down. Grandpa Dee dug in with vigor.

"Hey." She picked up his call as he stood in the hallway just outside the conference room.

"How's Cody?" Of course she would ask that before telling him what was on her mind.

"He's eating more dinner than any of us." O.D. leaned back against the wall, watching as nurses bustled down the hallway.

"Good. I just had to leave the house. I have never lived through such a quiet Thanksgiving morning." He could hear the tension in her voice.

"Must be hard without your mom." Might as well say it.

"Yeah. Besides that, Dad and Uncle Dub are sneaking off to whisper in the hallway every few minutes. I'm sure they're talking about the rodeo."

"Well, don't worry too much. The board still has to vote, right?" O.D. wasn't sure he could handle their family's politics while dealing with his own.

"I guess. You have enough to deal with. I shouldn't be talking about this to you." There she was, reading his mind again.

"No. Talk about anything you want. Are you still up at the old house? Does it look all right?"

"I just love it up here. You can see for miles. My family's house, your place, even Cedar Ridge Ranch. It's kind of chilly, but clear. I don't think we're getting any rain or anything for a while." He could sense her taking a deep breath.

"Well, enjoy that fresh air. Maybe when everyone goes home today, I can ride up there too." At the moment, nothing sounded better.

"I won't come after dark. Don't want Champ to trip or something."

"Yeah. Well, we'll meet up there sometime soon."

"Tell your family I said happy Thanksgiving." The wind whistled behind her.

"Okay. Talk to you soon. I'll lose the signal when I head back down the hill." Her words were choppy.

"Be careful. Happy Thanksgiving."

O.D. placed his phone back in his pocket. Funny how just riding up the hill could make a difference in the phone reception. They had the same situation at their deer camp over in the next county. The abandoned shack at the top of the hill was the best place to talk when he and his brothers went hunting.

The old shack? Why had he not thought of this earlier? He had driven out to the deer camp looking for John K., but he hadn't been up to the old shack. He hoped Grandpa Dee was almost finished eating. Once he was safely back at his room in the nursing facility, O.D. had a little drive out in the wilderness to look forward to.

22

Hope dropped her purple knit cap in her basket by the back door. Faith barely nodded as she carried a dish of corn casserole into the dining room.

"Timed that perfectly." Kayla removed a fruit salad from the refrigerator.

"Four cooks were plenty in the kitchen." She refused to let anyone make her feel guilty about escaping for a few minutes. Dad, Uncle Dub, and Uncle Bill had been doing it all morning. Junior was stuck, but he usually sat mesmerized in front of the Macy's parade every year anyway.

"I wish I'd gone with you." Aunt Tina whispered in her ear as she hugged Hope. "It was tough here without your mom choreographing us."

Hope glanced at the list she'd created for Faith on Mom's whiteboard. Her contribution, a pumpkin pie, was checked off before she went to bed last night. Even after the whole horse rescue adventure, she had done her part.

"Okay. Looks like our ladies have performed their usual magic." Dad slipped into his preacher voice as he stood at the head of the table. "I don't think Catherine would mind if we skip the sharing of each one's blessings this year. We all miss her. For sure."

Junior's crutches clanged to the floor as he plopped into a chair at the other end of the long table.

"We have all learned that God blesses us in His own way, in His own time. Let's give thanks together." He reached out his hands to link with Faith on one side and Aunt Tina on the other.

Hope reached for Junior and Kayla's hands, bowing her head. She breathed in one leftover trace of outdoor freshness before starting off with her own prayer. *Thank You, Lord, for the ability to ride and for friends who answer the phone when I need to talk.*

"Heavenly Father, we are truly thankful." Dad gained confidence with every word. "For family that travels from far away, for those who are nearby. For the wonderful food that has been prepared. For healing in Junior's body. Even Lord, for —" he paused, cleared his throat, "for taking Catherine to be close to You, instead of leaving her to suffer here with us. We know that Your plan is perfect. Help us in the days ahead to learn to let go of the reins a little bit. Help us to be still and truly know that You are God. Amen."

Hope opened her eyes, expecting Dad to be staring directly at her. Let go of the reins? Easy to say. But what did that mean? He wasn't looking at her. He reached for the carving knife to tackle the turkey. Was there already a deal with the casino owner?

She smothered her turkey, dressing, and potatoes in gravy, passing Mom's old gravy boat to Junior. The future of the rodeo wasn't even talked about. For as long as she could remember, they had lived from one performance to the next. Uncle Dub had always reported on the stock, which bulls were ready, which ones were retiring, how many calves were available for the roping events. Should she try to bring it up?

"Hope, how was your ride this morning?" Dad may have been a little clairvoyant, for real.

"Great. I took Champ up to the top of the hill. It was a little chilly, but at least it wasn't raining. The fog lifted early." She buttered a roll. If she hurried, she could go out again after helping with dishes.

"Belle would enjoy a ride too. Maybe I'll sneak off in a little bit." Faith dabbed her mouth with her napkin.

"You girls deserve a break after all of this." Dad reached over to squeeze her hand. "The men-folk will take over cleanup. Right, guys?"

"Sure." Uncle Dub reached for the piece of pie his wife was offering.

"Won't be hard. Junior will finish the rest of the food. Plates will be nearly clean already!" Uncle Bill jabbed Junior with his elbow.

"Just doing my part." Junior plopped another pile of mashed potatoes on his plate.

So, maybe she was the only one worried about the rodeo. Funny how everyone else continued in this strange new world. If Mom were here, she and Hope would probably head for the office after dinner. Mom knew what it took to keep a business going. The rest just sat back and took it all for granted. Hope folded her napkin beside her plate. Let go of the reins. Really?

"Hey, sleepy!" Faith poked Hope's arm. "Want to go out and shoot some hoops with Kayla and me?"

She heard Mom's voice in her head again. "You kids go outside. Get some fresh air." It was just a ploy to get a quiet minute with a cup of coffee and gossiping with her aunts. Maybe she should stay inside for the gossip.

What about Granny? She didn't see her very often. She

glanced over to where her dad's mom was sitting with a photo album in her lap. Granny glanced up.

"Go, get some fresh air, kids." Dad's ESP was hereditary.

"Okay, let's go." She followed the other girls to get their jackets,

"I'm coming!" Junior yelled from the living room.

"Okay. You can referee. But behave. No falling on that ankle." Faith went back to help him stand up.

Hope found Junior's blue jean jacket on a hook and tossed it to him. He struggled for a minute to balance with his crutch while putting arms in sleeves. They had been spoiling this kid. He'd have to fend for himself a little bit every now and then.

Hope tucked her phone down into her blue jean pocket. She really should call O.D. to see how their dinner at the hospital had gone. No, he said he was bringing his grandpa from the nursing facility, so he wouldn't have much time to talk until later.

"See if you can make one from here." Kayla stood past their free-throw line and lofted a ball toward the goal. Faith rebounded as it bounced off the backboard and dribbled it to the spot Kayla had chosen.

"Nothing but net!" Junior cheered as Faith's ball met the target.

"Time out!" Kayla stepped aside, pulling her phone out of her pocket. "Y'all have terrible reception here. I'm getting a whole string of messages from this morning all at once."

"Watch out for Junior!" Hope stood next to her wobbling brother as Faith ran past with the basketball.

"Wow." Kayla walked over to show Faith a text on her phone.

"Oh, man. That can't be good." Faith took the phone and shook her head.

"What?" Hope left Junior and deflected the forgotten basketball with her foot.

"Maria, that girl that has been seeing John K., just posted something weird about her friend Lissa." Kayla brought the phone to Hope.

"Can't understand parents who would kick out flesh and blood. Remember I'm always here for you, Lissa." Hope read.

The comments were popping up quickly under Maria's post.

"*What?*"

"*She told me she was talking to her Mom about the baby. You'd think they'd be excited about a grandbaby.*"

"*You know her dad. Only thing he's excited about is Jack Daniels.*"

"Man. Some things don't need to be shared on social media. I feel sorry for Lissa." Hope handed the phone back to Kayla.

But you didn't see the first part." Faith took the phone again, moving close to Hope. "Read this."

"*Lissa said her Mom went ballistic, but she told her it was all okay. At least the Billings would be good grandparents.*"

"*I heard O.D. gave her the money to go to the doctor. He said he'd help her with whatever she needed.*"

Hope's mouth went completely dry, and she thought her knees would buckle under her. No way. Not O.D and Lissa. She'd seen her trying to cozy up to him, but he'd always sort of pushed her away. At least when Hope was around.

Hot tears stung her eyes. Faith stood silently next to her, and Kayla picked up the basketball.

"What? What's going on?" Junior hobbled to them on his crutches.

"I'm going for a ride." Hope ran to the barn. Inside, Belle

stomped and snorted. Champ peered over the stall door, hoping to get out.

"Okay, you two." She opened Champ's stall, "Want to go up on the hill again?" She spoke softly to the big bay, but her hands shook as she gathered his tack and secured it. Maybe she shouldn't ride until she calmed down a little. But she couldn't stay here while everyone put two and two together.

Why did she care so much about the trouble that O.D. found himself in? Seems he had been living a double life. The secret was about to become very apparent to everyone. Not her business. So, why did her stomach feel like lead? What was making her heart pound? Tears stung her eyes as she fastened Champ's cinch before opening the stall door. Why was this news about Lissa affecting her so much?

She led Champ to the gate on the other side of the corral, allowing him to walk through before she latched it behind them. They headed for the top of the hill. But what would she do when she got there?

With no urging from Hope, Champ took the lead. His pace was steady but determined as he tromped through the crunchy leaves on the edge of the land Dad had mowed. As they reached the rocky trail to the top of the hill, Hope's eyes stung with tears. Idle gossip. Why did she allow a bunch of silly girls texting to control her feelings? But it wasn't idle. Lissa had told more than one person about her baby. Why would she lie about the connection to the Billings family? It was totally possible that O.D. had paid for a doctor visit. She'd seen those big eyes of Lissa's. If she was in trouble, she could easily convince someone as generous as O.D. to help her. Especially if he was the cause of her trouble.

Hope nudged Champ around an overhanging branch ahead that was too low to duck under. She tried to blank out her mind, just enjoy the ride. The breeze brushing her cheeks was a little moist. November couldn't decide if it was part of autumn or winter. She pulled her cap down around her ears, nudging Champ's flanks. Best to get up and down this hill before some kind of storm blew in.

At the crest, Hope dismounted. She handed Champ the small handful of oats she kept in her saddlebag, patting his neck. The view from here made life look normal. A couple of extra trucks in the yard, Faith and Kayla watching Belle in the corral. Junior must have hobbled back inside.

She turned to face the old house, listening as the wind rattled a piece of metal somewhere on the roof. What was it about this place that drew her? O.D.'s grandparents had not lived here long. Her memories were of summer days after chores were done, with six kids looking for mischief.

Champ snorted, walking closer.

"Yeah, buddy. Not a lot of point staying up here. No one's around."

Hope remembered the last talk she'd had here with O.D. He'd promised they'd meet here, maybe ride together. No hint of trouble brewing in his life. Did he think he could just pay Lissa off to keep her quiet?

Her cell phone displayed a new message from O.D. Her eyes stung with tears again.

Hey, what's up?

Of course. He was trying to strike up a conversation, make believe nothing out of the ordinary was happening.

She turned off the sound on her phone and shoved it back into her pocket. She had no idea how to respond to such an innocent question. *How about you tell me what's up, Mister hot shot future father?*

Another message, this one from Faith, popped onto her screen.

Hey, the wind is picking up. It's starting to rain. You coming home?

Maybe

She mounted Champ. No use getting wet up here. Strange how just this morning, she had ridden up to this old house to talk to O.D. Now, he was the last person she wanted to hear from.

She guided Champ down the Caldwell side of the hill, pulling her fleece collar around her neck, tying the string from her hoodie. The rain on her cheek was much colder than just a few minutes ago. Miserable, cold, damp weather. Perfect for her mood. Maybe she'd just hole up in her bedroom and watch something mindless on television for the rest of the night.

"There she is!" Kayla's voice reached her from a small clearing about halfway down the hill.

"What do you mean, 'Maybe'?" Faith rode up on Belle, passing the all-terrain vehicle Kayla was riding.

"Y'all didn't have to come get me. Champ knows the way home." Hope rode around them.

"Sure he does." Faith and Belle pulled alongside again. "But we thought you could use some company. You've got a right to feel hurt."

Hope stopped to allow Champ to nuzzle his stable mate for a minute. "I don't know if I'm hurt, or angry, or what I am. Why do I care if O.D. went and did something stupid? He hasn't made any promises to me about anything, at least besides this crazy contest thing y'all came up with."

"We're not blind." Kayla turned off the ignition of the noisy vehicle she was riding. "Everybody knows you two are meant to be together."

"Hmmph. Really? 'Everybody' doesn't know anything." Hope was through talking about this. She prodded Champ with her boot heel. They continued toward the barn as the cold November rain picked up in earnest.

"Well, I know one thing. I hope O.D.'s Mom and Dad are not looking at social media. The comments on Lissa's post are getting pretty crazy." Faith stuck her phone back in the pocket of her blue-jean jacket before following Hope.

"Serves him right." Hope allowed Champ to pick up the pace. They reached the dry safety of the barn in just a few minutes. Maybe she'd just bed down in the barn with the horses tonight and throw the phone in the garbage can. What a Thanksgiving this had turned out to be.

23

"Don't move." A camo-covered arm pinned O.D. from behind. He felt a gun barrel in his back.

"It's me." Had he spoken aloud, or were his words only inside his head? His heart pounded as the gun barrel eased off a little.

"What the—Dee? For the love of all that's holy. What are you doing up here after dark?" John K. spun him around.

"Looking for you. We need to talk." Yes. He could hear himself speaking now.

"Oh, good grief. Can you not get the message? We don't need to talk. Just leave me alone. I have never seen such a stubborn ..." John K.'s words retreated into the darkness as he strode away, toward the old shack above them.

"Stop. Really." O.D. bounded toward him. "You need to listen to me." He reached for his brother's arm and jumped back as John K. spun around to face him.

"No! I don't *need* a lecture about why I *need* to come home. I know about Cody. I've been checking on him. Mom and Dad know that I'm old enough to take care of myself. Why can't you get that through your thick, addled brain?" John K. squared himself up, a few steps away from O.D.

"You don't know what I've been dealing with. There's so much going on." O.D. spoke up with increasing confidence. How could he make his brother listen?

"Oh no! Little Dee is finally forced to be a man! I thought you might grow up while I was away. But no, when I come home, you're still following me around." John K. turned his back, stomping up the dark trail toward the shack. "Come back, John K! I need you, John K! I can't figure anything out on my own." He affected a whiny, high-pitched voice as he got closer to the top of the crest.

O.D. tried to follow, stumbling on rocks that his flashlight didn't uncover in time for his boots to miss them. "Who's acting like a child here? You're just running away!"

"Deal with it!" John K. had reached the shack and ducked inside.

Rain soaked O.D.'s face as he stood peering into the darkness. He scrambled up the hill, his flashlight clattered to the ground, the lamp breaking against the rocks. Still he pushed ahead, touching what must be the door to John K's hiding place.

"Big mistake." John K's voice filled O.D.'s right ear with a low rumble. That iron grip surrounded his chest again. "I am dead serious, little brother. Get. Out. Now."

After a hard push from behind, O.D. flew back into the night, landing on his knees outside. He struggled to stand in the total darkness. What a failure he was. Would he have to go home, tail between his legs, without even delivering the news he had come to tell his brother about Lissa?

"Yeah, it's dark!" John K shouted from inside the shack. "But it will be a lot quicker going back down this hill. Get moving. I can give you a kick-start if you need it."

O.D. moved forward. The grade was going downward. If he didn't try to hurry, maybe he could get to level ground to his truck. His arms flailed in front of him, hoping for something to help him stay upright.

His boots made their way down the steep hill. A cloud scampered across the moon. At least the rain had stopped for a bit. He spotted John K.'s truck and headed toward it.

A booming rifle shot echoed from the old shack.

"If he wanted to hit you, he could." O.D. stood tall, speaking to the dark trees around him. This was just his sharp-shooter brother's way of making him move a little faster.

"Okay." Hearing his own voice convinced him he wasn't dreaming all of this. "I get it. Just give me a minute to get back to my truck. What a pain you are, hero or no hero."

He tried picking up his speed a little, following familiar landmarks along the trail, until he stumbled against the driver's side of his truck. He stopped long enough to take a good deep breath, climbed in, turning on the ignition and the heater. No need to sit here for very long, but he wanted to warm up while he planned his next move.

His heart raced as the cab of the truck grew warmer. Why did he continue to get himself into such messes? John K. was right about one thing. O.D. could not resist the urge to follow his older brother, no matter the consequences. If their mom had not broken down in tears when he broached the idea, he would have taken the army recruiter up on his offer and ended up on the other side of the world himself.

The rush of warm air promised to lull him to sleep if he sat here very long. There were actual beds inside the cabin. Should he just give up and drive all the way home? Should he stay here to take a stab at talking to his idiot brother again in the morning?

His phone pinged in his coat pocket.

Everybody okay?

A text from Dad.

Yeah.

He did owe them an update. Okay? Well, they were both alive.

I found John K. in the little shack above the deer camp.

Good. I'll tell Mom. Stay safe.

O.D. chuckled at that one. Stay safe.
Funny how the messages arrived in a bunch out here.

We need to talk.

This one was from Hope. Strange she should choose the same words that made his brother want to shoot at him.

Okay.

He responded. Probably some news about their rodeo. He wasn't in the mood for worrying about that right now.

He put the truck in reverse, backing slowly down the hill toward the cabin. One last glance up the hill revealed smoke still rising from the chimney of the shack, but no lights. With no electricity up there, he wouldn't be able to tell if his brother was still watching him. Might as well stay in the more equipped cabin for the night. He could easily make it to work for his Black Friday deliveries from here.

Tired of texting. Can you call?

This message arrived as he stopped in front of the cabin. The reception was doubtful down here, but he'd try from out here in the truck.

"What's up?" He didn't feel the need for preliminaries when she answered. She was the one who had asked him to call, right?

"So much." Her voice was tired and emotional.

"Yeah." She didn't even know the half of it. "But you asked me to call." He took a deep breath, remembering the crack of the rifle all over again. He pulled his coat a little tighter around him. *Go ahead, Hope, what it is it?*

"Faith asked me to call you. She and that marketing guy at your dealership have some crazy stunt cooked up for tomorrow to try to get more entries for the truck give-away."

Just as he thought. Caldwell Rodeo business. "I have to work tomorrow."

"I thought you might. But Faith thought you might know how to get ahold of Tara at the TV station."

"We have a group text somewhere from the day we went on her show. I'm sure she will help with whatever Faith has in mind." Somehow, he sensed there was something Hope was not saying.

"It's good to hear your voice, though." He sat in the cold pickup cab outside the cabin. There was usually no cell service inside at all. Maybe he should bring her up to speed. "You won't believe what I've been up to tonight."

"You are full of surprises." What was this tone in her voice? She wasn't kidding.

"Somehow, I think you need to go first." There wasn't much use in explaining to her, anyway. He had gotten himself into this ridiculous spot, he would just have to get himself out of it.

"I guess you haven't seen anything that's going around on social media." She still sounded so serious, so resigned. What in the world was eating at her?

"No. My reception has been in and out. There's no Wi-fi for miles." He wasn't sure he wanted to continue this conversation. He had more important things to think about than the nonsense the world loved to chatter about.

"Well, let's just say that we're all learning there's more to O.D. Billings than meets the eye. Some secrets become very hard to hide." Now, there were tears in her voice.

"Hope, you need to just tell me ..."

His truck sputtered, then died. What? Had he forgotten to fill up with gas before this foolhardy trip? There was a supply in the shed behind the cabin, but—good grief.

He unplugged his phone from the charger. Dead. Wow. Would she think he hung up on her? He stared out the window of his truck, struggling to see anything but darkness. Rain pelted his windshield. A new tic-tic of ice joined in.

O.D. heaved a huge sigh. Tears burned his eyes. Why did he constantly run off half-cocked on these crazy missions? He didn't have survival training like John K., wasn't a daredevil like Cody. No, he was just boring old Orville Dewayne, always trying to fix things. Why couldn't he leave well enough alone, live his own life?

He pulled his coat around him. The cab of this truck wouldn't provide a great place to sleep without heat. The cabin was only a few hundred yards away. Get soaked on the way to a warm bed? Or stay dry but cold right here until morning? What a mess. What a terrible mess.

He reached behind the seat of the truck. There was usually a blanket of some kind. Yeah, a rough army blanket. Better than nothing. He covered himself, closing his eyes. Might as well try to sleep. The icy rain pelted and pounded. Wind rocked the side windows. Nope. No sleep.

"God? Are you out there?" O.D. had not prayed in a long time. "Do you listen to fools? Because I am the stupidest. I don't know what I expect you to do here, but I'm out of options. I guess I'll just wait to see what happens. I could use a sign of some kind, but I don't deserve it. I'm just tired of pretending I have everything figured out when you know I don't." He took a deep breath. Were his prayers going past the icy windshield?

A faint beep prompted him to look at his phone.

Still here.

O.D. dropped the phone, staring straight ahead. Did that just happen? Did the creator of the universe have time to send text messages to stupid guys sitting in stranded pickups? What had he done to deserve attention like that? A shiver rocked his core. He tried to start the truck again. Should he ask God for another sign? Better not press his luck.

Behind him, a floodlight shone from the front of the family's cabin. No use freezing out here when warmth and safety were so close. As the rain slackened, he stuffed his phone into his jacket pocket, pulled out his keys, and jumped out of the driver's side of the truck. With the army blanket over his head, he must have looked like some sort of camouflaged ghost. He ran for several steps as the phone buzzed in his pocket.

Was it God again? He stopped under a spreading cedar tree, pulled the phone out to answer the call.

"Hey!" Hope's voice both comforted and puzzled him. How was she getting through?

"Can I call you back?" Not a great time or place to carry on a conversation.

"Sure."

He had disappointed her again. He held the phone, trying to decide what to do next. Another rifle shot rang out.

"He's shooting again!" O.D. yelled, stuffing the phone back into his pocket before running toward the back door of the cabin.

24

"Shooting? Who's shooting?" Hope held the phone in front of her to check the signal strength. Live conversations were better than texts on the front porch, but O.D. had abruptly cut this call off. Maybe she hadn't heard him correctly. Where could he be that someone was shooting at him? He'd said 'shooting again,' as if it had already happened before. With Lissa's recent news, she didn't know why she bothered with this guy anyway. Whatever crazy mess he had gotten himself into was none of her business.

Just forget it. Like that was going to happen. She wondered how the police tracked down a caller's location. In all the old movies, you had to keep the person on the line while they did whatever they did. Out here in the country, the connections could drop without warning.

"Did you talk to O.D.?" Faith walked out holding her laptop, the screen door slammed behind her.

"He said we have a group text with Tara from the day y'all went on her television show. But Faith ... " How much should she tell her sister about this. She didn't even know where to begin.

"Sure, I should have looked through my old texts." Faith set the computer down on the padded porch swing, pulling her phone out of her pocket. "That calf roper's got a good head on his shoulders. You need to keep him around." Somehow, she managed to pick up the laptop while she scrolled through her phone messages and opened the screen door with her hip. "Better come inside. It feels like a storm's blowing in."

Hope stood looking at her phone as Faith left her standing there. Shooting. He said someone was shooting. That wasn't the kind of thing you could just ignore. Should she call the police? But what would she tell them? She didn't even know where O.D. was. She remembered what he always said to her when her mind was going in ten million different directions at once. 'Where are your feet?'

Right now, her feet were on the front porch. It was almost ten o'clock on Thanksgiving night. The north wind was picking up. Raindrops started a slow rhythm on the metal porch roof. Better get inside. She could use the landline to try to call that crazy calf roper again.

"Yeah, I know my surgery is tomorrow." Junior was leaning on the bar in the kitchen talking to their dad while he scrubbed the kitchen sink. "But I don't have to be at the hospital until 1:00. Why can't I go with Faith for a little bit in the morning?"

"Son. Use your head for something besides a hat rack. You are not even supposed to be standing on that ankle. We've been working all week to keep the swelling down. Come on. Get back in your chair. I'll pop some popcorn." Dad steered him past Hope toward the recliner.

"Sure. See you at 5:30." Faith hung the old land-line phone back in its cradle on the wall. "The marketing guy, Clark, called his friends at the radio station since we couldn't get Tara. He has the greatest idea for a Black Friday promotion. Dave Billings gave him permission to drive the truck they're giving away around town tomorrow while everybody's out shopping. Whenever someone spots it, they can get two entries in the drawing for the price of one donation to Cedar Ridge. He says we need to get the number of entries up because Mr. Billings is worried the whole promotion will be a joke if only two or three names are in that hat on giveaway day."

"So, what about the radio station?" Hope was having trouble keeping up with Faith's chatter.

"They are going to follow us around in a remote truck. They said it will be a good way to get folks to shop at some of their sponsors, as well as bring good publicity for Billing Boys. I've got to go see what kind of Rodeo Queen outfit I can find to wear." She ran toward her bedroom.

Shooting. O.D. said someone was shooting. Hope stood in the empty kitchen holding her phone. What a chaotic night. Right now, it was hard to remember that this was the first Thanksgiving without Mom. It wasn't ending like any holiday she remembered.

How could Faith be running on about some Black Friday promotion after the news that Lissa was spreading on social media? Hope's legs shook. She sank onto a barstool. O.D. had been a rock for her in the past few days. Even though they'd known each other since they were kids, there was something special happening between them. His secret life was about to be painfully obvious to everyone, and he didn't even know it. Now, someone was shooting at him.

Be still and know that I am God. Whose voice was whispering in her ear? The television was on in the living room, where Dad and Junior were catching up on the late football game. Faith was rattling clothes hangers in her room. *Be still.* She closed her eyes, remembering Mom's face, just above her, kissing her goodnight after a nightmare. If only she'd been able to return those words to her mother during those terrible last few weeks. *Be still.*

She walked down the hallway to her room, closing the door behind her. She pulled up the quilt, perched cross-legged on the bed before pressing O.D.'s phone number.

"Where are your feet?" She wasn't sure why she said these words as he answered.

"What?" He sounded out of breath, but at least he was alive.

"You are always telling me to get my head where my feet are. So, where are your feet?"

"Inside the cabin at our deer camp. The gas can is out in the shed, but it's raining hard again, and ..."

The gas can? He was talking gibberish again. "Now, who is shooting at you?" Hope's heart raced as she tried to follow her own advice. *Be still.*

"John K. was shooting. But I think he has stopped now. He was just trying to get me to go away. I will have to be at work at about 7:00 in the morning, but I don't want to leave when I just found out where he has been hiding." O.D. sounded a little calmer.

Hope took a deep breath and blew it out slowly. He was not in immediate danger. Okay.

"Okay. First. Remember you are not alone." Where were these words coming from?

"Thanks ... You just don't know how much ..." His voice faded, then stopped completely.

Hope checked her phone. No signal. How did this happen? She had not moved, they had just been talking. Sometimes cell phones were not worth anything. One thing she and her mom agreed on. Landlines were worth paying for, especially out here in the country. She opened the door to head up the hallway toward the living area.

"What do you think?" Faith emerged from her room in black jeans, pink plaid flannel shirt, and gray fleece vest. The latest tiara perched on her severely tousled hairdo. "Picture the hair looking much better. I plan to get up at 4:00 to fix it."

"Maybe change jeans. Do you have a faded denim pair that is not completely ripped up?" Hope worked to keep the tone of her voice sounding normal.

"Yeah, I was sort of thinking the same thing. Oh, Hopie, this is going to be so much fun. Clark thinks we can sell lots of chances for Cedar Ridge tomorrow." Faith pulled her into a hug.

Faith's giggle sounded more like a fourteen-year-old than someone headed for her third year of college. "I've got to get a few hours of sleep. Try to come by one of our stops tomorrow. They'll be all over social media. Goodnight, Dad, Junior!" She pecked Hope's cheek, stepped back into her bedroom, closing the door.

Hope reached the living room as Dad was turning off the television.

"Everything okay, Punkin?" He set the remote control down on a table before switching on a lamp.

"Yeah, I think so. I was talking to O.D. The cell connection fizzled. Glad we still have a real phone." She turned on the light over the kitchen stove.

"Any news about Cody?" Dad helped Junior tuck a blanket around him on the couch.

"He's okay, I guess. Probably worn out from their Thanksgiving dinner at the hospital."

"Does that fancy coffee maker do hot chocolate?" Dad turned the light out in the living room and headed for the kitchen. She wanted to call O.D. back. Was she going to have to serve her dad a midnight snack?

"I think we have some new pods in the pantry. I'll look." She plugged her cell phone into a charger.

"Just fix whatever's handy. Coffee, tea. Maybe decaf. We both need to sleep tonight. One for each of us. That is, if you've got a minute to talk."

"Sure." Hope found two decaf hazelnut pods, checking the water level in the coffeemaker. What was up with her dad? Was O.D. wondering why she wasn't calling him back? The machine warmed up, she placed Dad's favorite cup in its spot to start his coffee.

"Okay." She placed his steaming cup in front of him at the kitchen island and started her cup brewing. She'd rather just call O.D. *Be still.*

"To begin with, I need to tell you how proud I am of you. Faith gets her accolades for being our barrel racing princess, and Junior certainly commands attention, but I don't give enough credit to Hope Catherine. You are my rock, sweetie." He sipped his coffee calmly.

Her eyes filled with tears as the warm mug filled her hands. His rock? She was more like a leaf floating down the creek.

"I don't feel like anybody's rock." She stared into the steaming mug.

"Well, your mom used those words about you all the time, especially toward the end." Now he was talking about Mom? How could she talk with Dad about Mom? She stood, picking up her mug.

"I really need to go get some sleep."

"Punkin, sit down." He rarely got stern with her. She hadn't needed that tone much over the years. She sat, facing him again.

"You are the strength of this family. We all have our own

agendas. We depend on you to keep a handle on everything. Your mom told me you were the one she could depend on. While everything around us was caving in, you were steady. Your name fits you. You give us all hope."

A hard lump filled her throat, but she cleared it long enough to speak. "Thanks, Daddy. It is not easy."

From out of nowhere, her mom's pain-filled eyes flashed into her mind. "But I don't think Mom thought I was very much help to her. She usually sent me out of the room on some errand. Like she couldn't stand the sight of me." Her voice was growing louder. No reason to wake the house.

"No!" Dad stood up, walked around to her side of the island, wrapping her in a hug. "She was too hard on you. When it was down to just the two of us after you left at night, she always told me how much she treasured each of you kids, and she would always start with you. She expected more from you because you could handle more."

"Yeah. I was great at bringing her a glass of water or talking to the doctors about her treatment. But I couldn't do anything important. She said I was useless. I failed her."

Dad released his hold, using his rough finger to turn her chin toward him. Hope turned to see tears filling his eyes.

"She told me about that." He whispered. "She said she asked you to go get a gun. That was so unfair. She wanted to apologize but couldn't find the words. So, I'll do it for her. Honey, your mama did find peace. No one but Jesus gave that to her. Not the doctors, not me, not any of you kids. She had Him by her side and in her heart at the end. I guarantee you."

25

O.D. stared at the cellphone in his hand. With the charger connected, he had plenty of signal strength for the moment. But Hope had been the one to disconnect this time. Maybe she was tired of talking to him. He couldn't blame her. She had a brother, too, but he never used her for target practice. He didn't need to whine to Hope about this crazy rescue mission he had concocted.

The little cabin was plenty warm. He could still hear the wind rattling the roof, but at the moment, there was no rain falling. Maybe he should get the gas can to fill up his truck.

John K. had not intended to shoot him. For the first time, he wondered if his brother was having post-traumatic stress issues. He had a lot to learn about the after-effects of serving in the military. John K. had always been comfortable around guns. Now he was using his skills to remind O.D. that he could take care of his own problems. At any rate, maybe he would not tempt fate by going back outside right now.

'You're not alone.' He remembered that was the last thing Hope told him before she hung up. Right after she reminded him to find his feet and get his head to the same spot. He smiled and blinked back tears.

He was more convinced than ever that he should consult the wisdom in that honey-blonde head before running off on his next foolhardy adventure. She was becoming Jiminy Cricket to his Pinocchio. Now, there was a story he'd forgotten about. Was this whole thing about changing from a wooden puppet to a real man?

"God, I'm so confused." He sank into the old leather couch, his head in his hands. "Why should anybody care what I do? I am so busy trying to fix things with John K., when he doesn't want fixing. I tried to help Faith and Hope with their rodeo, but that seems to be falling flat. I turned down a great job opportunity. None of my plans come to anything. My dad doesn't even remember he has three sons most of the time. There's nothing I can do to help Cody, either. What if he never walks again? How can I fix that?"

From the kitchen cabinet where he'd left his phone charging, a notification beeped.

O.D. stood up slowly. His wet boots were heavy as lead as he crossed the small room to pick up the phone. Nothing new on the screen, just the last message he'd received.

Still here.

He brushed away the tears that were washing his cheek.

"Okay, God." He whispered. "I get it. I'm not alone. I don't know why You care, but evidently You do. So, I'm turning this over to You. For real. I'm done trying to fix everything. You can take over now."

———

The front door was banging, rattling. This time, it wasn't the wind. Someone was trying to get in.

O.D. crossed the room in his stockinged feet. The sun was coming up. He must have fallen asleep on the couch in the cabin. *Oh, man. Late for work on Black Friday.*

"Come on, Little Dee. I won't try to kill you. Just let me in." O.D. opened the door. John K. stopped before coming in, his hand stretched forward. "Truce?"

O.D. shook his brother's hand with no hesitation. What had changed overnight? "Yeah, man. Of course."

"I killed a deer as soon as the sun came up this morning. See?" John K. gestured to the yard, where a carcass hung in the tree. "I could have processed it up at the shack, but you've got electricity, water, and coffee. Hey, is the coffee ready?"

"I just got up. I'm late for work." O.D. pulled his boots on.

"Work? Then why did you come out here last night? You enjoy being shot at?" John K. took off his camo jacket and opened the cabinet above the coffee maker.

"No. Listen. I have something to tell you." O.D. pulled on his jacket on the way to the kitchen.

"Now, don't start that business about coming back to help Dad. You have the thickest skull ..." John K. wheeled around to face him.

"No!" O.D. threw his hands up, ready to fend off an attack again. "There's something else. Lissa told me about the two of you. She's pregnant, John K."

"Lissa? Maria's little friend? What? Lissa and me?" John K. set the glass carafe on the counter, doubling over laughing. "Of all the crazy ... Honestly, there's not even any chance. I haven't gotten that close to any girl since I've been home. Not even Maria. What in the world?" He stopped laughing and raised his hands to the ceiling. "Lissa?"

"For real? Well, why would she tell me that? She said her parents would kick her out of the house. She couldn't tell

Maria because Maria loves you. She didn't want an abortion, but she didn't have money for the doctor."

"And the Billings boys could come to her rescue." John K. fixed O.D. with a level stare. "She just wants money, Dee. I was a convenient scapegoat since nobody but Maria knew where I was. Claiming I was the father triggered your sense of responsibility and bought her some time." John K. turned back to the coffee maker, scooping the fragrant grounds into the filter.

"Wow. Do I feel stupid." O.D. stood at the door. "I'm sorry, John K."

"Hey. I've done a lot of rotten things, but when I get a girl pregnant, it will be after the wedding ceremony. After I've figured out who God wants me to be." John K. poured water into the top of the machine, pushed the power button.

O.D. swallowed a lump in his throat. What a total idiot he was. Lying was not in his brother's DNA. Lissa acted out of desperation, using O.D.'s reputation for helping folks out. He should have known better.

"Coffee will be ready soon, then we can get that deer processed. It will be like old times, but without Dad telling us we're doing it all wrong." John K. retrieved two mugs from the cabinet.

"No. I need to make deliveries today. But hey ..." He crossed the small room and surrounded his brother in a bear hug. "I'll quit bugging you about the dealership. Just come home. Mom and Dad and Cody need you."

"Yeah. We both need to quit sneaking around in the middle of the night." John K. stepped back to shake O.D.'s hand again. "I'll be down after I get this deer stabilized. Love ya, Little Dee. And ... you know you are the one that needs to step up at the dealership. You need to graduate from driving that delivery truck and wearing short pants all winter. You've got a pretty good head on those shoulders if you can just keep it somewhere near your feet."

O.D. bounced down the short stairway. He ran to find the can of gas in the shed. His boss deserved his time for at least part of a busy Black Friday.

He aimed a quick prayer at the sun shining above the pine trees. *Thanks. Glad You are still around after all my foolishness.* A beep from his pocket made him laugh.

Great timing, God.

26

Hope's tires threw muddy chunks of gravel as she rounded the last curve before the service road. Faith had already posted about two different stops on their Black Friday tour. At least there would be a few more entries in the truck give-away. The month leading up to Christmas was usually packed with activity. At this moment, she was not excited about any of it. She shook her head, trying to dispel the last glimpse of O.D.'s eyes, looking so sincere the last time they had been together. She reminded herself that it was all an act. He evidently practiced that look often with Lissa, and who knows who else.

A little bit of extra activity near the Billingses' barn caught her eye, and she stopped for a minute when she had a full view of Ms. Felicia's huge canvas. O.D.'s mom was picking up extra paint cans and stepping back to admire her creation.

Hope recognized the image. It was the same as an oil painting that hung over the Billingses' fireplace. The three boys were easily recognizable, even as they moved away from the viewer. John K. was in the lead, his legs pumping hard on his bicycle. O.D. ran along behind, waving a lariat rope over his head. Last, but not least, Cody brought up the rear on a tricycle that was too small for him, with cowboy boots that were too big.

Her eyes teared up, realizing how important this choice of subject matter was to Felicia. They all longed for a repeat of this scene, but with Cody walking.

The sun glistened on the wet road. Hope scanned it for tricky spots of black ice on the pavement. The instability of the road matched her current situation.

Would O.D. call again? With all the talk of his brother shooting at him, she had never gotten the chance to confront him with Lissa's news. His social media connections might be in and out at the deer camp, but surely he had seen some of the talk buzzing around Crossroads. The consensus was that Lissa would become an official Billings very quickly. After all, everyone reasoned, O.D. had too much decency to leave her out in the cold. Baby news before wedding bells was totally accepted these days.

Hope's stomach churned. She couldn't tolerate breakfast this morning. The rest of the world could accept this turn of events, but she didn't have to be happy about it. Even with all of his grandstanding, she had trusted O.D. She'd even believed that maybe the two of them might move past next-door neighbor status to something more. No matter how silly that dream had been, it was hard to shake.

She guided the SUV into the drive-through line. Maybe a sausage biscuit and a mocha latte would perk her up. Next, the routine task of balancing the monthly bank statement for the rodeo. Ten-key by touch was better than trying to figure out a certain calf roper's mind.

Why had she forgotten to find out whether Junior would spend the night at the hospital after surgery? Dad would have had enough of her rowdy brother very soon. She'd end up with overnight duty if it were required.

She sighed, remembering the ride she'd taken in O.D.'s truck. Even in the dark, with deer popping out of the fog, she had felt like there was very little that the two of them couldn't handle. Too bad that wouldn't happen again.

"Thanks for dropping by. Would you like a deluxe breakfast this morning?" The speaker under the menu played a recorded suggestion.

"No, thanks." Hope leaned out her driver's side window to place her order. A familiar delivery truck was two vehicles behind her in line. So, he was working this morning. There might not be a chance to talk about Lissa's news before Junior's surgery this afternoon.

The driver of the old car directly behind fumbled for change in the console. Might as well be helpful. She could afford to pay for two breakfasts.

Get his too. Where had that thought come from? He didn't deserve a break. Not today.

"What may I get you today?" The live voice on the speaker jolted her back to reality.

"A sausage biscuit and a mocha latte, please."

"Coming right up. Please drive around."

The lady behind her ordered, pulled up, then O.D. leaned out slightly to place his order. Hope leaned toward the middle of her vehicle, hoping he wouldn't recognize her.

"That will be six fifty-five."

Hope found two twenty-dollar bills in her billfold. She had only remembered having one. Okay. She heaved a huge sigh.

"Please pay for the two people behind me as well."

"I like this pay it forward thing." The young lady with pink hair smiled as she took the bills from Hope, handing her a bag. "The next two? Most people just do one."

"Yes. The car and the delivery truck. If there's any change, keep it for yourself."

"Wow! Thanks, ma'am." The girl waved at a co-worker, who was coming over to watch the reaction of the lady in the old car when Hope pulled away.

Tears filled Hope's eyes. He didn't deserve that. No way. So why had she done it? *Yes, you are a strange one, Hope Catherine Caldwell.*

She decided to eat the sandwich while the latte cooled. The traffic ahead of her slowed as they approached an inflatable waving sign in front of the Seventh Heaven store. Already a popular place for finding bargains of all kinds, the parking lot was full this morning. In front of the store, a familiar rodeo princess waved at passing motorists in front of the radio station's remote truck.

"Hope!" Faith waved frantically. Hope pulled into the parking lot, watching for an empty parking space between the radio station's truck and the front of the store.

Faith met her as she stepped out of the driver's side of the truck.

"Hey! Glad you came. Did you see our tweets?" Hope hadn't seen her sister's face so animated in months.

"No. I was just heading to the office for a bit. How's it going?" Behind Faith, a line of people waited to fill out entry forms.

"The radio station is giving away donuts and coupons for Seventh Heaven. Folks can't wait to find out about the truck giveaway. We're telling them about Cedar Ridge and our rodeo too. We've had at least twenty more entries already this morning." Faith stood near the driver's side of the truck.

Hope left the remainder of her sausage sandwich, grabbing her latte. Finally, some good results for this contest of theirs.

"Mr. and Mrs. Jennings are going to hang out here this

afternoon while we're with Junior at the hospital. Come on over, you can talk to people about what you do at the rodeo. They are really interested, Hopie!" Faith ran ahead.

"So, Faith, come tell us again about the purpose of this whole pickup truck giveaway." The deejay waved Faith over, holding a microphone near her.

"Well, my sister Hope just got here. She might like to tell your listeners more." Faith pushed her from behind.

"Ah, folks. There are two pretty Caldwell sisters. I hope they'll pardon me for saying this, but they're like the city mouse and the country mouse." The loud man guided Hope closer to his partner standing near the truck, who placed a headset on her so she could hear the radio.

"Yeah," the deejay winked at her. "It's like we have both Taylor Swift and Carrie Underwood right here in Crossroads. I wonder if they can sing?"

"Ha! That might be asking a lot, buddy. But they can tell us what this pickup truck giveaway is all about. Right, Hope?" He held the microphone up to Hope as Faith smiled at her.

"I guess." Hope swallowed. What madness. She just started out to balance a bank statement this morning.

"So, tell us why folks should come to the rodeo next Thursday to buy a chance on this pickup truck." He nodded at her.

"Well, the rodeo is fun for everybody. And Cedar Ridge Ranch is a great place that helps all kinds of people." Really? They wanted her to talk on the radio, with no advance warning?

"Hey, Ty, what's up!"

Hope blinked her eyes in the dim light under the tent. She recognized the broad shoulders of the guy walking toward them. The confident walk was unmistakable.

"Hey, it's our favorite delivery driver. O.D., you may need to get some longer pants soon. It's almost wintertime." The deejay named Ty waved in his direction. O.D. slid up next to Hope. She took a deep breath. No problem. She'd let him do the talking.

"So, Billings Brothers is giving this pickup truck away. Why, praytell?" The microphone shifted from Hope's face to O.D.'s.

"We've always seen our dealership as more than just a place that sells trucks."

"Yeah, they have cars, vans, S.U.V.s too, right?" Ty prompted.

"No, I mean, we want to be part of the community. That's why we've been a sponsor of the Caldwell rodeo for such a long time. We love Crossroads. We believe in her future."

"Whew. Cue up the violin music. Or I guess it would be a fiddle for these sappy cowboys, right?" Everybody around the tent laughed.

"Yeah. Call me sappy and sentimental, but it's true. The young people in this town deserve some wholesome activities like the rodeo. Along with that, Cedar Ridge Ranch is doing a wonderful job of keeping folks of all ages healthy enough to participate. It's a win-win." O.D.'s hand slipped around Hope's waist. She tensed up, stepping away.

"Okay. So, everybody come on down to Seventh Heaven this morning and buy a ticket to get into the great Billings Boys Truck Giveaway. For $50.00 your name goes in twice. If my math is correct, that means for $100 your name goes in four times. Then, on the last Tuesday before Christmas, come to the Caldwell Rodeo, and you just might drive this big black beauty home!"

Ty waved at a producer, who started music blaring through the speakers. He reached to shake O.D.'s hand.

"Thanks, Buddy. Great to see you today." He smiled at Hope. "You, too, Miss Carrie—I mean, Hope."

Hope moved to her left while watching for the large cables that were everywhere under her feet.

"Hey." O.D. followed, catching her arm. "Good to see you this morning. Thanks for talking to me last night. Can we sit down somewhere for a minute?"

Without his cowboy hat, his dark eyes shone even more. So strange how they lit up from inside.

"We do need to talk. Have you checked social media at all?" Hope pulled her arm away. Boy, did they *ever* need to talk.

"No. I was a little busy. I have to work this morning. I'll be at the hospital this afternoon checking on Cody. I guess you'll be there with Junior. Maybe we can sneak off for coffee."

"Maybe. I ..." Hope stepped away.

"Well, look who's here!" Tara Williams swooped in from the edge of the crowd. Her cameraman ran to catch up.

"Can we do a quick lead-in for our news break? Good promo for the contest."

"I guess." O.D. reached in Hope's direction, but Tara pulled him into place for her interview.

"Okay, we're live in three, two, one ..." The cameraman pointed at Tara and her microphone.

"Folks, we're at Seventh Heaven, where everything is seven dollars or less. On this Black Friday morning, you can get a great jumpstart on your Christmas shopping." She motioned for the cameraman to pan towards the store then back to her.

"And there's more! While you're here, you can also buy a chance on the great pickup truck being raffled off just before Christmas at the Caldwell Family Rodeo. Here's O.D. Billings, middle son of the Billings Boys, to tell us all about it." She held the mic in his direction.

"Now, before we start, you know my first question. You've

always used initials. But what in the world does O.D. stand for?"

"Well, Tara. I want to start a little differently. I want to first say God is good."

As if they had expected it, the crowd standing around the tent piped up their response. "All the time."

O.D. beamed. He had them eating out of his hand again. Hope's feet shifted, but she couldn't look away. Why had he mentioned God?

"But to answer your question, today, I am Openly Devoted. There's a beautiful young lady standing just out of your camera angle ..." His eyes trapped Hope's again.

No way. He was not going to use her as part of his act.

Hope pushed her way past the people who had gathered. She stumbled toward her S.U.V.

"Sorry, Tara." She heard O.D.'s voice behind her. "Hope!"

She was grateful that her S.U.V. was on the edge of the crowded parking lot. Reaching it just a few steps ahead of O.D she jumped in. She started it before he could reach the door handle.

"Hope! Wait."

She tried to look straight ahead, but those eyes. There was a new desperation as he placed his flat palm on her rolled-up driver's side window. Nope. She would not be part of the spectacle. When he found the real O.D. Billings hiding somewhere, they could talk. But not before.

She turned her head away, slowly moving forward. Maybe he had enough sense to step back before she ran over his foot. That was his business at this point. Faith waved at her just before she left the parking lot. Someone would fill her in. If not in person, on social media. The tweets would soon be flying.

"Did you see O.D. on TV?"

"I think he was about to propose to Lissa."

"No, somebody told me he was talking about Hope Caldwell."

Hope's phone rested on the seat beside her. She considered throwing it out the driver's side window. No. That would be foolish. She drove the short distance to the arena, parking behind the main building just in case he decided to follow her here.

Inside, she barely got started on the bank statement before tears clouded her eyes. Ridiculous. If he was going to be a father, why wasn't he spending time with his future wife instead of declaring his feelings for Hope on television? It just proved that the O.D. Billings she thought she knew didn't exist. He was all show. If there was a real, solid character under there, he hadn't revealed it to anyone yet.

She left her desk, walked out toward the arena, flipping the huge light switch along the way.

Silence reigned in the dusty but neat-as-a-pin enclosure. The buzz of the lights was part of the ambiance. Usually, she stood here for deep breaths, closing her eyes to imagine the events that would unfold, remembering past ones.

Today, there was a strange emptiness. Was she the only one in her family that still cared about this place? Faith was traipsing around doing publicity spots. Junior would have to stay at home to recover from surgery. Even Dad was moving on, concentrating more on work around the ranch than preparing for the upcoming rodeo.

"Mom? Have I failed you?" She whispered, afraid to disturb the routine pops and creeks as the arena came to life. "I've tried so hard to keep things the same. It's like the whole world is falling apart."

The sound of a ringing phone intruded in her thoughts. Her cell was turned off. It had to be the office phone. No one would assume she was working on Black Friday. But Dad did know she was coming down here. Had something changed with Junior's surgery?

She ran the few steps to the office door, her boots throwing up dust, then echoing on the concrete floor near the office.

"Hello," she was out of breath when she answered.

"Hey. I am so sorry."

How did he know to call her here?

"I'm busy." She tapped a pencil on the desk.

"Yeah. I know. But I just had to tell you that. I want to talk more, but I'm working right now too." His voice had a different sound. No teasing or joking at all. More serious.

"Whatever." She hated when people said that. But at this moment, it was all she could summon.

"I will be at the hospital this afternoon to check on Cody. Is it okay if I look you up while you're there with Junior?"

"I don't know …" She didn't want to talk at the hospital.

"Oh. Okay. Well. I'll see you sometime. We'll talk."

Was he at a loss for words? Now that was a new development.

"Okay." She disconnected the phone.

27

O.D. reflected on his day as he drove on autopilot. John K. was almost back to normal. He'd been in his element, processing the fresh deer kill at the cabin when O.D. left. O.D. had promised to quit bugging him. The boss was a little upset he'd arrived late to start his route, but O.D. could make up the time and keep everything running. Then, Tara's interview messed everything up.

Face it, Little Dee, it was not Tara's fault. Once again, you had to jump in to rescue Hope instead of letting her flounder. Then what was that business about Openly Devoted? Were you about to propose on live television?

O.D. stopped at the next four-way intersection. Why did a microphone make him lose his mind? Sure, he wanted to tell Hope how he felt, and he wanted her to know about the new connection he had with God. But for cornbread's sake, why did he try to do that with the whole tri-county area watching? She may have bought his breakfast, but that didn't mean she was ready for a marriage proposal.

Someone behind him honked. He pulled ahead, then

navigated a roundabout on the way to his next stop. "God, are You still there?" He prayed aloud as traffic passed to his left. "I don't need another text this time. I know You are." He smiled. It was cool to know he could pick up the conversation where he'd left off.

"I messed up again. I think I need someone to guide me through this. Thanks for being there. We'll talk again soon. Amen." He jumped out to make the next run to a porch, dodging an overly friendly yellow cat. "Sorry, buddy. No time for an ear-scratch today." Maybe he was just plain losing his mind. Talking to God like He was riding along in the truck? Now carrying on a conversation with a cat?

He checked the address for the next stop, guiding his truck around the cul-de-sac. He needed some help with this getting connected with God thing. He'd look up Smiley Caldwell when he got to the hospital this afternoon. Hopefully Junior's surgery would go off without a hitch, so Faith and Hope could handle things for a little bit. Smiley would know what to do next.

He actually sang a little as he finished his route. The happy songs he'd learned as a kid in church rang in his head and poured out of his mouth. Yes, this was a pretty good day. If he could only have a few minutes with Hope to get her on the same page.

"Yeah. I'm finished." He checked the clock in his truck after dropping off the last package, then called in.

"Hey. That's great." The dispatcher sounded distracted. "Could you possibly come back to pick up another quick run this evening? Today has gotten crazy busy."

O.D. frowned. He had really wanted to take Hope out tonight. But at the moment, she wasn't speaking to him anyway.

"Maybe after supper? Is there anything that has to be

delivered by a certain time today?" He pulled into a parking spot at the hospital while talking on the hands-free phone.

"No, it's really just getting a head start on tomorrow. But it would help a lot." The dispatcher adopted a pleading tone.

"Sure. I'll come in about eight for a couple of hours."

"Thanks, O.D. You're a good egg."

"Just slightly cracked." Uh-oh. There was the stand-up comic coming out again. *Control it, Dee.*

He entered the hospital, went straight to the elevator, pressing the number for Cody's floor. He hadn't even scanned the parking lot for John K.'s truck this time. Mom and Dad would be glad to know their oldest would start coming during regular visiting hours very soon, now that O.D. was not nagging him so much.

"Hey!" Smiley Caldwell met him as the doors opened.

"Hi!" O.D. held the elevator door, allowing him to step in instead of getting out. "You're the man I need to see. How's Junior?" The door closed. O.D. pressed the button for the top of the hospital.

"He's great. They'll be sending him home to recover this afternoon. But what's up with you?" Smiley still held his cowboy hat in his hands.

"I've been doing some thinking for the past day or so. Is there a place we can talk for a minute? Like, I mean, have a serious conversation?" How should he lead up to this?

"Sure, son. There's a chapel on the second floor that is pretty quiet." Smiley's voice was quieter, gentler than his usual bravado. "Something wrong?"

O.D. swallowed. "No, actually, I think something is very right. I think God and I have come to an understanding."

"Fantastic!" Smiley clapped him on the shoulder. The door opened on the top floor, where two nicely dressed older ladies joined them.

"Could you press the ground floor, please?" The ladies stepped to the far right. They probably wondered why neither of the men had gotten off.

"Of course." O.D. took his cap off, nodding at the ladies.

"Drop me on four so I can check in with the girls, then I'll meet you on two." Smiley rocked from one boot to the other.

O.D. pushed the buttons to start the elevator down. What would the preacher say? Would he think it was crazy to believe that God would send texts while your brother was shooting at you? Well, it was a little crazy.

The ladies were more nervous after Smiley stepped off on the fourth floor. He smiled at them, managing a weak "have a good day" as he got off on the second floor.

The chapel was tucked between the Employee Activity center and the Human Resources office. Inside, dim lights and a stained-glass picture of Jesus led him to the front of the room. He sank onto the front pew.

I have no idea how to do this. O.D. sat staring at the picture. *But hey. Thanks for sending Smiley Caldwell. Seems like you use that family pretty regularly.* The quiet in the room invaded his brain. He sat for a long moment, just absorbing it, taking one deep breath after another.

Eyes closed, he sensed another person in the pew behind him. He turned to see Smiley Caldwell with his eyes also closed in prayer. He waited for them to open before breaking the spell.

"Thanks for coming."

"Of course. Now, tell me what's on your mind, young man." Smiley came around the wooden bench to sit next to O.D.

"Well, over the past couple of days, I've realized I've been going about this life business all wrong. I've been busy trying to be some kind of hero. I just can't do it. Not by myself." O.D. focused on a candle to the right of the picture in front of him.

"And there's no need to." Smiley waited for him to continue.

"The problem is, I don't know why God would care enough about some overgrown kid who keeps messing up. No matter what I do, I keep making a complete fool of myself. I don't think I'll ever change. Why would He listen to me?" He turned to face Smiley, wiping away a stray tear.

"I can't answer the why part." Smiley focused on his own hands in front of him. "But I know God does care. The Bible is full of verses that assure us He loves us. He created us, then spent hundreds of years arranging the perfect conditions for sending His son to save us. It's a wonderful day when we start to believe that and accept it in our hearts." He turned his head to look into O.D.'s eyes. "Is that what has happened to you, son?"

"Yes, sir. I need His help, if He'll have me. I am ready to quit trying to save the world on my own." O.D. stood up. "What comes next?"

Smiley stood before him, reaching out to clasp his right hand. "You answer this question. Do you believe that Jesus is the Christ? The son of God?"

"I do." O.D. had known this was true for years.

"And you've been baptized?" Smiley shook his hand vigorously.

"I was dunked on the same day John K. was. I've spent my whole life following after him like some kind of forlorn hound dog. Now, I need to let God know I'm serious, on my own."

Smiley checked his watch. "Our church has a little prayer service tonight at six o'clock. You could come for that, to make your decision public. Congratulations, Dee. I'm so proud to help you out with this." Smiley's voice sounded a little too loud in this super quiet chapel. The simple handshake was turning into a full-on pump handle exercise.

"Thanks. I'll see you at six."

"I want you to do a little reading this afternoon. There's someone in the Bible I think you should meet." Smiley scribbled on a notepad he had in his pocket. "Paul was the apostle that brought the Good News to the world, but he started out on a totally different path. I think you will identify. See you soon. Welcome to the family!"

O.D. hadn't realized they were walking out of the little chapel until they emerged into the brightly lit hallway.

"See you soon." *Welcome to the family? Oh. The Christian family.*

O.D. pushed the glass door under the drive-through awning open, taking a step out, trying to remember exactly where he had parked his truck.

Angry Spanish words bombarded his right ear. His cheek exploded with the pressure of a fist. He retained his balance, instinctively raising his right arm to defend himself.

"What the—? Who?" before he could see his attacker, another blow caught the left side of his face. This one knocked him to his knees. Lissa's boyfriend Billy stood over him, fists at the ready.

"Stand up, coward. You can't hide behind your rich family forever." Billy shouted.

"Hey, what's the deal?" O.D. stood but backed away, keeping his arms up.

"Oh, like you don't know. Your baby. That's what is the deal." Billy moved in again.

O.D. lowered his fists, trying to stop Billy with a punch in the gut. Billy reached around him. They both fell at the door of the hospital.

"Call 911!" an older lady with her hands full of potted flowers ran back into the lobby.

"Stop this. I have a taser, if I need to use it." A burly security guard struggled to separate the combatants.

"Talk to her, man!" O.D. yelled at the squirming Billy. "She told me it was my brother's baby."

"Liar! It's all over town. It's you. You ..." The torrent of hateful words resumed.

"Hey. We'll let the judge sort this out." Another uniformed man held O.D's arms as the guard took control of Billy.

O.D. closed his eyes. Was this real or some kind of nightmare? Maybe the part where he gave his life to Jesus was a dream, and his real life would always be one punch in the face after another. *God, help me.*

28

Hope followed the Caldwell entourage out the front door of the hospital. Junior's freshly repaired foot led the way, propped up in front of him in the wheelchair. The male nurse who pushed him had stopped a couple of times to rest his hand on her brother's shoulder.

"Really, buddy. You've got to sit still in this thing. You could tump us all over in the hall, then you'd have to be admitted again until they made sure you were okay." The dreadlocks on his head bobbed as he stood upright again, turning to face Dad. "Is he always this fidgety, or do they have his medicine whacked out?"

"That's how we know he's gonna be okay. It's the Junior we know and love." Dad smiled. "Behave, son." That stern tone, usually so rare, was back.

Through the glass doors leading out of the lobby, she spotted Faith in Dad's truck. She hoped dad's front seat would move back enough to make Junior comfortable on the way home. Faith couldn't get near the drive-up exit because a police car had it blocked. *What was happening here?*

"Talk to Lissa! Get the truth! I had nothing to do with this." That voice sounded familiar. But surely ...

"Mr. Billings, you've got to quit shouting at that guy." The policeman was using all of his strength to restrain O.D. "I don't want to have to taze you, really."

Hope stopped dead in the doorway of the hospital. What crazy trouble had he gotten himself into now?

To the right of the doorway, another policeman was talking to a much calmer Billy Gonzalez, who was in handcuffs. The officer held one hand over the top of Billy's head as he placed him in the back of his cruiser.

"Officer, I know this young man. What happened here?" Dad approached the policeman, who waved at him to step back.

"I'm sorry, sir. Unless you witnessed this incident, I can't discuss it with you. We're taking both subjects in on a charge of public disturbance. It will all get sorted out at the police station." He opened his back door for O.D. "You'd best just keep quiet right now, Mr. Billings."

Hope's boot kicked something in front of her. She bent down to retrieve O.D.'s cell phone. His message screen lit up as she held it. He had been sending her a text. "Will you be with your Dad at six? Please? I really—"

Tears filled her eyes. Dad told her O.D. wanted to talk. Now, he was in the back of a police car. How did he continue to get himself in such messes?

Faith jumped out of Dad's truck.

"Hope!" Faith shouted at her. "You need to go back up and tell O.D.'s parents what's going on. His dad can come down to bail him out."

"What *is* going on?" Hope's voice sounded shrill even to her own ears.

"When I came down to get the truck, O.D. and Billy were

fighting right over there." She pointed to the flowerbed near the hospital entrance. "The hospital security guy was on the phone with the police."

"Fighting? Like yelling, or what?" Hope couldn't believe O.D. had just come from his brother's hospital room to start a fight on the way to his truck.

"No, Billy was flailing away at O.D., and he was defending himself, trying to push him away. Billy was saying. 'I believe her. Why would she lie? She says her baby is going to be a Billings.'"

"And what was O.D. saying?" Hope still held the phone as the police cars pulled away.

"He said, 'But it wasn't me. And it wasn't John K.'"

"Ma'am," The nurse turned to speak to Faith. "You can pull up now."

Faith ran back to the truck.

"I guess Faith is right. You'd best go back up to fill the Billingses in." Dad hugged her. "God's still got this, Hope. O.D.'s a good kid. It will all work out."

———

Felicia Billings leaned against the wall outside Cody's room as Hope approached. "How are you, sweetie?"

"I'm fine. But I have something upsetting to tell you about O.D."

"What? He just left ..." Felicia stood up straight, holding Hope's hand.

"He's okay. But he is on his way to the police station." There was no good way to say it.

"The police station? What?"

"He dropped his cell phone." Hope handed it to O.D.'s mom.

Felicia held the phone with a lost expression on her face.

"Apparently, a guy was waiting when O.D. left a while ago and started a fight with him at the door of the hospital." Hope didn't know what O.D. had told them about Lissa.

"That boy." Felicia shook her head. "No matter what happens, trouble seems to track him down. I hope you can help him stay away from it in the future." She hugged Hope.

"Me?" How had this conversation turned to her?

"He shared two pieces of news with us just before he left here." Felicia brushed a stray lock of hair off Hope's forehead. "One, that he had given his life to Jesus today, and two, that he didn't know if he could keep going without you by his side."

Hope swallowed a lump of tears. *Oh, my goodness.*

"I'll tell his dad. I can stay with Cody while they get all of this straightened out." Felicia stepped toward the hospital room, cracking the door enough to peek in.

Hope headed down the hallway toward the elevators. Two of the nurses behind the desk were putting the finishing touches on a small Christmas tree. She had not learned to be comfortable in a hospital, but she did admire those who were.

Stepping up into the driver's seat of her SUV, she shook her head. What a crazy, mixed-up day. But what O.D.'s mom said kept coming back into her head. O.D. had given his life to Jesus but couldn't imagine going forward without Hope. She smiled. The same thought had been haunting her too. She tried to give him up to Lissa for the sake of a new little family, but the pieces of that picture just wouldn't come together. She had never known someone so right. No one else could complete her sentences, understand what she was thinking before she herself fully knew. O.D. Billings was made for her. If she could just get past the dread of the next crazy adventure he might embark on.

She drove past the Billings Boys dealership, where a crowd

gathered around the truck they were giving away. Evidently, Santa Claus had joined Tara there. She was furiously passing out ink pens so the parents could buy a chance at the truck while the kids told Santa their desires. The banner above read, "Win This Truck for Christmas!" Had that been O.D.'s idea?

She honked her horn, waved, but continued toward the Billingses' barn, to the turn that led to her own house. Felicia's new mural was glistening in the evening sunshine. What must it be like to be the mother of three adventurous boys? O.D.'s mom took the news of his latest trouble in stride. It looked like she was confident that things were going to turn out okay. Hope would love to have that much peace in her heart.

She took a deep breath. Right now, she just wanted to get Champ and take a ride. The shadows around the out-buildings were already lengthening. It wouldn't be light for much longer.

Faith met Hope at the back door.

"You okay?" Faith hugged her tightly.

"Me? Why wouldn't I be okay?" Hope tried to calm her jumping stomach.

"We haven't had much time to talk about this O.D. and Lissa thing. Apparently, now Billy knows. He was plenty mad." Faith moved into the kitchen, handing Junior's lemonade jug to Dad.

Dad held the jug, shifting from one leg to the other. "You two girls come to Junior's room for a minute. I want to talk to the three of you before he goes back to sleep." He strode away with purpose. Hope wondered what in the world was on his mind.

"So, you're not upset about O.D. and Lissa?" Faith came closer, leaning in to speak softly.

"I don't believe there is an O.D. and Lissa." Hope stood up. "O.D. said he had nothing to do with this. I believe him. I'm not sure why, but I do." She wasn't trying to keep her voice down. At this moment, she needed to be sure of something.

"Okay, then. I hope you're right." Faith walked ahead of her to their brother's room down the hall.

Dad perched on the edge of Junior's bed, gesturing to the little loveseat, usually covered with discarded clothes. Hope longed for the days when Junior was able to get around well enough to mess up his room.

Dad walked to the bedroom door before turning to face them. He stared at his boots. "There's no easy way to say this. I've been talking to your Uncle Dub, and it will take an official board meeting, but ..."

Hope's stomach churned. She reached for Faith's hand.

"The rodeo before Christmas when we give away the truck will be the last bi-weekly rodeo at the Caldwell arena."

"What?" Junior winced as she sat up straighter in bed. "What are you talking about, Dad?"

"You're selling out?" Faith squeezed Hope's hand.

"Uncle Dub is selling his rodeo stock. He and Aunt Tina want to spend more time with Kayla Grace before she goes to college. They will be busy on weekends. He has more than he can take care of with their own cattle business. The rodeo animals are just too much."

"We could find another stock supplier." Hope's mind was racing. How could this happen? They had tried so hard to keep things going. Then the thought she couldn't chase away blurted out of her mouth. "What would Mom say? We have to keep this going for her."

She stood up, facing her dad.

"Before your mom got sick, we were talking about moving on. The rodeo has been our life for a long, long time. But it does keep us tied down." Dad stood a little taller now. "With her gone, my heart is honestly not in it. That will begin to show. I'd like to spend more time with the church, helping young people in a different way. You kids need to get your own lives going. Faith will be in nursing school, Junior needs to finish high school, and Hope ... you can do anything you set your mind to, and then some."

The three siblings sat silently. There was no reason to say anything further. Hope felt like the floor had just fallen out from under her feet. No rodeo? Now what?

29

O.D. rubbed his stubbly chin, squirming on the metal chair. He rehearsed in his head the speech he needed to make. *Yes, sir. I've learned my lesson. Next time someone comes up from behind me and starts punching me, I will not react. I will step back and politely say, 'Please stop that.'* It was no use. He couldn't be convincing. After years of tussling with his brothers, he would always defend himself. He hadn't meant to hurt Billy, just to get him to stop fighting. If that hospital security guy had waited another minute or so to call the police, the whole evening would have gone better for all of them.

"Orville Billings." The well-dressed man at the table in front of the room tapped a pencil on a stack of papers.

O.D. sat taller with a jolt. Orville. That was him.

"Yes, sir." He managed to find his voice.

"Come up here, son. We don't have all day." The other people waiting laughed. They clearly knew this routine better than O.D. did. "So, did you have time to do some thinking last night?"

"Yes, sir. Thinking and quite a bit of reading. I found out

that the one thing it's really easy to get in jail is a Bible." O.D. placed the tiny copy the jailer had given him on the table in front of the judge.

"Well, I'm glad we could accommodate you." More giggling. O.D. noticed that Billy was leading the merriment.

"Okay. Settle down. Mr. Billings and I need to talk." The judge adjusted his reading glasses. "Since no one has filed anything additional, you are only charged with disorderly conduct. Since the hospital is a public place, intended to be a quiet location, it is a given that scuffling and shouting at each other is not appropriate."

"Yes, sir." The judge didn't want to hear his side of the story, which was fine, since it sounded pretty lame even in O.D.'s head.

"I talked to your family's attorney last night. He said your dad had always told you boys that if you found yourself in jail, you would spend at least the first night there." The judge paused. The giggling in the room stopped. "I think that's a pretty good policy. Actions have consequences."

"Yes, sir." O.D. was relieved he wouldn't need to say much more.

"Okay. Collect whatever you brought in with you from the officer over there," he pointed to a desk behind a window. "Report for court next Tuesday. Stay away from the young man you were scuffling with at least until then, okay?"

"Yes, sir." O.D. turned to look at Billy, who was staring at his hands. As long as Billy stayed away from him, things should be fine.

He picked up his jacket, belt, and wallet from the man behind the desk. "No cellphone?"

"Sorry, you didn't bring one in, and we don't keep them in stock." The smirk on the guy's face made O.D. wonder if he had been giggling along with everyone else. This guy must really enjoy his job.

"Did I use my only phone call last night, or could I try to get a ride home?" O.D. had almost reached the door before he remembered that his truck was not parked outside.

"You watch too much TV." The female officer that had escorted him from lock-up pointed to a phone on a desk. "Just dial nine to get an outside line. It won't connect to anything but local numbers." She turned away without another word, leaving him in the spotlessly clean lobby.

"Dad," O.D. said as the phone was answered on the first ring. "I'm ready. I have to be in court on Tuesday."

"Okay. Sorry about what happened. But you know …"

"Yeah. I get it. I will think a little longer before reacting like I did. The accommodations were definitely not five-star down here." O.D. rubbed his chin. He needed to go home to shave.

———

"Thanks for telling me to read about Paul," O.D. said to Smiley Caldwell on speakerphone in his truck the next day. "I understand why God had to strike him down to get his attention. But even after that, he had to constantly remind himself about what he should be doing. Stubborn old cuss."

"And one of God's greatest evangelists. I'm glad you spent some time in the scriptures. See you tomorrow at church?"

O.D. sighed in satisfaction. He had been impressed with what he read at the jail, especially when he realized Paul mainly wrote in prison.

He and Hope still had some talking to do. Right now, though, alone time was necessary. Maybe he'd volunteer to spend some time at the hospital tonight, get some more reading in. He had a funny feeling she would approve.

———

Hope watched the scenery go by as she and Dad returned from the grocery store. So familiar, so ordinary. But as they passed by the Caldwell Arena, she felt like she was entering an unknown land. What would be next? She hadn't even asked Dad about the arena. Uncle Dub was selling the rodeo stock, but what about this building?

"I talked to Randy Jennings last night." Dad's mind was headed down the same road as Hope's. "He said it will take a board meeting on their end, too, but we may be able to work out a deal with the Cedar Ridge ranch to take over the arena."

"Really?" He wasn't selling to the casino?

"Well, there was one condition." Dad checked the traffic at the next intersection before continuing the drive home. "He said he offered you a job a while back, yet you never answered. They will need a new office manager when Ms. Genevieve retires. Since you know everything there is to know about the arena …"

Hope pressed her lips together to keep from reacting. When had all these plans been made? Had no one thought to ask her?

"I guess …" She didn't know what to say. All this time, she thought she was fighting to keep the rodeo alive for the rest of her family. Had they been playing along just to humor her?

She'd always admired the Jennings family and Cedar Ridge Ranch. Would her volunteer gig become a real job? Funny, she had the strange urge to bounce this idea off O.D. She should be able to think this through on her own, but it was a lot all at once. Too much to think about by herself.

30

O.D. turned down the loud country station he was listening to as he drove to the hospital. He tapped his fingers on the steering wheel as he waited on the traffic at the stoplight to move. Was that John K.'s truck at the post office?

His brother emerged from the front door, waving at him before opening the driver's door of the old green truck. Instead of driving through the intersection, O.D. pulled into the space beside John K.

"What's up?" John K. came to his open window.

"I'm headed to spend the night with Cody. Mom and Dad can really use a break tonight." O.D. was pleased to be having a calm, normal conversation with his brother for a change.

"Hey, I was thinking of doing the same thing. There's no room for both of us. Why don't you go on home?" John K. flipped through the letters in his hand.

"Getting your mail here instead of at our house?" O.D. shut off his engine.

"Yeah. I'm grown now. I need my own address. Hmm." John K. held up an envelope with a large pink seal on the back.

"This is definitely not mine. I don't plan on entering a Rodeo Princess pageant any time soon."

"You would certainly stand out from the other contestants." O.D. laughed.

"Well, I guess Miss Faith Caldwell needs her own space too. She has the P.O. box next to mine." John K. left Faith's envelope on the top of his stack. "Seriously. Go on home, Little Dee. I'll take the Cody watch tonight. Tell Mom I'll be home for breakfast in the morning."

"Will do." O.D. reached out his window to shake his brother's hand. "Tell Cody I said hey."

John K. walked back into the post office as O.D. headed toward home. It would be sort of nice to have an evening off.

His phone started ringing just as the truck pulled back into traffic. He looked down long enough to see the name of the caller: Q. Heston. Had he not made his answer clear about the casino job? He navigated to a nearby bank parking lot, heading to the back, out of the way of anyone driving through.

He managed to pick up just before the call rolled to voice mail.

"Have you ever been to the National Finals Rodeo?"

What? My goodness.

"No, sir."

"I'm taking all of my top staff to Vegas for a crash course in rodeo betting. I know you said you weren't interested in this job, but why not join us, no strings attached?" Heston was definitely on a speakerphone. O.D. wondered who else might be in the room.

"Sorry, the dates conflict with the Caldwell Family Rodeo. Our dealership is giving away a truck." O.D. had a feeling Heston would have an answer for this.

"Yeah, I have heard rumblings about you and the younger Caldwell girl. I have a private jet. We can get the two of you back in plenty of time for your little giveaway. Perfect chance to impress the country mouse. They even have wedding chapels out there if things get serious."

O.D. pressed his lips together. Talk about overstepping.

"Mr. Heston. I appreciate the offer, but I'm not your man. Seriously."

"Offer stays open. Trip stays open. Just let me know. The Caldwell Rodeo is a remnant of the past. DownRiver Casino is the future." Heston hammered the last word. "We'll talk again."

O.D. disconnected, leaving the bank parking lot. Vegas, National Final Rodeo. Goodness, it was getting harder and harder to hold back the 'sure, why not' that threatened to pop out of his mouth.

Hadn't there been something in those scriptures he'd read about not conforming to the world? More reading would be a good way to occupy his mind tonight.

31

Hope turned around in her seat at the front of the sanctuary. She should have known O.D. would not be here this morning. She'd been surprised that he hadn't texted her with some sort of excuse. Had he gone chasing after John K. again? Had he gotten into another fight with Billy?

She checked her phone again before turning it off. Lissa had posted pictures of herself with Billy, looking very happy. Hope couldn't help chuckling when she scrolled past again.

"Everybody better mind their own business and quit spreading rumors. My baby is going to have the best Daddy. Me and Billy don't need any of you." Did Lissa think they would forget who had started those rumors?

Regardless. It was time to concentrate on the worship. Time to move on with her own life. O.D. was a grown man. She needed to let him take care of himself. She had just dropped her phone in her purse when someone bumped her right shoulder.

"Mornin'," O.D. whispered as the first song brought them to their feet.

Hope couldn't restrain a smile of relief. She had to admit, he did have a way of following through. She struggled to keep her mind on the songs and prayers in the worship service.

O.D. stood quietly next to her, gripping the back of the pew. His rough fingers rested over hers, squeezing them now and then when Smiley's message made a point that resonated. She smiled at him once, but he was listening intently, only releasing her hand to look up a scripture on his phone. Hope sighed. Maybe he was serious. This new, calmer O.D. was a welcome change.

"Before we go home, I have some very good news to report." Dad addressed the congregation after the last song. "Our friend and neighbor, O.D. Billings has rededicated his life to Jesus. He plans to worship with us more often. After the final prayer, you are invited to come over to give him an official welcome to the family. The angels are already rejoicing! Let's pray."

Hope met O.D.'s glance as he smiled. Yes. There had definitely been a change here. Her heart raced. What a loving Father they served.

"Amen." The congregation ended their prayer in unison. O.D. was surrounded by people wearing blue jeans and newly shined cowboy boots.

"Hey!" He reached out as she started past him. "Want to go to Amy Lou's for lunch?"

"Don't you have deliveries to make?"

"No." He leaned closer. "I sort of got fired. Something about not calling in yesterday when I couldn't report for my shift."

His crooked smile made losing a job seem like not very bad news. What a crazy guy.

"Hey, Hope, come on, we're going to the cemetery, remember?" Faith whizzed by, not waiting for an answer.

"Well, I'm not sure about lunch." Why did her sister assume what Hope wanted to do?

"Well, give me a call later. Maybe we can go get a piece of pie or something." His gentle squeeze caused a tiny tingle in her fingers,

"Sure. See you later." He accepted a hug from a gray-haired lady in a long skirt, then turned to wink at her before heading out the door.

"Earth to Hope," Faith bumped her arm. "Let's go get something for lunch."

"Where's Dad?" Hope scanned the front of the auditorium, finding their dad deep in conversation with a teenager she didn't recognize.

"You girls go ahead. I've got my truck." He waved at them, "I'll make sure your brother and I get something to eat." He sat in a seat at the front, holding both of the girl's hands in his with his head bent toward hers.

"He's so in his element here." Faith led the way out the front door.

Hope nodded, grabbing some quick hugs from the members on her way to catch up. Dad was an expert rodeo announcer for sure, but here, he was so comfortable, much more real. He'd said his heart was not in the rodeo anymore. It was here with these people, serving as God's outstretched hand.

As they reached the freshly washed ice blue pickup, Hope noticed that the area behind the truck seat was packed with artificial poinsettias, holly, and fir branches.

"I thought we might take away the fall décor at the cemetery and fix Mom up for Christmas this afternoon." Faith slid behind the steering wheel. Hope settled in next to her, snapping her seat belt.

"Sounds good. But can we get a cheeseburger on the way?"

Hope wasn't sure whether the churning in her stomach was entirely hunger. She would have to get used to the new aura that surrounded O.D.

"I don't know how you keep from ballooning up to 300." Faith laughed. "But yeah. I'll drive through somewhere."

Hope pulled out her phone to send a quick text to O.D.

It may be close to 2:00 when we get back home.

K

Funny how short responses didn't seem rude when you were on the same wavelength.

———

"There, now it looks better." Faith straightened up after securing the faux-evergreen decoration to their mom's headstone. "Mom loved Christmas."

"Yeah." Hope sighed. She remembered Dad had seldom been able to stop Mom from turning their house into a winter wonderland even before the Thanksgiving leftovers were put away. "It was the one time of year she was peaceful." Tears stung her eyes as the wind whipped through the thin jacket she'd worn to church.

"Hey. I need to share something with you." Faith dropped Hope's arm, taking a couple of steps toward the truck.

"Sure, what's up?" Hope couldn't imagine what was on her sister's mind. They hadn't talked beyond day-to-day stuff in quite a while.

"I'm thinking I might start entering some Rodeo Queen pageants. There's good scholarship money for the winners. I just haven't had time with the rodeo coming around every two weeks." She adjusted some flowers that were falling off a headstone nearby.

"I guess it has held all of us back a little." Hope pulled her jacket tighter.

"I might need some help. Someone to sort of be my manager on the road. Costume changes, keeping Belle healthy and happy. I don't know if I can do this without you, Hopie." Faith turned on her blue-eyed charm.

"Of course you could. But I will think on it. I haven't told the Jenningses anything firm about working for Cedar Ridge." Hope blinked to keep her head from spinning. Would she ever really get to make her own choices, or would she always be holding extra costumes and leading horses around for Faith?

"This is a really big change for all of us." Faith hugged her. "I know Mom would just encourage us to do our best and keep going. Right?"

"Of course." Hope pasted on a smile, trying to hold back tears. "One boot in front of the other." Dad was happy with extra time for the church, and now Faith had plans. Junior would have to concentrate on finishing high school, but what would she do? Mom's advice sounded good unless you weren't sure how firm the ground was underneath those boots.

———

"You know I'm always up for a piece of pie," O.D. handed the menu to his Aunt Candace. "Just bring me whatever looks the best today."

"You got it," Candace laughed, turning toward Hope. "He's too easy. How about you, sweetheart?"

"Do you have ice cream?" Hope also closed her menu. "I know it sounds strange, being so cold outside, but ..."

"Actually, we do. We have a luscious peppermint, just in

time for Christmas. No pie under it?" Candace made a note on her pad.

"Nope. Just a double scoop of the peppermint, with some chocolate syrup if you have it."

Hope grinned at O.D. "What?"

"Nothing. You just continue to amaze." He reached across the table for her hand as Candace walked away.

"Thanks for coming out with me. I have needed to say something to you for a few days now." O.D. sat back, fiddling with his napkin.

"Can I go first?" Hope sat up straighter. She needed to clear the air.

"Sure. What's up?"

"I need to apologize." Hope leaned back in the vinyl booth.

"You? For what?" O.D. leaned forward, his dark eyes focusing on hers.

"I never should have believed those rumors about you and Lissa. You've never been anything but upfront with me." She met his eyes, instantly regretting mentioning the other girl's name.

"Hey. I don't blame you for wondering. I made the same mistake, believing her story about John K. I guess she just knew our family's reputation for being generous. I was the most convenient Billings Boy to use to finance her first trip to the doctor's office. She must have been pretty desperate." O.D. sat back, fiddling with his fork.

"O.D. to the rescue." Hope nodded. "She knew you wouldn't tell anyone. I'm sorry she took advantage of you."

"Thanks. You're the only one who could ever see through all the smoke I was sending up. Until recently, I wasn't completely sure about me, either." O.D.'s thumb made circles in her palm.

"Here you go, a thick slab of coconut meringue pie." Candace set the plates between them. "Two scoops of peppermint ice cream for you, hun. Y'all want coffee with that?"

"Maybe later, Ann-Ann." His face flushed a little as he released Hope's hand.

Hope sat quietly. It had bothered her to distrust him.

"I just need a sounding board today." O.D. picked up a healthy piece of his pie with his fork, chewed, and swallowed before speaking again. "Mmm. I do love me some pie. But here's the thing."

She couldn't remember many times he had been at a loss for words. She waited until he finally spoke.

"I've had a job offer. From that casino owner, Mr. Heston." He focused directly on her.

"Yeah, I remember." Hope tried to keep her voice even.

"Nothing about that job was right for me, at least not for the man I want to be. But it is hard to get that 'no' through Heston's head." O.D. took another bite of pie.

Hope breathed a huge sigh. "I guess he's used to having what he wants."

"He even called me last night, offering me a trip to Vegas for the National Finals. A trip for two, in fact." O.D. peered up again.

"For two?" Hope swallowed hard.

"Yep. I told him 'no' again. I hope this time it sticks. I don't need any of that 'what happens there stays there' jazz in my life." He smiled, reaching for his Coke.

Hope nodded but couldn't find the words. She had doubted him but should have known better.

"Anyway, John K. made it very clear that he doesn't want to work with Dad at the dealership, so I'm thinking of applying for the General Manager job. Like I said, lately you are about the only one who seems to get where I'm coming from. What do you think?"

"You would be great! You know everything about every part of the business, even where to find the gadget that loosens ropes to rescue trapped horses!" Hope laughed.

"I wanted to run it by someone before I talk to Dad. It sounds funny when I say it out loud." O.D. laughed.

"Doesn't sound funny to me." Hope lowered her voice. This was a no-brainer. O.D. could take a huge burden from his dad while Cody was still in the hospital.

"Good." O.D. leaned closer, touching her cheek with his finger. "After all that's happened, I think you understand better than almost anybody else. Well, you and God. But I'm still getting used to talking to Him."

"He's a great listener." Hope took his hand. "You're not the only one needing career advice."

"You mean, if the casino buys the rodeo?" O.D. popped another bite of pie in his mouth.

"It's not an 'if' anymore. Uncle Dub is selling the rodeo stock. Dad said there won't be a Caldwell Family Rodeo after Christmas." Hope said the words softly,

"What?" O.D. popped up and moved over to her side of the booth. "Just like that? So, the casino is taking over?"

"Not completely. They might be buying Uncle Dub's animals." Funny, she hadn't even asked Dad who was buying the rodeo stock. "But not the arena. Dad is working out a deal with the non-profit that runs Cedar Ridge."

"Wow. How are you feeling about all this?" He reached behind her, his arm putting gentle pressure on her shoulder, his left hand patting her arm.

"I just feel lost. Dad said Randy and Sue want me to come work for Cedar Ridge, but I just don't know. Then, today, Faith came up with an idea for me to follow her around the Rodeo Queen Circuit to help her with costumes and take care of horses. I know she would really appreciate my help, but I just don't know." Hope looked down at her hands.

"Hey. Things will work out. You've got your whole life in front of you." O.D. used his finger to turn her face toward him, then tilted his head down so that he could look into her eyes. "You can do anything you want. It's your life. Not theirs."

"It's just kind of like somebody let all the air out of me." Hope leaned back a little, fiddling with her ice cream. "We worked so hard on that contest, trying to get attendance up. But the whole time, Dad was thinking about ending the rodeo. He said he and Mom had talked about it before she got sick."

"Lots of things are changing." He pulled his pie over in front of him. "But if I've learned anything over the past few days, it's that God doesn't intend for us to try to do all of this on our own."

"You're right. He's always there." Hope smiled. She liked this new O.D.

"And so am I." His voice was so sweet, so soft. If they weren't in the most public place in Crossroads, this conversation would probably end with a kiss.

"Thanks. We've got lots to think about, but it's all doable. As long as we can keep our lame-brained brothers out of trouble." Hope picked up her jacket to signal that it was time to go home.

"Nope. I'm for letting them take care of themselves from now on too!" O.D. signaled Candace. "Looks like table five today." He handed her several bills.

Candace turned to look behind her. "The one that told me her coffee tasted like lukewarm dishwater?"

"That's the one." O.D. smiled, grabbing Hope's hand as she stood up.

"What am I going to do with you?" Candace walked away, shaking her head.

———

"Hey!" Faith ran up with her phone in hand as O.D. opened the truck door for Hope in front of the Caldwell place.

"Hi, O.D." Faith shoved the phone in front of Hope. "Look, here's a local pageant I can enter right after the first of the year. It leads to a regional one, where the prize money is even bigger. I can fill out the application and send it in, but I might need some help getting my wardrobe together."

"Wow. Give me a minute!" Hope held on to O.D.'s arm as she stopped next to the truck. Probably more for moral support than anything. "We'll talk inside. I'm not sure I'm up for this 'pageant mom' thing. Maybe you can get Kayla to go with you."

"Oh. Okay." Faith looked from Hope to O.D. and back again before walking off.

"There you go. Good job." He whispered in Hope's ear. "It's your life. Not hers."

"Thanks." Those hazel eyes might make him melt into a puddle right here in their front yard.

"See you soon." He placed a brief kiss on her forehead, turning to walk around to the driver's side. He couldn't help wishing her life might be connected to his for a long time to come. At least he hadn't blurted out a proposal this time. That moment would need to be special.

———

Hope stood in the center of the arena with tears in her eyes. They had made it through the last bareback ride, the last calf roping, the last barrel races, even the last bull ride with no injuries. Up until now, things had been routine, though Dad had tweaked at her emotions a few times with his extra special announcements and expressions of gratitude.

O.D. was in his element, guiding the nervous finalists to stand next to the gleaming black truck under the announcer's stand. He raised a "thumbs-up" signal to his dad, who was taking over the announcing duties for the truck giveaway.

"Okay, folks. Davis Billings, here. The owner of Billings Boys. We'll get right down to business. Five lucky participants are ready with keys in their hands. Only one will start this truck. That winner will drive it away after signing over whatever he or she drove to the rodeo tonight to Billings Boys. I'm hoping none of them rode up on a mule." The crowd laughed in approval. "Let's not make them wait a minute longer."

Hoots, hollers, and applause echoed from the metal roof of the arena.

A twenty-something man wearing blue jeans, tennis shoes, and a baseball cap opened the driver's side door of the truck to climb in. He fidgeted inside for a moment, then shook his head, raising his hands before climbing out.

O.D. assisted an older man as he tried his key, then jumped back down next to him on the dusty floor.

"Okay, here we go." A willowy gray-haired lady jogged over, opening the door confidently and waving off O.D.'s hand. In less than a second, the mighty engine engaged.

The crowd cheered wildly. Tara Williams ran over to meet the winner as she turned the engine off and climbed out.

"Hey! It worked." Hope's dad was applauding wildly behind her.

"Yes, sir. A great way to end the night." Hope hugged him. They expanded to a group hug as Faith and Junior walked closer.

O.D. wrapped his arm around Hope's shoulder as she moved away from Dad.

"The winner of that truck certainly looks happy." Tara pushed a microphone in front of O.D. as the cameraman gave her a signal.

"Yes. The Billings Boys are tickled." He pulled Hope closer, supporting her as she got a little wobbly with the spotlights aimed her way. "We raised over $10,000 for Cedar Ridge ranch, and a sweet lady got a pretty good Christmas present out of it."

"So, it's the last night of the Caldwell Family Rodeo, right?" Tara moved the microphone toward Hope. "How do you feel about that?"

She swallowed hard. There was no way she would be able to put any thoughts together right now. Her dad, Faith, and Junior stood just to their left. Maybe O.D. would steer Tara in their direction.

"Hey, you forgot to ask your standard question, Tara!" He saved the day again.

"Oh yeah! Are we finally going to learn what O.D. stands for?" Tara turned to be sure the television camera was rolling.

"As a matter of fact, it stands for Orville Dewayne."

Hope laughed out loud.

"I was named for my two grandfathers. I'm super proud of both of them. Orville Billings, Retired U.S. Marshall, who lives in Montana, and Dewayne Tolliver, Army Special Forces veteran from right here in Crossroads."

"Well!" Tara turned toward the camera. "You heard it, folks. We have an exclusive on KRVA. Mystery solved."

"Come see us down at the Billings Boys dealership!" O.D. waved at the camera. "We would love to show you our new truck and van conversion center for folks who need modifications to make life easier."

"I guess your brother Cody's injury sparked that idea." Tara aimed the microphone back at O.D. but Hope sensed that he wasn't prepared to talk about Cody right now.

"Tara, could I have a word or two?" Hope summoned her courage. "I want to say thanks to all who entered this contest on behalf of Cedar Ridge Ranch. They are looking forward to some big changes. Now they will be able to help lots more people in our community. Merry Christmas!"

"There you have it," Tara turned to face the camera. "The Caldwell Family Rodeo is history, but I have a feeling we haven't seen the last of Crossroads's new power couple, O.D. Billings and Hope Caldwell. Back to the studio now for the Christmas forecast."

Tara hugged Hope as the cameraman turned off his light.

"See you soon! Y'all have a wonderful holiday." She waved at O.D., running off with her microphone and a small bag the cameraman had left behind.

"Power couple?" O.D. chuckled as he pulled Hope closer. "Good job promoting Cedar Ridge tonight. You shouldn't be so timid about speaking up."

"Some people have to stop to think for a minute before they speak." Hope smiled at him.

"Okay. Yeah, that will be your job from now on." O.D. pulled her close, warming her lips with a kiss.

32

"How do you think he is, really?" O.D. stood next to his dad in the hallway of the hospital.

"They don't pay me to be a doctor, son." Dad ran his fingers through his hair. "It's a waiting game. They are fighting infection, making sure things don't move backward, even though we don't see much progress."

"He has told me he doesn't need somebody here 24/7." O.D. set his backpack down on the floor.

"Yeah, that's mostly your mom's thing. She wouldn't rest with her baby up here alone."

That could have gone unsaid, but O.D. knew how true it was. Their mom loved deeply.

"Son, I've had a lot of time to think while I sit here." Dad turned toward him. "You know how worried I have been about the future of the dealership. Smiley Caldwell's decision about the rodeo made me realize that change is not entirely bad."

"Not bad, but it certainly affects a lot of people." O.D. thought of Hope's hesitation, Change was hard for her.

"Well, John K. has made it clear that my plan for turning

the day-to-day stuff at Billings Boys over to him is not happening."

O.D. nodded. That was an understatement.

"So, rather than placing an ad in the newspaper, what would you think about coming up to let me show you the ropes. You really know most of it already. Everybody down there has a lot of confidence in you. Unless you're thinking of hitting the pro calf roping circuit?"

O.D. cleared his throat, hoping he could summon words that sounded coherent. First things first. He closed his eyes, sent up a quick prayer. *Thank you, Lord.*

"Dad, you know how I feel about Billings Boys. I would be honored to have a part in keeping it going strong." After all the struggle to force his older brother to step up, relief washed through him like a wave. "You've got yourself a new GM, Dad. Let's do this."

Dad laughed. "Well, now! That was easier than I thought. Yeah. I think we can make this happen." Dad's shoulders relaxed as they hugged. "Enjoy your night watch with Cody. I'll see you in the morning."

O.D. walked into the hospital room, placing his backpack under the side chair. Cody slept more now than when he first arrived at the hospital. He missed the constant ribbing his little brother used to dish out.

He walked over to the window overlooking the parking lot where Billy had jumped him. So much had changed since that day. If only Cody's progress could be that quick.

A soft but persistent knock echoed from the door to the tiny room.

"Come in." O.D. couldn't imagine who would be visiting. That was another thing that had changed. At first, Cody's friends had crowded his bedside. Now, with too little changing, it was down to the family and Junior when he could get a ride.

Aunt Candace pushed the door open.

"Hey, Tough Guy, what's shaking?" O.D. loved the nicknames she always used. John K. had been Superstar, he was Little Dee. Cody had picked up Tough Guy during his toddler days.

"I guess he's catching up on his beauty rest." O.D. walked around to hug her.

"Shouldn't take long. He's always been the prettiest of you boys." Candace kissed his cheek. "But I actually came to talk to you. Can you step out into the hallway for a minute?"

"Sure."

She closed the big metal door, leaning against the tiled wall outside,

"What's up?" O.D. stood next to her, both hands in his back pockets.

"Your mom and I had a long talk last night. Besides the fabulous news about you coming to an understanding with God, she said that you were thinking of asking Hope to marry you." Candace reached into the pocket of her apron.

"I have this feeling that Hope is the one, but I don't know if she'll have me. After all, I haven't acted the part of a responsible husband-type lately." O.D. stared down at his hands.

"Well, when you get up the courage to find out how she feels, maybe this will help her to realize you're serious." She held her right fist toward him, and he placed his hand under it. The delicate gold ring with one simple diamond that fell into his palm had Hope's name written all over it.

"Was this yours?" O.D. held it up to reflect the fluorescent lights. Aunt Candace didn't talk a lot about her marriage to

Uncle Duke. They married in their early thirties. His motorcycle crash had taken him far too soon.

"No. Your Grandpa Dee gave this to our mama over fifty years ago. She gave it to me not long before she died."

O.D. waited for the rest of the story. It was so hard for his family to talk about his grandmother.

"I told your mom right after the funeral. It made her so sad. She said we should have recognized the signs. Giving away prized possessions ..." Candace looked away, brushing an errant curl off her forehead.

"The signs?" O.D. had never been told what happened when he was just a small boy.

"Felicia found her in the house on the hill during our dad's last assignment. Dad had promised he was retiring after the contracting job. We all tried to go up there when we could, invite her to come stay with us. But nothing helped. She was so lonely, even in a room full of people. She wouldn't talk, barely ate anything. But she wouldn't go to a doctor ... wouldn't try." Candace used a lacy handkerchief to blot her eyes. "When we finally convinced her to go and get some medicine, she took the whole bottle at once, along with the only bottle of whiskey they had in the house. I thought we would lose your mom, too, when she found your grandma and the note she left."

"This ring was meant for happiness. Our mom wasn't happy. I think that's why she gave it to me. When Duke came along, he bought me my own ring." She held her right hand up to allow her diamond ring to catch the light. "So, I hung on to Mama's ring for just the right time. I think this is it. What it needs, what we all need, is Hope."

O.D. held the ring in the palm of his hand. It couldn't be more perfect. Simple, beautiful, one of a kind. But was Hope ready for this? He had to do this right. He couldn't risk her thinking he was being impulsive and reckless again.

"Well?" Aunt Candace tucked the handkerchief back in her blue-jean jacket pocket to stand near the door to the diner. "I haven't known too many times when you were at a loss for words, Little Dee."

"It's perfect. After all that has happened in the past few days, I am scared to death to mess this up." He clutched the ring in his fist. "I just don't know what she'll say. What if she still thinks I'm being immature?"

"You may have the rest of the world convinced of that, but Hope knows better. Give her some credit." Aunt Candace pecked him on the cheek. "Pray about it. I'll do the same." She waved as she walked toward the elevator.

O.D. reached inside his jacket for the breast pocket he usually forgot. The little diamond would be safe there until he figured this out.

Okay, God, I promised not to do anything on my own anymore. Are You with me? He laughed as a notification buzzed on the phone in his pocket. Okay. This was doable. But there was one more person he needed to talk to. First, he'd go sit with Cody until Mom showed up to stay for a while.

A ring? For real? He walked into Cody's room to find him snoring. "You're missing all the fun, little brother."

———

"You need a shave." Grandpa Dee shook his hand when O.D. found him sitting in the lobby of the nursing facility.

"You're right. But I came by to share some news with you." He helped Grandpa Dee move his wheelchair around to face the little loveseat near the window.

"You won the calf ropin'."

Well, at least he seemed to know which brother was visiting him this time. Better talk fast before he forgot.

"No, sir. But I came close." He smiled. "The other day, Smiley Caldwell helped me come to an understanding with God. I found out I'm a lot like the apostle Paul, flawed but useful to God."

"Well, now!" Grandpa's voice boomed through the lobby. He reached for O.D.'s hand. "Good job, son."

"Thanks. There's one more thing." He tried to lower his volume, hoping Grandpa would take the hint. "I've decided to ask Hope Caldwell to be my wife."

"All at the same time? Don't get too swept away, now. Stop and ask God for directions, son." Grandpa did become quieter.

"That's what I think Hope will say, so I'm taking a minute to think about it. But your daughter sort of gave me a push this morning." He reached into his breast pocket to find the ring.

"Your Mama stopped trying to push you long about the time you learned to run off on your own."

"No, this was the other one, Candace."

"She pushes pie and coffee." Grandpa's dark eyes sparkled.

O.D. was so glad he'd come by at this moment. He hadn't had such a rollicking conversation with his grandpa in weeks.

"She gave me this to use when I'm ready." He held the little ring in front of him, and Grandpa took it between his thumb and forefinger. The cloud that came over his face was balanced by a tiny smile.

"Yes. Yes." Grandpa nodded, giving the ring back. "A simple, beautiful ring for a simply beautiful girl. What it needs now is Hope."

Exactly what Aunt Candace said. O.D. swallowed hard and tucked the diamond back in his pocket.

"Where will you live? I don't think it's good to stay with parents. Especially not when you're grown." Grandpa rubbed his chin.

"Well, she loves the old house on the top of the hill. The one you and Grandma lived in."

O.D.'s mind was racing. The wrap-around porch begged for new chairs to watch the sunrise and sunset. There was enough flat space next to it for a new barn. They'd be close to both families but still on their own.

"Yep. It's not going anywhere. It was built to last. Needs a new coat of paint." Grandpa's eyes were lighting up. O.D. thought he'd probably had lots of plans for the place before Grandma passed away. It needed lots more than paint, but that would be a good start. He patted Grandpa Dee's hand then stood to put his hat back on. Everything was in place. Now, to convince the potential bride.

———

"So, how does the tree look?" Faith put the finishing touches on the Christmas tree in the front window.

"Okay, I guess." Hope laid her phone face down on the coffee table. Everyone was showing off their decorations, sharing plans for the coming holiday. She just couldn't get in the mood.

"Wow, Sis." Junior hobbled in from his bedroom. "That looks like a big city Christmas tree."

"Thanks. Might as well bring a little city to the country." Faith laughed.

"What's for supper?" Junior opened the door to the refrigerator, poking his head inside.

"Well, you're certainly back to normal." Hope stood up from the couch. After Faith did all the decorating, the least she could do was try to rustle something up for her starving brother.

"Dad fixed a crockpot full of pinto beans." Faith snapped the lid on a plastic tub.

"Here," Hope handed Junior a potato peeler. "If you peel, I'll fry some potatoes."

"I'll start a pan of cornbread." Faith carried the tub full of decorations towards the garage.

Hope's phone buzzed when she picked it up from the table. O.D.'s texts arrived in a series of short bursts.

Hey

Want to hang out with me for supper?

Nothing fancy. Maybe pizza?

Sure.
What time?

Sort of early if it's okay. About 5:30?

No, wait. I'll pick you up at 4:37.

Four thirty-seven? What in the world? Hope chuckled. Never a dull moment with this guy.

Okay

It was four twenty now. That didn't give her long to clean up and rebraid her hair.

"Faith, I'm sorry, but can you fry the potatoes? O.D. wants to take me for pizza at 4:37."

"What? Oh, yeah!" Faith pulled out an iron skillet and set it on the stove. "What a dunce! I almost forgot he was taking you out tonight."

"He just asked me." Seriously, what was going on here? "How did you know?"

"It's not like it's a surprise or anything. Way to go, Faith." Junior peeled furiously, dropping the naked potatoes in a bowl.

"Are you wearing that?" Dad stepped back to look at Hope as he walked in the back door.

"How did you know I was going anywhere?" Butterflies invaded Hope's stomach.

"I ran into O.D. a while ago. He said he might ask you out." Dad opened the refrigerator for the iced tea pitcher.

Junior's attention was focused on the potatoes. Faith poured oil into the skillet. Hope had never seen three people try so hard to act unconcerned.

"I guess I'd better go change." Her heart pounded as she went to her closet to find something a little nicer. She hoped her evening would be as exciting as her family expected it to be.

———

"There you go." O.D. opened the passenger side door of his truck at exactly 4:37.

Hope stifled a giggle as he ran back around to his side. She climbed up into a cab filled with warm pizza odors.

Her mouth was open to ask what in the world was going on when O.D. started whistling. Whistling.

What was that tune? It was familiar, maybe an old hymn? As he resumed, the words popped into her head. 'Farther along, we'll know all about it.'

The branches of the trees that lined the road brushed the

top of the truck. The gravel under the wheels grew thinner. Rainy days would make this road hard to navigate.

"Oh, man." O.D. pulled over to the right to accommodate an old pickup truck headed the other way.

"Was that your mom riding with John K.?" Hope couldn't keep quiet a moment longer. His family was acting stranger than hers.

"He never has been very good at staying on schedule. Probably why he went MIA in the army." O.D. turned toward her with a tiny smile. "Just hang on for another minute. Okay?" Hope turned around to watch John K.'s truck bounce down the narrow dirt road with paint cans and a ladder jumping crazily in the bed. She faced front again as they continued up the dirt road and caught O.D. looking in the rearview mirror as the sun's reflection lit up the inside of the truck.

"I've never come up here from this side. Always through the woods on a horse." Hope broke the silence as the truck stopped in front of the old clapboard house. "Hey, it's been painted."

"Yeah. That was Grandpa Dee's suggestion. Mom said it needed primer first, so it will look better when we put the real coat on. Can you climb out on your own? I need to get a couple of things from behind the seat." O.D. opened the driver's side, Hope climbed down on the passenger side. It was amazing how nice the old place looked with a fresh coat of paint. The sun glinted off the metal roof as if the house knew it was on display.

She followed O.D. around the north side of the house to find him placing the pizza box next to a vase of flowers on a rickety old table. Nearby, a small fire pit held a healthy blaze between two brightly painted Adirondack chairs.

"Not too fancy, but I hope this will do." O.D. held his hand out to her as she got closer. "Before you sit down, turn around this way." He took her hand and pulled her closer to his side facing the setting sun.

Below and in front of them, the sky was painted shades varying from brilliant orange to deep purple. Hope gasped. A light breeze brushed her eyelashes. She felt a hint of the cool moisture that always teased them just before Christmas.

"It's beautiful." She took a deep breath. When she sank back against O.D.'s shoulder, his heart was beating into her back.

"Best view anywhere." Placing his hat on the table next to the pizza box, his bright eyes sparkled as he turned her to face him. "Don't want the pizza to get cold, but I have something to say first."

Hope swallowed hard, fighting tears. "Dee ... I ... "

"Sorry. I really need to go first this time." He placed his finger against her lips. "I sort of know what you're thinking. Grandpa Dee told me that I should take a little time after coming to an agreement with God, to keep this separate, so I waited a bit. But the truth is, it's all too connected." She was facing him now. He pulled her in so that their noses almost touched.

"Ever since John K. came home, I've been struggling to figure out who I am, how I fit into this world. I'd spent years putting on a show, trying to create an image of some hot-shot showoff that didn't need anyone. You are the one who saw through that. You helped me realize that I didn't have to impress anybody. I didn't have to fix the world all by myself. It's sort of like this old house. A coat of paint helps, but down deep, it's just the same old house, not fancy, but not going anywhere. I'm here to stay too. Everything I love is right here. I have my faults, do some stupid things, but God is still here with me. He understands. And you are a big part of keeping my head where my feet are."

Hope was dumbfounded. How could he give her credit for any of this?

"The thing is, now that God's in my corner, I think I can keep my head and my feet in close proximity. But without you, there's no heart. You have that, Hope Catherine Caldwell. So, I need you right here, with me. For every sunset. And on the other side of the house, for the sunrises too."

He released his hold on her and dropped to his knee. From somewhere, he pulled out a tiny diamond ring. The sun caught it, making it sparkle with the last rays of the day.

"You can set the timetable. I won't have this house livable for a while, but this ring, this house, and my heart are yours forever. Will you stick around with me?"

"Of course!" For once, she didn't think before blurting out the words. This crazy, mixed-up man wanted her to live in this beautiful spot with him? Right now, she couldn't imagine being anywhere else.

He stood up and pulled her against him, kissing her gently at first, then with everything he had. She reached up with both hands to pull his face even closer, kissing him until her knees were weak.

"Really?" He took a step backward, almost pulling them both over.

"Yes, you nut. Really!"

He kissed her again, guiding her to one of the chairs. "I'd better light a lantern. It will be dark soon. Here, eat some pizza." He shoved the box into her hand.

"Wait. What did you do with the ring? You didn't drop it, did you?" Hope's belly was doing flips. She wasn't sure eating pizza was the wisest thing right now.

"No, it's still right here." He retrieved the little ring from his breast pocket and placed it on her finger. "See. That's why I need you. I can set up a pretty good show, but it's those details."

"And if it weren't for you, I'd plan the details forever, and nothing would ever happen." She held the ring where the campfire made it shine again. "I guess God meant us to be a team." Grease was starting to make the pizza box hard to juggle, so she placed it back on the little table as O.D. ran to light a lantern that was hanging in a nearby tree.

"I'm not very hungry." She peered under his hat when he came back. His smile started in those miles-deep eyes before spreading to his lips.

"Me neither."

They stood facing each other in front of the two chairs. There was so much they should talk about, but words would ruin the moment.

O.D. reached behind her head, moving his fingers through her hair for a moment before pressing her cheek against his. His breath was soft against her skin. She felt, more than heard, his huge sigh.

"I used up my turn to talk. Did you start to say something?" He whispered, guiding her over to one of the chairs again. He sat and pulled her down with him, settling her on his lap in the sturdy wooden chair.

Hope cleared her throat and settled against his chest, facing what was left of the picture-postcard sunset.

"I guess I want to say thanks for always being you, underneath the show. I was a little jealous for a while."

"Jealous?" O.D. sat back, turning her to face him.

"Tara ... the other girls who worshipped you." She tried to focus on those sparkling, unwavering eyes.

"There weren't that many. Tara is just an old buddy from school." He spoke softly.

"Who happened to be your prom date after you had both

graduated." This shouldn't bother her so much after so long, but it did.

"Yeah. That was crazy." O.D. smiled. "Her station wanted a story about prom, so she asked me to come along. She said she didn't think the cameraman would want to double as her date." He reached for her hand again. "I remember how pretty you were that night. But you were buzzing around, acting all 'in charge' and stuff. Didn't seem to have time to dance."

"Yeah. I guess since I didn't have a date, I didn't want to just stand around, so I volunteered for the prom committee." Hope's cheeks were on fire. "What about all of your groupies?"

"Groupies, for a calf roper?" O.D. guffawed, his chest bouncing with laughter. "They didn't know anything about the real O.D. They never will."

"I guess I should have brought some more wood for the fire. It's getting a little chilly up here." O.D. pulled her against him. "We shouldn't stay too long anyway. There are two whole houses full of people down there waiting to see how this all turned out." Hope snuggled into his shoulder, inhaling the freshly washed scent of his shirt.

"No need for a fire." This time, she turned her face up toward him, kissing his stubbly chin, then his welcoming lips. If this moment lasted forever, it would be fine with her.

"Well, the lantern may run out of fuel before the night's over. We'll have to come back when the porch is safe to sit on. Maybe we'll even have electricity." He kissed her again, his hands pressing against her back, his heart beating against her chest.

She took a couple of shallow breaths, waiting for him to claim her mouth again.

"I think we need to take it a little easy here." He said softly. "That's my common sense, not my heart, talking."

"Your common sense?" Hope laughed. "That will take some getting used to."

He doused the embers of the fire with water, stirred it with a shovel, doused it again. She held his hand as they walked to the tree to retrieve the lantern.

"Wait." He stopped in his tracks before opening the passenger side of the pickup.

"What now?" Hope was afraid to move.

"I forgot! I brought some sparkling grape juice and a couple of Mom's pretty glasses. Just in case you wanted to 'cheers' after you said yes." He reached into an ice chest in the bed of the truck.

"Sure!" Hope laughed. "Why not?"

"Here's to Crossroads's newest power couple." O.D. opened the bottle. She held the glasses as he poured.

"Here's to never trying to go it alone." Hope raised her grape juice. Glasses clinked. The last gleam of daylight reflected on a window of the old house behind O.D.'s head. With no idea what would happen next, Hope couldn't have been more confident.

EPILOGUE

Hope released Faith's hand as they stood together on the newly-floored front porch.

"Here he comes." Faith pecked her on the cheek before walking down the short ramp toward the driveway. "I'll make sure the photographer hangs back while y'all talk."

O.D. stepped out of the passenger side of John K.'s truck, standing still for a moment before walking toward her.

She fluffed the billowing skirt of her beautiful dress, resisting the temptation to sit on the porch swing. Surely her knees would hold her up long enough to speak to him before the ceremony started.

O.D. walked up the ramp, clasping her left hand while removing his hat with his right.

"Have you ever seen me speechless?" His dark eyes bored into hers. "You look incredible."

"Not often." Hope examined her hands, her heart pounding. "I feel the same way. We have both been so busy the past few days, we haven't talked much."

"Yeah. I was worried about getting the house and the barn

ready. I just hope the toilets flush and all the lights come on when they are supposed to. Having an outdoor wedding in Arkansas in April can mean iffy weather. Tara's station said the storms should hold off till tonight."

"Slow down, cowboy. That's a lot of details to think about." She detected the spark in his eyes that she loved so much.

"Right. I told you I'd quit worrying about details. That's what I have you for." O.D. took both of her hands. His lips trembled as he pulled her closer for a kiss.

Hope wished for the security of a seat behind her again. He pulled away, resting his cheek against hers with a sigh.

"Okay, what's wrong?"

"I made sure that everything was accessible for Cody, and I think he will be here today." He turned to stare down the road. "But Grandpa Dee won't be. I really wanted him to see the happiness that lives in this place these days."

"The nurses said the excitement would be too much for him. He's more content with his routine where he is. I'm missing Mom too. But we'll make it." She blinked back a tear.

The photographer moved a little closer. Faith and Kayla followed behind, whispering to each other.

"We'll have time to talk later. Are you sure you want to do this?" O.D. bent down to peer into her eyes.

"Absolutely." This time, she kissed him. "You planned the start time for exactly 6:55. So we need to get with it!"

"We need to have the sunset as a backdrop!" O.D. laughed, backing away with a huge bow. "See you in a few."

Hope's heartbeat sped up. His theatrics had annoyed her so much in the past. Today, she couldn't be more grateful.

O.D. jogged away as his dad's freshly washed truck arrived with the rest of their family.

She moved toward Faith and Kayla, glancing toward the guests seated in front of a wooden deck located in the spot O.D.

had used for his proposal. The clouds added a layer of dark purple to the glorious colors overlooking "their" valley. Her boots crunched on the new gravel walkway. O.D. had done such a good job supervising the projects needed to get their new home and wedding venue ready. She didn't know how the day could be more perfect.

A gust of wind flirted with her skirt, and she held it down over her boots.

"Hey, Faith!" John K. yelled from the platform, where the vine-covered archway he had built swayed crazily.

Faith lifted her skirt to run toward him.

"Bring another of those weights from the back of the truck." John K. knelt near the back of the arch as blossoms from the garlands decorating it brushed the top of his head.

Kayla stood near Hope, grasping her hand as John K. continued to work. "I guess we put too many flowers on it."

"No. It's perfect. At least it's not raining." Hope smiled at her cousin.

A rumble of thunder rolled through on cue, and they both laughed nervously.

"Let's go. Your dad is ready to start the ceremony. He may just have to hold the arch with one hand and his Bible with the other." Kayla led her toward Junior, who was waiting to escort Hope up the aisle.

Faith waved as she ran back to take her place in line. She aimed a quick thumbs-up toward Hope.

Hope closed her eyes. *Thank you, Lord. You have given us a wonderful day for a wedding. Help us all remember Who is really in charge here. Your plans are perfect. Amen.*

ABOUT THE AUTHOR

Jenny Carlisle has been writing stories since she learned to hold a pencil.

Raised with her younger sister in Southeast Kansas by a divorced Mom, letters to their Daddy helped Jenny develop her writing voice. After her mom's remarriage added 4 new siblings and a move to Arkansas, she graduated from high school in her new home. She studied journalism in college but left her studies when she married her best friend and began a career with the State of Arkansas. Story-telling continued in spiral notebooks while she waited for their three kids at scout meetings and band practices.

Membership in Fiction Writers of Central Arkansas led to awards at local conferences. A group led by Linda Fulkerson that soon became the Arkansas Chapter of American Christian Fiction Writers provided her with a writing home. She served in each of their offices over the years and gained lifelong friends.

Preparing the bulletin for her congregation led to sending articles to Gospel Tidings, a nationally published magazine associated with the Churches of Christ. For over 10 years, she was a monthly columnist for Ouachita Life magazine, which is distributed all over the southwest region of Arkansas. She makes presentations to local civic groups, encouraging others to tell their own stories.

Britta Meadows at Peas in a Pod Publishing helped her create her first non-fiction book in 2017 and a second one in 2021. *Turn, Turn, Turn* and *To Everything a Season* encourage readers with a mix of nostalgia and hope for the future.

She continues to inspire with blog posts and monthly newsletters while enjoying the process of writing and publishing the stories that fill her heart.

Jenny's goal is to use the talents God has blessed her with to reach out with hope and a wistful smile to all who read her work.

MORE CONTEMPORARY WOMEN'S FICTION FROM SCRIVENINGS PRESS

Perfectly Arranged

Book One of the Hopeful Hearts Series

Liana George

Short on clients and money, professional organizer Nicki Mayfield is hanging up her label maker. That is until the eccentric socialite Katherine O'Connor offers Nicki one last job.

Working together, the pair discovers an unusual business card among Ms. O'Connor's family belongings that leads them on a journey to China. There the women embark on an adventure of faith and self-discovery as they uncover secrets, truths, and ultimately, God's perfectly arranged plans

———

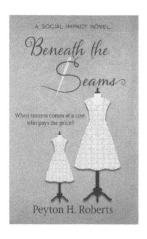

Beneath the Seams

Peyton H. Roberts

Fashion designer Shelby Lawrence is launching her mother-daughter dresses nationwide when she receives a photo of the girl who will change her life forever. Runa, the family's newly sponsored child, is a clever student growing up near Dhaka, Bangladesh. Shelby's daughter Paisley is instantly captivated by their faraway friend. As the girls exchange heartwarming messages, Shelby has no idea that a tragedy in Runa's life is about to upend her own.

Dresses are flying off the racks when a horrifying scene unfolds in Dhaka that threatens to destroy Shelby's pristine reputation. Even worse—it sends Runa's life spiraling down a terrifying path. Shelby must decide how far she's willing to go to right a tragic wrong.

Both a gripping exposé of fashion industry secrets and a heartwarming mother-daughter tale, Beneath the Seams explores love, conscience, hope, and the common threads connecting humanity.

———

Scrivenings
PRESS
Quench your thirst for story.
www.ScriveningsPress.com

Stay up-to-date on your favorite books and authors with our free e-newsletters.

ScriveningsPress.com

9 781649 171894